OFFed Stage Left

JOANNE SYDNEY LESSNER

Dulcet Press

Also by Joanne Sydney Lessner

The Temporary Detective
Bad Publicity
And Justice for Some

Pandora's Bottle

ISBN-10: 0-9981332-0-5
ISBN-13: 978-0-9981332-0-1

Printed in the United States of America
Cover design by Linda Pierro

Published by Dulcet Press
New York
www.dulcetpress.com
info@dulcetpress.com

For my sister

ONE

"*BE KIND TO YOUR WEB-FOOTED FRIENDS, for a duck could be somebody's mooo-ther,*" Sunil Kapany sang under his breath to the tune of "The Stars and Stripes Forever."

"Shhh!" Isobel Spice elbowed him. "There's a rehearsal going on, in case you hadn't noticed."

"You have to admit, it's better than the lame words we're being forced to sing," Sunil grumbled. He sank further into his cushioned seat in Livingston Stage Company's darkened theater, drawing up his knees against the scratched donor nameplate on the seatback in front of him. "Seriously, who thought it was a good idea to write lyrics to Sousa marches?"

"I don't see how you can have a musical about the March King without using his music," Isobel said. She shifted the bustle of her pale-blue and white muslin gown, her act one costume for *Sousacal: The Life and Times of John Philip Sousa.*

"Easy," Sunil replied. "You hire a composer with a sense of the period to write the book songs, and use Sousa's marches for the gazintas and gazoutas."

Isobel frowned. "The what?"

"The underscoring that *goes into* one scene and *goes out of* another. Gaz*intas* and gaz*outas.*" He looked askance at her. "Have you never done a musical before?"

"Plenty." She bristled. "And I've never heard anyone use those words. You are totally making that up."

"I am not," Sunil said, affronted. "Hey, Kelly!"

Several rows in front of them, Kelly Jonas, the stage manager, held court behind a large wooden plank balanced across the seats, which served as a makeshift control center for tech rehearsals. She looked up from her prompt book, a three-inch binder stuffed with script pages and scenic renderings, fastidiously divided by brightly colored tabs. Pushing aside a long strand of graying hair, Kelly squinted at Sunil through her wire-rimmed glasses.

"Yeah?"

"What are gazintas and gazoutas?" Sunil asked.

"The play-ons and play-offs before or after a scene," she answered distractedly. A movement onstage caught her attention. "Are we ready to move on?"

Sunil turned triumphantly to Isobel. "See?"

Isobel sighed. "This is going to be a long day."

"They don't call it a ten-out-of-twelve for nothing."

"Is there anything more tedious than spending ten hours waiting around while they set lighting and sound cues?" Isobel whined.

"Um, yes. Doing the actual show."

As much as Isobel hated to admit it, Sunil was right. From day one, it had been clear that *Sousacal* was a dog. There had been a buzz of anticipatory excitement in the air when the company assembled for the first read-through in the third-floor rehearsal studio of the sleek, state-of-the-art performing arts complex in downtown Albany. In addition to hosting the century-old Livingston Stage Company, relocated from its charmingly dilapidated (some said haunted) prior home in an old vaudeville house, the building had a black box theater and a café that served light meals before and after performances. Everything about her surroundings made Isobel feel like a working theater professional.

Everything, that is, except the material. Sunil had politely informed her after the read-through that his shin was black and blue from her kicking it under the table. But having taken out her frustration on his tibia, she resolved to relish her first regional theater job rather than let the disappointing quality of the show get her down. Since moving to New York a year and a half ago, when she'd met Sunil at her very first audition, Isobel had learned that most acting work was to be found in summer stock or regional theaters. Isobel had resigned herself to the conundrum of living in New York in order to get work out of town, which was the best way for a young performer who was not yet a member of Actors' Equity Association to build her resume. Despite Sunil's increasingly steady stream of snarky comments, she had thrown herself enthusiastically into her small role as John Philip Sousa's first love, Emma Swallow, while assiduously preparing the larger role she was understudying: Jennie Sousa, the composer's wife.

Isobel sighed again and flipped open her script to a scene between Jennie and Sousa, running her finger down the neon pink highlights. "I may as well use my downtime to memorize lines."

Sunil jerked a thumb at the stage. "You really think Arden is going to miss a performance?"

Isobel followed his gaze. Arden Claire was stalking the proscenium like a tiger that hadn't had its morning coffee. A statuesque, auburn-haired beauty, Arden had once represented New York in the Miss America pageant and was hailed as a minor celebrity, even though she hadn't made it past the swimsuit competition. So far, her portrayal of Jennie Sousa was not living up to expectations. Throughout the three-week rehearsal period, Ezra Bernard, the director, had pushed Arden to suppress her natural hauteur and find Jennie's quiet strength and self-deprecating humor. Their struggles swallowed up rehearsal hours, and the more Ezra tried to mold Arden's characterization, the more fiercely she clung to the glamour that had guaranteed her past successes, which didn't exactly endear her to the rest of the company.

Chris Marshall, the charismatic, square-jawed actor playing Sousa, found her completely intolerable. All Arden's scenes were with him, which meant her epic ego flashes impacted him more than anyone else. Initially, Chris had struck Isobel as the sort of galvanizing personality who stepped up to lead the company, but after three weeks of Arden, he had withdrawn into sullen, stormy silence. Lately he had stopped addressing his leading lady directly and had taken to routing all his communication through Ezra, a gently bearish man who was growing increasingly frazzled as opening night approached. Isobel was surprised now to see Chris saunter onstage and whisper something in Arden's ear, prompting her to glower at him and retreat to the wings.

"Even divas get sick," Isobel remarked. "Better safe than sorry."

Sunil gave Isobel an appraising look. "If I didn't know you as well as I do, I'd warn that girl to watch her back."

Isobel flicked her eyes toward him. "Are you being purposely obnoxious today?"

"I assure you, it's completely accidental."

"Ha ha."

"Trust me, you're better off playing Emma."

"Jennie is the lead. She's Sousa's wife. Emma is a passing fancy. I'm only in act one," Isobel griped.

Sunil raised an eyebrow. "Let me get this straight: you think the show is a piece of crap, but you're complaining your part isn't big enough?"

Isobel crossed her arms defiantly. "What if I am?"

He laughed. "You are so predictable! Look, Jennie is your typical ingénue. Emma has, if you'll pardon the expression, spice." Isobel glared at him, but he went on. "Plus, you get to come back at the end as the hotel maid who finds him dead."

"I have two lines and a scream," she said. "About what you have in act two as the Indian chief who makes Sousa an honorary chieftain."

"I don't scream—I chant." Sunil twirled the walking stick that rested horizontally across his knee. "Isn't it time someone told Felicity she hired the wrong kind of Indian? I'm pretty sure the Pawnee Nation doesn't have a Delhi tribe."

Isobel resisted the urge to look several rows behind her, where Felicity Hamilton, artistic director of Livingston Stage, was sitting. Felicity was in her late fifties, short and stocky with impeccably coiffed black hair, a deceptively warm smile, and a calculating gaze. She had never married, but despite an apparent absence of maternal warmth, she treated her nephew and godchild Jethro like a son. It was Jethro Hamilton, a self-described Sousa fanatic, who had written the book and lyrics to *Sousacal*. The musical was Jethro's baby, and, in his way, Jethro was Felicity's.

"She thinks she's getting points for non-traditional casting," Isobel said. "Don't kill the dream."

"Where she's really getting them is casting a brown person to play Philadelphia gentleman and man of the church Benjamin Swallow, your...gulp...stepfather."

Isobel knew that Sunil, an Indian Jew, was perennially frustrated by the inability of directors to see past his ethnicity and hire him for the beautiful tenor he had inherited from his cantor father.

She patted his hand. "It's utility casting. They had to give us small parts because we're covering the leads." She eyed him curiously. "You are looking over Sousa's stuff, right?"

Sunil pulled his hand away. "I've glanced at it."

"Glanced...?" Isobel's jaw fell open. "It's huge! Sousa carries the show."

"Eh, it's pretty much sunk in by osmosis. Besides, you know actors. They'll drag themselves onstage coughing and hacking rather than turn their creation over to a scheming understudy. You know, I'm not even the—"

"What if something serious happened to Chris? And what if there were a Broadway producer in the audience and you had to go on?"

Sunil snorted. "As if Broadway cares a hoot about what happens in the boonies."

"Last I checked, Albany was the state capital."

"Like I said, the boonies. Theatrically and politically," Sunil cracked.

"Plenty of Tony winners are launched in regional theaters like Livingston," she reminded him.

Sunil unbent his long legs and stretched them out under the seat in front of him. "Let's review all the reasons that's never going to happen with *Sousacal*. Number one: the show sucks. Number two: the show sucks. And number three: it's not very good."

Isobel turned a page with a dainty finger. "Then you won't be interested in what I heard from Thomas in the costume shop."

"Probably not." Sunil yawned ostentatiously and tipped his straw boater over his face.

"Arden, back onstage, please." Kelly's voice echoed over the God mic. "We'll finish the duet and move on to the wedding without stopping. Ensemble, please be ready for your entrance."

Isobel set her script on the seat next to her and nudged Sunil. "Come on. Time to make the donuts."

He righted his hat with a groan and led her down the aisle. They skirted the orchestra pit via a set of narrow utility stairs and took their places offstage left.

"So, what did you hear in the costume shop?" Sunil asked casually.

"I thought you weren't interested," Isobel teased.

"I'm not. I'm bored."

Isobel's eyes darted around the wings. Three chorus women, locals whom Isobel didn't know well, were fussing with their costumes, which they were all wearing for the first time. One of the ensemble men was trying to draw out the shy little boy who played young Sousa, while two others were engaged in a quiet but intense conversation. Satisfied that nobody was listening, Isobel returned her attention to Sunil.

"Someone from the Donnelly Group is coming opening night."

"The Broadway producers?" Sunil waved her off. "I don't believe it."

"Thomas says all they have in the pipeline is revivals, and they're scouting for something new," Isobel insisted. "And you know as well as I do, if you want to know what's going on, ask the costume shop."

"Still don't believe it."

"And…continue," Kelly called.

Chris and Arden picked up, rather mechanically, in the middle of act one, scene seven. Isobel watched them intently, mouthing Jennie's lines while Sunil eyed her in amusement.

"You're really taking this seriously," he whispered.

She ignored him and continued, but stopped abruptly when Arden veered from the script.

"I can't sit on the gazebo bench if that spotlight is right in my eyes," Arden announced.

"We'll adjust it on the break," Kelly said. "If you stand on six, you should be in the clear."

Arden shuffled over a few inches. "Now I'm in the dark."

"Those are your choices right now. We'll fix the cue later," Kelly said.

Chris reached for Arden. "Oh, Jennie, you've made me the happiest man on earth. Please? Not just a tiny kiss?"

Arden stepped forward and shaded her eyes from the bright stage lights. "Ezra, I need a fan for this scene. It's summer and she would have one."

"Jesus Christ," Chris muttered.

"We'll get you a fan," Ezra boomed from the back of the house. "Go on."

Chris repeated his line. "Not just a tiny kiss?"

"Not until I have a fan," Arden said.

"Something I'll never be," Chris retorted.

"Ooh, snap," breathed Sunil.

Arden shot Chris a murderous look.

"I will get you one for tomorrow's dress," Ezra shouted. "Finish the goddamn scene!"

Arden turned to Chris and batted her eyelashes unconvincingly. "Not until we're married," she said with a tight-lipped smile.

From the orchestra pit, the piano launched into the intro to Sousa's famous march, "The Washington Post." Chris dropped to one knee, flung his arms wide, and sang in a lusty bari-tenor:

> *I'll probably die if you don't kiss me,*
> *Yes, that's what I most want you to do,*
> *You simply have got to see it through!*

As Chris pulled Arden onto his knee, Sunil continued the verse, singing his own lyrics into Isobel's ear:

> *I'll die if I ever have to sing that!*
> *I'll fall off the stage and land on my head,*
> *And then I'll be just as good as dead!*

Isobel let out a squawk of laughter, which was topped by an even louder shriek from the stage, where Arden was jumping up and down, clutching the back of her thigh.

"Stop!" Kelly called out over the mic. "Are you okay?"

"There's a wire sticking out on this stupid bustle!"

"Thomas? Are you in the house?" Kelly asked.

"Coming!" The lean, blond costume designer loped down the aisle and took the utility stairs by twos. "Okay, princess, let's see what the problem is."

He led Arden into the wings next to Isobel and Sunil. Arden spun around, allowing Thomas to hike up her skirts and examine the bustle, which was knotted around her waist under the candy-cane-striped dress.

"Yeah, I see it. Heather, do you have pliers or something?"

The mousy, wide-eyed assistant stage manager hopped down from her stool, rummaged in a box on the floor, and retrieved a slightly rusted pair of pliers. Arden turned around, hands on hips, facing Isobel, while Thomas adjusted the padded wire contraption.

"Those things are a pain in the ass," Isobel said sympathetically. "Literally."

Arden's lip curled. "Oh, look, it's my stalker. Probably wishing the wire had hit an artery."

"I'm just doing my job," Isobel said defensively.

Thomas released Arden's skirts and let them fall to the floor. "You're fixed."

"We're good," Heather reported into her headset.

"Back onstage, please," Kelly called over the mic.

With exaggerated courtesy, Isobel pulled aside the black masking curtain. But as Arden flounced toward the stage, the entire length of material came down from the ceiling, burying *Sousacal*'s leading lady under its heavy folds.

TWO

ARDEN THRASHED AROUND trying to untangle herself, her cries muffled under the drapery. Heather and Thomas managed to unwrap her, while Isobel stood rooted to the spot, staring uncomprehendingly at the length of masking still in her hand. With a start, she let it fall, just as Arden emerged from the mass of felt, her face crimson, panting with fury.

"You bitch! What the fuck was that?"

"It was an accident! I hardly touched it." Isobel looked up at the bare pipe swaying high above their heads.

Sunil knelt down and examined the top of the curtain. "The ties aren't torn."

"I don't see how it could have fallen," Heather said nervously. "We tied them pretty tight."

"They must have gotten loose somehow," Isobel said, turning her hands over as if trying to determine whether she could possibly have developed superhuman strength without realizing it.

"What happened?" Ezra arrived in the wings with Kelly on his heels.

"Isobel moved the masking aside and it came down," Heather explained.

Kelly consulted her stopwatch. "We're due for a break anyway. Heather, get Dan and check the rest of the masking. Everyone else, back in twenty."

Thomas put up his hand for attention. "I've taken my notes, so change out of costume, please. We still have work to do." He laid a gentle hand on Arden's shoulder. "Any damage?"

"No." Arden looked daggers at Isobel. "Despite her best efforts."

"I told you. It was an accident," Isobel said, tearing up in spite of herself.

Sunil took her elbow. "Come on, let's get changed."

Isobel shook him off and wheeled on Arden. "How can you think I pulled it down on purpose?"

Arden's blue eyes were icy. "You're always in the wings mouthing my lines and mimicking my moves. You'd love to get me out of the way so you can play Jennie."

Isobel let out a gasp and pointed to Arden's chest.

Startled, Arden glanced down. "What?"

"Your paranoia is showing," Isobel spat and stalked off.

"Oh, man, you took that over the line," Sunil said, catching up with Isobel as she stormed up the stairs, holding her skirt up.

"She's crazy."

"Look, whoever hung the masking obviously didn't tie the ties tight enough. She should realize it wasn't you, but you can't blame her for thinking it."

Isobel paused on the landing. "If Arden is so insecure that she's threatened by my learning her role—which, by the way, I'm being paid to do—then I'm the least of her problems." She thrust an accusing finger at him. "And *you* should be learning Sousa. What happened just now is proof of that."

"Yeah, that's kind of my point."

"I don't like your point."

"Where are you going? Thomas told us to change."

"I want to see Hugh."

They emerged onto the third floor, where the orchestra was having their first rehearsal. Even better than sharing her first regional theater job with Sunil, Isobel's boyfriend Hugh Fremont had been hired as the show's musical director. Isobel pushed open the door to the large studio with more force than she intended, and it slammed against the wall with a bang. Fortunately, the rehearsal was over and the musicians were packing up, filling the air with chatter. Hugh stood on a small podium, speaking to a trumpet player. Isobel liked observing him from afar. He was handsome in a bookish way, with wavy chestnut hair and green eyes behind tortoiseshell glasses. Perhaps because he was British, his gestures both on the podium and in life were elegant and restrained. He adored her, and even if she wasn't quite as head over heels with him as he was with her, the sight of him calmed her.

"Hugh could have done it," Sunil said, jolting her out of her silent admiration.

"Why would Hugh rig the masking?"

"No, I mean he could have written a delightfully witty original score for this show instead of leaving us singing Jethro's cringeworthy lyrics to recycled Sousa marches."

"You're right." Isobel flushed with girlfriendly pride as Hugh came toward them. "He's a brilliant composer."

"Talking about me again, are you?" Hugh gave Isobel a kiss.

"Actually, yes. We were agreeing that you should have written the score," Sunil said.

"Oh, I was joking," Hugh said, flustered at having unintentionally paid himself a compliment.

"Sunil's right," Isobel said. "You'd have written great music, not to mention superior lyrics."

"Oh, I don't know. I've grown rather fond of 'It's time that I start my own band' as an alternative to being kind to our web-footed friends," he said with a mischievous grin.

"Shhh!" Isobel giggled. "Jethro is right over there."

"Oh, yes, lucky me," Hugh said. "He's been running up and down between your rehearsal and mine, driving me absolutely bonkers with meaningless orchestration questions. Oh dear, now he's tackled poor Woodiel."

Isobel and Sunil followed Hugh's gaze. Jethro Hamilton was blocking the path to the coffeemaker, gesticulating wildly at the bewildered trumpeter. If Isobel hadn't known better, she'd have pegged Jethro as one of those overgrown, socially awkward, unformed men of thirty-five who fritter their lives away in the family basement hacking the Minecraft servers of unsuspecting middle schoolers. In fact, Jethro was an adjunct history professor who had parlayed his lifelong obsession with John Philip Sousa into a musical. He had also self-published two historical mysteries and sang in a barbershop quartet called the Sundaes.

Hugh gathered the pens and pencils scattered on his music stand and tucked them into his shirt pocket. "Let's escape while we can."

They hurried out of the room and pulled up short in front of the stairwell.

"Where to?" Isobel asked. "We're only on a twenty, and we still have to change out of costume."

"We could run out to the 7-Eleven and get sandwiches," Sunil suggested.

"It's too cold to go out," Isobel protested. "Let's just get a quick snack in the café."

They returned to the main floor, where the expansive seating area was occupied by quiet clusters of cast and crew. At the table nearest the door, Arden was chattering at top speed to Marissa Doyle, who doubled as Sousa's stoic, German-born mother and his business partner's litigious widow, Mrs. Blakely. Marissa was in her late twenties, roughly the same age as Arden, but her plump frame, frizzy hair, and belty alto had already relegated her to character roles. Isobel found Marissa funny and down-to-earth, but only when Arden wasn't around. The two were housed together with Ezra and Chris in one of two condos provided for the out-of-towners, and they seemed to have struck up a friendship. Isobel was shrewd enough to realize that Marissa's intermittent frostiness was a show of loyalty to Arden, but still, it upset her.

"And then that little bitch pulled the whole damn thing down on me," Arden finished breathlessly.

Marissa had the grace to blush, but the trio couldn't escape before Arden spotted them.

"Speak of the devil," she said waspishly.

Before Isobel could frame a response, Sunil pulled her back and led the way toward the theater lobby.

"Anyone want to tell me what that was all about?" Hugh asked.

As they continued down the hall, Isobel filled him in on what had happened backstage.

"That's unfortunate," Hugh said. "Arden is not untalented, but she's hopelessly miscast. She probably knows as well as the rest of us that you would have been much better in the role."

"Then why didn't I get it?" Isobel plopped sulkily onto an upholstered bench.

"Darling, we've been over this. Felicity had to cast a union actor in the lead. That is absolutely, positively the only reason you didn't get it. I was at the callbacks, remember? They all went nuts over you. Especially Jethro."

"He told me to look up photos of Jennie Sousa online," Isobel said. "He said I looked exactly like her, and he's right. It's a real resemblance. It's not superficial."

"Look, Arden is the kind of person who's going to feel threatened whether or not she has a reason," Sunil said. "She probably thinks she lost Miss America because Miss South Carolina stole her butt glue."

Hugh laughed. "Butt glue?"

"Yeah, it keeps their swimsuits in place," Sunil said.

"I'm not even going to ask how you know that," Isobel said.

"I dated a pageant girl in college," Sunil explained. "I can also tell you about nipple covers, duct tape, and spoons. But I digress. My point is, all you can do is keep your head down and do your work."

"Ah! So now it's okay that I'm taking my understudying obligations seriously?"

"All I'm saying is that you should just do your job. No more, no less."

"He's right. It never hurts to be discreet," Hugh said. "Wait…spoons?"

"Cold spoons on your eyes," Sunil said in confidential tones. "Gets rid of the bags in no time." He snapped his fingers for emphasis.

Isobel gave an exasperated sigh and turned to Hugh. "How did your rehearsal go? Better than ours, I hope."

"Well, nobody got beaned by falling scenery. There were a few surprises in the parts, and as far as the drummer was concerned, time is a magazine. But all the cuts worked, which was what I was most concerned about. Oliver and I spent hours marking them all in, and we were so bleary by the end it wouldn't have surprised me if they'd been a complete disaster."

"Too bad Oliver got stuck accompanying our tech rehearsal," Isobel said, thinking of Hugh's unfailingly eager assistant.

"That's all right. He'll get to hear the orchestra at the dress tomorrow. You all will."

"Dress!" Isobel sprang to her feet. "We were supposed to change. Come on!"

She planted a noisy kiss on the top of Hugh's head and sprinted toward the stairwell, Sunil on her heels. In her dressing room, Isobel divested herself of her elaborate costume as quickly as she could and hung it on the rack next to her name card. Comfortable once more in jeans and one of Hugh's sweaters, she returned to the theater feeling more sanguine. The anticipation of singing with the orchestra for the first time had jolted her out of her doldrums. So what if the show was terrible and she should really be playing the lead?

Her script was lying open next to the seat she'd inhabited earlier. Isobel gasped and snatched it up.

In crude block lettering, someone had scrawled, "Die, bitch!" with an arrow pointing to one of Jennie's pink highlighted lines.

THREE

ISOBEL RIPPED THE OFFENDING page from her binder, crumpled it in her hand, and furiously thumbed through the rest of her script looking for more graffiti. Arden must have written it as a warning to back off learning her role. Isobel paused. But if that were the case, why not scribble across the whole page, totally defacing it? She uncrumpled the paper and examined it again. The arrow was pointing very precisely to the name Jennie, the point colliding with the J. Maybe she was wrong. Maybe whoever wrote it was trying to make it look like Isobel had it in for Arden. But who would go to that kind of trouble? And why?

She looked around the theater. Cast and crew members were scattered around, both on and offstage. Breaks were determined according to Equity rules, which meant that the crew generally worked through them. Furthermore, some actors might have changed their costumes and returned more or less immediately to the house. Whoever had defaced Isobel's script had done it brazenly, with plenty of witnesses. On the other hand, nobody would think twice about an actor or even a crew member picking up a script, and if the scribbler had been seated, he or she would have been well hidden from prying eyes.

"Are we picking up where we left off or—" Sunil appeared at the end of the row, slightly out of breath, and caught the distress on her face. "What's wrong?"

She pulled down a seat for him and handed over the script page.

He scanned it, his brow creasing in concern. "You have to show this to someone."

"I can't," she said. "Don't you see? It looks like I wrote it about Arden."

He looked up. "What? No, it doesn't. Why would you write 'Die, bitch!' in your own book?"

"Shhh! Because she *is* a bitch."

"Yeah, but you don't need to make a note to remind yourself. And you don't actually want her to die." He hesitated. "Right?"

She smacked his arm. "Don't be ridiculous. You don't think someone is trying to make me look bad?"

"I think you're being paranoid. Someone is threatening you. Probably Arden. I mean, it's *your* script."

"That was my first thought," Isobel admitted. "If that's the case, then it's best to pretend I didn't see it and act like nothing happened."

"I think you should show it to Kelly. She's experienced and not easily ruffled. Not Heather. She strikes me as pretty green."

"I refuse to acknowledge Arden's grandstanding by showing Kelly or anyone else. And what if we're wrong and Arden didn't write it, and I accidentally show it to the person who did?"

"You're reading way too much into this. You pissed off Arden when you pulled the masking down on her. You heard her in the café. Of course she wrote it."

Isobel sat up. "What if the masking wasn't an accident? What if someone rigged it for me to bring down on Arden?"

"How many times have you moved the masking aside for Arden?"

"I've never had the opportunity before."

"Exactly. And it was sheer chance that you happened to do it today. Let's say someone did loosen the ties on the masking on purpose. How could they predict it would be you who brought it down—and how could they know it would be on Arden?"

"I guess you're right," Isobel said uncertainly. "You don't think somebody is going out of his or her way to frame my conscientiousness as something more sinister?"

"I think you've developed a tendency to infer malice aforethought because you solved a few mysteries last year. But you're looking for meaning where there is none."

"You're sure?"

"I'm sure."

Isobel wasn't convinced, but she stuffed the page into her pocket and put the matter out of her mind for the rest of the afternoon rehearsal.

By the time the company broke for dinner, the general consensus was that things were moving more quickly than anticipated. Isobel, Sunil, and Hugh decided to splurge at a nearby Chinese restaurant. When they returned for the evening rehearsal, Isobel had a long stretch when she wasn't needed onstage, so she joined Hugh in the pit to help him and Oliver touch up the few mistakes Hugh had identified in the orchestra parts that morning. Over the monitors, they heard Marissa and Chris rehearsing the scene where Mrs. Blakely threatens to ruin Sousa if he doesn't pay royalties to her husband's estate.

"I need higher stakes from you both," Ezra instructed them.

"It's a friggin' tech rehearsal," Chris said.

"And you may as well use it to work on the scene. Which needs work," Ezra snapped.

"Ezra does not sound gruntled," Hugh remarked.

"It's not their fault," Isobel said, shaking a bottle of Wite-Out. "There are no stakes. Sure, they squabble over the band's royalties, but it's not exactly the stuff of great drama."

"Ezra is well aware," Hugh said. "That's why his only hope is to get them to commit one hundred and ten percent."

"It's a losing battle."

"You know what's a losing battle?" Oliver piped up. "Trying to get Jethro to fix the story. It's not like John Philip Sousa's going to see it and complain that the details of his life are wrong. If it isn't dramatic, rewrite it. Change it. Add some tension, manufacture conflict. But don't put the audience to sleep for the sake of historical accuracy."

"Hear, hear," Hugh concurred.

"And that's exactly why screaming at Marissa and Chris isn't going to help the scene. Or the show. It's a fundamental flaw in the narrative." Isobel screwed the top back on the Wite-Out. "This is empty."

Hugh yawned and pushed away the second trombone part he was working on. "I don't know about you, but I could use a cuppa."

"There's coffee in the green room," Isobel said.

Hugh gave her hand an affectionate squeeze. "A cuppa is only ever tea. And that's what my sleepy British soul is craving. Hold the fort, Ollie, there's a good chap."

"You know, he doesn't always talk like Lord Grantham," Isobel told Oliver. "Only when he's making fun of himself."

She linked her arm through Hugh's, and they exited the orchestra pit into the vom underneath the stage, so named for the vomitoria in Roman amphitheaters. Stairs on either side of the curving passage led to stage level and the wings, and offstage left, a second flight continued up to the dressing rooms and the green room. Despite the fact that every backstage lounge was called the green room, Isobel had yet to be in one that was actually painted green.

Livingston Stage Company's non-green room was empty at present, but the coffeepot on the sideboard was full. Isobel poured herself a cup as Hugh microwaved water for tea. Leaning against the counter, she felt the crumpled script page in her pocket and suppressed a fleeting impulse to show it to Hugh.

"This isn't ideal, you know," he said, indicating the humming microwave. "As my Irish friend Niall says, 'ye can't make tea unless it's bailin'.'"

"Two minutes on high isn't close enough?"

"No, and neither are you." He pulled her toward him and kissed her. She melted at the warm softness of his mouth. "You're not on for a while, right?" he murmured.

"Mhm."

They maneuvered to the lumpy couch, a green room staple, and made themselves comfortable. The microwave beeped, but Hugh ignored it.

They were interrupted by Sunil not long after. Isobel and Hugh sprang apart, grinning sheepishly.

"We're on a five," Sunil said, unfazed. "I thought I'd give you a heads-up before the rabble descends."

"You're a pal," Isobel said.

She and Hugh pulled themselves together as the other actors invaded, in various states of grumbling and exhaustion, heading straight for the kitchenette. Isobel glanced at her watch. Nine thirty. They were called until midnight. She left Hugh and returned to the sideboard to retrieve her cup.

"Hey, somebody took my coffee," she said.

Heather set the empty pot back on the hot plate after pouring out the last cup for herself. "I'll make more."

"Thanks, but at this point, I probably shouldn't. I'll be up all night." Hugh's water was still in the microwave, so Isobel programmed another minute to reheat it. Heather rinsed out the coffeepot and measured heaping tablespoons of dark roast into a new filter.

"How far did we get?" Isobel asked.

"Not far enough," Kelly said, coming up behind them. "We finished with Marissa and Chris, but the touring medley is next, and that will take a while."

After the break, Isobel followed the others back into the theater and took her place onstage next to Sunil. Most of the company doubled in this scene as Sousa's band, wielding dented brass instruments on loan from a local high school. She mimed playing trombone, while Hugh and Oliver banged out "King Cotton" on the piano four-hands. Chris, as Sousa, shifted his weight from side to side as he pretended to conduct.

"And...hold," Kelly called.

Chris mumbled something and dashed offstage.

"I want to spike that bench," Kelly continued. "Heather?"

Isobel glanced into the wings, but the assistant stage manager was not at her desk.

"I don't see her."

"Dan?"

When Kelly got no response from the tech director, she clambered over Ezra, who was folded into his seat, and jogged down the aisle to the stage. She climbed the utility stairs, then knelt down and made a tiny L in bright green tape on the floor by the front right corner of the bench.

She rose and looked around. "Where did Chris go?"

"He said he'd be right back," said Talia Romano. Talia, a dark-haired, alabaster-skinned soprano, was playing Marjorie Moody, the opera singer who soloed with Sousa's band. "Can I mark my aria when we get to it? I don't want to sing full out this late."

"Yeah, whatever. We can't wait for Chris. Sunil, can you cover?"

Sunil started in surprise, and Isobel gave him a push forward. He took his place and raised his arms to conduct, flashing Isobel a smile, as if to say, "No worries. I've got this." Hugh and Oliver started to play again, and Kelly trotted back down the steps.

"Talia's right. It's getting late, so let's skip to the—" She looked around. "Where's Ezra?"

"He took off like a bat out of hell a minute ago," Thomas called from the back row, where he was basting a hem.

"Where is everyone?" Kelly asked. Suddenly, her face went white. "Oh, shit!"

And she, too, was down the aisle like a shot and out the main exit into the lobby. Isobel scrambled down the steps and ran out after her. As she reached the lobby, she saw the door to the women's bathroom swing shut. She waited a moment and then followed Kelly in.

"Kelly? Are you okay?"

"Oh…man," Kelly groaned from inside a stall.

"Can I get you anything?" Isobel offered.

"Noooo…"

Isobel crept out of the bathroom and started back to the theater. On a whim, she crossed the lobby and inched open the door to the men's bathroom.

"Ezra?"

"Get the fuck out of here!" he bellowed.

She let the door slam, turned the corner down the hallway that led to the stage door, and hurried upstairs to the green room. Sunil was standing guard in front of the bathroom door.

"Chris?" she asked.

"Yup."

"It's like everyone has stomach flu or something," Isobel said. "Where's Heather?"

"Maybe the other bathroom?"

He followed her down the hall, and she jiggled the doorknob. "Heather?"

"Um…just a sec…"

Isobel turned to Sunil. "Jeez. Anyone else?"

"I hope not. We're running out of bathrooms," Sunil said.

"There's one in the vom, stage right."

They chugged downstairs and poked their heads into the pit, where Hugh and Oliver were chatting.

"What's up?" Hugh asked.

"Not sure," Isobel said. "A bunch of people seem to have been seized by a collective need to use the bathroom."

Oliver jerked his thumb to the right. "I saw Dan run past a while ago."

"We are now officially out of toilets," Isobel declared.

"Don't the dressing rooms have them?" Hugh asked.

"Some do, some don't." Isobel motioned to Sunil. "Come on. Let's see who else we've lost."

Marissa was in the bathroom in the dressing room she shared with Arden, and Talia was now occupying Sunil and Chris's.

Isobel and Sunil returned to the stage, where Arden was standing dead center, irate.

"Where the hell is everyone?"

"Bathroom," Isobel said.

Arden narrowed her eyes. "All of them?"

"Actually, yeah."

"Come on, chop, chop!" Jethro Hamilton strode down the aisle toward them. "We can't afford to waste time. We open tomorrow night!"

Sunil surveyed the remains of the decimated company. "Yes, but tech is for Kelly, Heather, Dan, and Ezra to work out the cues. It's their rehearsal, not ours."

The door to the lobby opened, and Kelly staggered down the aisle, her face drenched with sweat.

"Go home," she bleated. "We'll finish tomorrow." She waved at Jethro. "Find Heather, and if you can't, will you shut everything down? I just…can't."

"Stomach flu isn't this coordinated," Sunil whispered to Isobel. "It must be food poisoning or something. Did they all eat the same thing for dinner?"

"I don't think so. Everybody scattered." Suddenly light dawned. "But they all drank the same coffee."

FOUR

ISOBEL FOUND IT DIFFICULT to sleep, partly because she kept replaying the nine-thirty break in the green room, and partly because Talia, who had the room next to her in the condo they shared with Hugh and Sunil, spent most of the night making horrible noises in the bathroom across the hall. Isobel tossed and turned, reminding herself that tomorrow was a big day—dress rehearsal followed by opening night—but that only increased her anxiety. She kept coming back to the coffee. The more she thought about it, the more she was convinced somebody had put some sort of laxative in it.

She remembered watching Heather make the second pot of coffee, and she hadn't seen her add anything. More to the point, Heather had taken the last cup from the first pot and been sick, which meant that if the coffee was indeed the culprit, it was the first pot that had been tampered with. Isobel had poured herself a cup from that pot, but had left it untouched on the counter when she and Hugh had repaired to the sofa. Whoever had stolen her coffee saved her from a night of cramps and diarrhea. Ha! Served them right. Somebody must have slipped into the empty green room during rehearsal earlier and stirred the laxative into the pot.

But who? And, more importantly, why?

By the time Isobel dragged herself out of bed at ten the following morning, she had come to a disturbing conclusion, which she voiced to Sunil and Hugh over breakfast in the condo's airy kitchen.

"You really think someone is trying to sabotage the show?" Sunil asked, generously cream-cheesing a bagel.

Isobel drummed her fingers on the pine table. "It's three things, isn't it? The masking, the note, and the coffee."

Hugh looked up from his tea. "What note?"

Isobel sighed and handed him the crumpled script page, which was still stuffed in her jeans pocket.

"This isn't funny." He lifted his glasses off his nose and squinted at it more closely. "Who wrote this?"

"That's the question," Isobel said. "Was it Arden threatening me, or was it someone else trying to make it look like I wrote it about Arden? Sunil thinks the former, but given everything else, I'm starting to think the latter. Especially if the masking wasn't an accident."

"Perhaps the scribbler thought it was Arden's script and was threatening her," Hugh suggested.

"A quick glance would ascertain that it was my script," Isobel pointed out. "Emma's lines are highlighted in yellow and Jennie's are pink."

"Well, aren't you organized, Hermione?" Sunil ribbed her.

"Don't you think it's likely that the same person who wrote the note also loosened the masking and doctored the coffee?" She took a bite of Sunil's bagel.

"Hey, get your own!"

Hugh handed the page back to Isobel. "If you're right, then someone could be setting you up. You did pull down the masking, albeit accidentally, and you might have tampered with the coffee while my back was turned."

"You know I didn't. And besides, I poured myself a cup."

"Which you never drank." Hugh took her hand. "Look, I know you didn't mess with the coffee. And I know exactly what kept you from drinking it. But to anyone else, all three things combined with—and please don't take this the wrong way—your eagerness to step into the role, well, it does rather point the finger."

Isobel pushed away from him and stalked over to the refrigerator. She pulled a yogurt from the taped section on the bottom shelf marked "Isobel" and ripped off the foil top angrily.

"Not helpful," she snapped. "And besides, Arden didn't get sick. So can we please focus on who might have done it instead of talking about how everyone thinks it was me?"

"What was you?" Talia stumbled into the kitchen.

Isobel rushed to her, glad of the distraction. "Are you feeling better?"

"A little." Talia sank gratefully into Isobel's chair. "I don't think I can eat anything, though."

Hugh jumped up. "Tea and toast. That's the thing."

"If you say so," Talia said, looking distinctly green.

"I'm curious…did you have coffee on our break last night?" Isobel asked.

"Yeah. There was a cup on the counter that nobody claimed, so I took it."

That's one mystery solved, Isobel reflected and immediately felt guilty for having thought the coffee thief deserved what she got.

"And you're sure that was the one sitting there before Heather made the second pot?"

"I guess. I didn't know she made more. Why?"

"Don't you think it's a little strange that half the company suddenly got the runs last night?" Sunil asked.

"Coffee does make you go," Talia said uncertainly.

"Not like *that*," said Isobel, who had been privy to Talia's ordeal in the privy.

Hugh set some tea and dry toast in front of Talia.

"You think there was something in the coffee?" she asked, tentatively breaking off a corner of toast.

"There isn't anything else that so many people consumed last night," Isobel said. "Everyone split up for dinner. Where did you eat?"

"Marissa invited a couple of us over to the other condo and made a big stir fry," Talia said.

"Oh?" Isobel perked up. "Who went?"

"Me, Arden, and Thomas."

Isobel licked yogurt off her spoon. "Marissa's the only one besides you who was sick."

"I know she had coffee," Talia said. "I was talking to her while she poured it."

"What about Arden and Thomas?" Hugh asked.

"Arden doesn't do caffeine, and I don't know about Thomas."

"What about Ezra, Chris, and Kelly?" Sunil asked.

"Ezra for sure. He used up the last of the creamer. And Chris definitely had some"—Talia sat up, suddenly interested—"because I remember he commented that it needed more sugar because it was a little bitter. Don't know about Kelly."

Sunil threw up his hands. "That's a quorum. Somebody put a laxative in the coffee."

"What?" Talia gasped. "Why?"

"Someone hates ten-out-of-twelves so much they wanted rehearsal to end early?" Sunil suggested.

"Who would do that?" Talia asked, aghast. "We open tonight!"

"Maybe the same person who rigged the masking to fall," Isobel said. "I know we all think the show is flawed, but is there anyone who has that kind of grudge against it?"

Talia blew on her tea to cool it. "Geoff, obviously. But I can't imagine he would do anything like that."

The others exchanged a glance.

"Who's Geoff?" Isobel asked.

"Hugh knows," Talia said.

"You do?"

Hugh withered at Isobel's accusatory glare. "Sorry to disappoint you, but I really don't. Who's Geoff?"

Talia paused, her teacup in midair. "I can't believe you, of all people, don't know about this. I thought Oliver would have filled you in."

"Erm, he has not. Care to enlighten us?"

Talia set her cup down and looked around the table at her expectant audience. "Geoff Brown. Oliver's brother. He wrote the original score to *Sousacal*, and Jethro threw it out last summer."

"What?" Sunil, Hugh, and Isobel exclaimed in unison.

Talia looked at them, bemused. "The show started as their collaboration. Geoff was also supposed to be the musical director, but he walked when Jethro junked his score."

Isobel turned to Hugh. "Remember at my audition when Felicity said they'd recently lost their musical director? It's how you got the job."

Talia nodded. "That's why I assumed you knew."

"I'm surprised Oliver stayed on if Jethro screwed over his brother," Sunil said.

"Maybe Geoff wanted a spy," Talia said.

Or an accomplice, thought Isobel.

"But why would Jethro throw out an original score in favor of recycled Sousa marches?" Hugh asked. "He must have had to rework all his lyrics to get them to fit."

"Geoff's score was music and lyrics. Jethro wrote all new words to fit the marches," Talia explained.

"I can't imagine it's an improvement over Geoff's score," Isobel said. "How bad could it have been?"

Talia's face grew pale. "Um…I don't think I should have had that second piece of toast."

Sunil and Hugh edged their chairs away from the table to give her a clear shot to the bathroom, where loud, gastric noises erupted the moment she slammed the door.

"Well, that was quite a dump," Sunil said.

Isobel smacked him. "Stop that—she's suffering!"

He rubbed his arm. "I meant an information dump. Firing the composer? Talia just gave you a lot to work with."

"But it doesn't quite make sense," Hugh mused. "Musicals aren't written overnight. They must have been working on it together for a while, workshopping it, all that kind of thing. Why toss the score when it's finally been slated for production?"

"It's happened before," Sunil said. "*Little Women* got picked up after a workshop, and then they sacked all the writers before it went to Broadway. *Finding Neverland*, too. Makes you wonder what the producers thought they were picking up."

"The story itself, which is in the public domain, like Sousa's life." Isobel turned to Hugh. "You know Oliver best. Do you think Geoff put him up to sabotaging the show?"

Hugh shook his head vigorously. "I don't see it. For one thing, he's never mentioned Geoff."

"Well, he wouldn't, would he?" Isobel said. "Then you'd start asking questions, and you'd get suspicious as soon as stuff started happening."

"How does Talia know?" Sunil pushed away his empty plate. "Is she that plugged in? I got the impression she was primarily an opera singer."

"She is," Isobel confirmed. "She told me she's doing this to get some theater on her resume."

"In that case, it seems odd that she would know something like this, don't you think?" Sunil asked.

"She could have heard about it from someone who's more connected. In any case, she can't be the only one who knows about Geoff's score or that Oliver is his brother," Isobel said.

"True. And as soon as things started going amiss, anyone with half a brain would start asking questions," Sunil said.

Isobel smiled sweetly at Hugh. "You have half a brain. Will you start asking questions?"

Hugh swept Talia's toast crumbs into a napkin. "It's rather awkward."

"Unless you want Sunil or me to—"

"No, no, I'll do it." Hugh stood. "If an opportunity arises, I will engage Oliver on the subject of his brother's score."

"Thank you." Isobel rose and pecked him on the cheek. "It's best if I keep my nose clean. I don't want to get blamed for whatever happens next."

FIVE

EVERYONE MADE IT TO the dress rehearsal on time that afternoon, although Isobel noted that those who'd had the misfortune to drink the spiked coffee were looking the worse for wear. Arden, however, was raring to go. She stalked up and down the dressing room hallway in her corset and bustle, warming up with yowls, screeches, and tongue twisters.

Talia set her blush on the table in the dressing room she shared with Isobel and put her head in her hands. "I'm going to kill her if she doesn't shut up."

Isobel did up the last three buttons on her bodice as she walked to the door. "I'll take care of it."

Making a mental note to do her warming up in the rehearsal rooms upstairs, she gave Arden a wide berth and went in search of Heather. Isobel found her in the green room, examining the coffeepot.

"So you came to the same conclusion I did," Isobel observed.

"What?" Heather turned around, startled.

"Laxative in the coffee."

"Oh, yeah. I mean we all got sick right after the break." She held up the pot. "I rinsed it out, so today's coffee should be fine. I was about to make some."

"I'm pretty sure the people who got sick drank from the pot you finished, not the pot you made, though I could be wrong."

Heather gave her a curious look. "You've given this a lot of thought."

Isobel shrugged. "I couldn't help noticing. Listen, when you're done, could you politely suggest to Arden that she warm up in her dressing room? Preferably with the door closed. Talia is still feeling crappy, and Arden's singing isn't helping."

"I'll try," Heather said, although she looked cowed by the thought.

"Thanks."

Isobel left Heather spooning coffee grounds into the filter and descended the two flights to the orchestra pit. Hugh beamed with delight when he saw her.

"You look like you stepped out of an episode of *Masterpiece*," he said.

Isobel executed a graceful turn. "I have to say, the costumes are the one thing this show has gotten right. Thomas is a genius." She hitched her eyebrows in the direction of the piano, where Oliver was noodling quietly on the keys.

"Patience," Hugh counseled.

"Never my forte." She picked up the first trumpet part from the nearest stand and shivered with excitement. "Ooh! I can't wait to sing with the orchestra!"

Hugh frowned. "It's a shame we aren't having a *sitzprobe*."

"And why aren't we again?" Like most singers, Isobel looked forward to the *sitzprobe*, a special rehearsal for the cast to sing with the orchestra without the distraction of costumes and staging.

"It was a budget trade-off for five extra musicians. I'm grateful for the players, but it means the pressure's on this afternoon."

"But you said yesterday went well. It should be fine," she reassured him.

"It's more for you than for us. I'll keep the band volume down as best I can, but I don't want everyone to blow out their voices before tonight. Remind me to remind everyone during the warm-up."

"Somehow I doubt you'll need reminding." Isobel touched his arm. "You seem a little nervous. Are you okay?"

Hugh tugged down the cuffs of his plaid button-down shirt. "I always get a bit jittery when it comes time to put it all together."

She pulled him close and gave him a kiss. "Don't worry, you'll be brilliant. You always are."

HUGH WATCHED ISOBEL bounce away, her skirts swishing behind her. She was so lovely and artless, funny and endearing, and, if he was being completely honest, occasionally vexing. He wished he could confide the real reason he was on edge, but he'd been sworn to absolute secrecy. And if there was one thing he knew about Isobel, it was that keeping her mouth shut required a Herculean effort. Word of Broadway producers attending opening night was bound to generate something akin to hysteria among the actors, Isobel especially. Knowing her, she'd make the leap from producers scouting a potential property to being discovered in the supporting role of Emma Swallow. She would only be disappointed when, inevitably, it didn't turn out that way.

And there was still the problem of the show's embarrassing score. John Philip Sousa's marches were magnificent—as marches. They were never meant to be lyricized. God bless the cast for giving it their all, but they just sounded silly. Hugh feared the musical deficits would reflect badly on him, no matter how well he had prepared the cast or how good the orchestra sounded. Finding out that there had once been an original score was a blow. Whatever was wrong with Geoff's version, it had to have been better than what they were stuck with.

Well, there was no use dwelling on what might have been. It was time to employ the stiff upper lip that was his birthright and ensure that both cast and orchestra performed to the best of their abilities. He had been paid extra to reduce Sousa's orchestrations for their relatively limited forces, and he was pleased with the result. That was exactly the sort of thing a Broadway producer might take note of for future reference, but he sternly reminded himself not to get his own hopes up. Hugh was slightly concerned that some of the lighter voices might not be heard above the brass, but there was time to thin out the texture before the evening performance if the afternoon dress revealed problems.

Musicians drifted into the pit, finding their spots, setting down their instruments, and swapping out threadbare seats for ones that offered a little more padding.

"Need anything?" Oliver asked.

He hovered next to Hugh, his backpack slung over one shoulder. Oliver was six years younger than Hugh, twenty-two, with high color in his pale cheeks that contrasted with his straight black hair. He was quick-witted and a good musician, ready to help and happy to entertain himself doing crosswords in pen when he wasn't needed. No matter what Isobel suspected, Hugh couldn't imagine Oliver lurking in the wings plotting sabotage.

"Are all the parts out?" Hugh asked.

Oliver nodded. "I put them on the stands last night during tech."

"Perfect. You'll sit in the house and listen for balance, right?"

"Heading there now."

Hugh hesitated. With the pit filling with musicians, this probably wasn't the best time, but if Oliver could tell him something about his brother's score—for example, that it had been awful—Hugh might feel better about the hand he'd been dealt.

"Hold on." Hugh beckoned Oliver over to the piano, which had been rolled out of the way under the stage, since there was no piano part in the orchestration.

"I recently found out that your brother was supposed to be the musical director. What happened?"

Oliver shrugged. "He got another gig."

This wasn't the answer Hugh was expecting, but perhaps it was the official version.

"So it had nothing to do with his original score being jettisoned? You see, I just figure whatever he wrote had to have been better than this."

Oliver's lip curled slightly. "You can't believe everything you hear."

"Then it's not true?"

Oliver flicked the strap on his backpack. "I didn't say that. It's complicated."

"Places for act one." Kelly's voice came over the monitor.

"Anything in particular you're worried about?" Oliver asked.

"Sorry?"

"Any places where you're particularly concerned about balance?"

"Oh, right. The brass in 'Stars and Stripes' and 'Liberty Bell.' And 'Semper.'"

"Okeydoke."

Oliver waved cheery hellos to a few musicians as he left the pit. Hugh felt like he'd bungled his assignment. He should have given his approach more thought. At the very least, he shouldn't have initiated the conversation right before places. He suddenly had a new appreciation for Isobel's investigative forays. Discreet questioning was harder than he thought.

But not as hard as a full orchestra dress rehearsal without a *sitzprobe*. It was time to focus. He rallied his confidence and took his place on the podium.

"Good afternoon, ladies and gentlemen." He smiled at the assembled faces. "Great work yesterday. Today's watchword is *balance*, so you'll be seeing a lot of this." He lowered his left hand, palm down, to indicate that they should play softer. "Oliver is out in the house taking notes. As soon as the lights go to half, we'll start with the overture."

The house lights dimmed. Hugh raised his baton and concentrated on giving his upbeat in the correct tempo. Getting off to a good start was critical, and the dress rehearsal was the only time the musicians would be focused on him. Once they knew how it went, Hugh could conduct stark naked with a parrot on his shoulder and they'd bury their noses in their books and play on regardless. He knew that phenomenon well enough from his own time playing keyboards in the pit. He'd done one run of an Off-Broadway show for so long he'd taken to reading a magazine while he played the score from muscle memory. But this early in the process, he retained some control, and the truth was, he loved the dangerous feeling that it might not work and it was up to him to make it happen. The excitement of putting all the musical elements together for the first time was more thrilling than being in front of an audience. That was for the actors. This rehearsal was for him.

He brought down his baton, and the orchestra pealed out the beginning of "The Washington Post." For the overture, he didn't have to worry about balance, and he coaxed and gestured, encouraging his players to be bold with the dynamics. He was especially proud of the overture. He'd arranged a medley of Sousa's most famous marches, plus a few obscure ones that he was fond of, like "Nobles of the Mystic Shrine," which segued into...

He raised an eyebrow at the principal flutist, who had played her solo obbligato four bars early.

"Measure forty-six," he called.

She ignored him and continued playing. He was still trying to get her attention when the trombones clashed with the tuba. A few bars later, the horns and trumpets went astray.

"Stop! Stop!" Hugh waved his arms and the players obeyed, bewildered. "I don't know what happened. Let's go back and pick up at measure forty-six, please."

He gave the upbeat and the orchestra began again. To his horror, it sounded exactly the same. He rapped his baton on the stand and turned to the flutist.

"You're tacet. The obbligato comes in four bars later."

"I have forty-six to forty-nine marked as cut."

"That's impossible."

She pointed to her music. Hugh hopped down from the podium and looked for himself. There were pencil marks through the four bars in question, with the Latin word *vide*, meaning "see," divided up on either side as *vi:* and *de:*, the standard method of marking cuts when there was no time or budget to reprint the parts.

"There is a four-bar cut, but it's at the end, remember? Please put those measures back in. Anyone else have those four bars cut?"

"I've got fifty-two to fifty-five out," said the principal trombone.

"And I've got sixty-one to sixty-four," said Woodiel, the lead trumpet.

"No." Hugh tugged on a lock of hair in frustration. "There are only four bars out: ninety-seven to one hundred, and that's for everyone. If you have anything else cut, erase those marks."

"Can we go on, please, Hugh?" Ezra called from the house.

"Yeah, sorry. Just have to fix this."

"We don't have time."

"And I don't have another opportunity," Hugh snapped. "Skip ninety-six to one hundred, please. Everything else stands."

With some players still erasing their parts, Hugh raised his baton and got the overture back on track. He finished with a triumphant flourish, waited for a smattering of applause from the house, and then segued into the opening number, to the tune of Sousa's "El Capitan" march. The ensemble, costumed as the good citizens of Washington, DC, circa 1854, gathered and began to sing:

The Sousas' child is born—
It's a boy, and everyone's happy now!
Though girls are sweet,
Antonio is a happier pappy now.

Talia stepped forward for her solo and was met with a massive cymbal crash, followed by a full orchestral crescendo. She gave Hugh a reproachful look and shook her head to indicate that she had no intention of competing with the wall of sound. Instead, she mouthed the words and exaggerated her gestures.

Still keeping the beat going, Hugh called out, "Folks, that's too loud, and there's no cymbal there, Greg."

Hugh's arms were moving independently of his brain, which was trying to make sense of what he was hearing. They'd fixed every wrong note they'd found at yesterday's rehearsal, and he certainly didn't remember any mismarked cuts or stray cymbal crashes.

The opening number ended without further incident, and as the dialogue continued above him, Hugh leaned forward. "What happened at measure ten?"

"I've got it marked *fortissimo*," Woodiel said.

Several others echoed him.

Hugh felt his throat constrict. "It should be *mezzo piano*. And no cymbal crash." He thumbed through his score. "Looking ahead to the next number, does anyone see anything in his or her part that wasn't there yesterday?"

The principal clarinetist, acting as de facto concertmaster in the absence of a string section, frowned at her music. "I've got *vide* marks from measure twenty-four to thirty-two. I don't remember any cuts in this number from yesterday."

"That's because there aren't any," Hugh said grimly.

A hot flush overtook him as the realization sank in: someone had tampered with the orchestra parts. Which meant he had no idea what the musicians were going to play. His only chance to polish the musical side of things before they faced a paying audience would be a complete waste.

Using his high-backed stool for leverage, Hugh vaulted over the pit rail and dashed up the aisle. Oliver was already heading toward him.

"What's going on down there?"

"Someone messed with the parts. Added cuts, dynamic markings, all kinds of stuff that's not supposed to be there."

Oliver blanched. "We've got to fix them!"

"It's our only dress rehearsal. They can't stop for us," Hugh said. "Best we can do is go over the parts from the end of the show and fix things moving backwards. We won't get to go over the numbers we've already done, but this way at least we can meet in the middle and have a chance of hearing some of the show intact."

"What if we get to a song before we're ready?"

Hugh's stomach sank. "You'll have to play it on the piano. It's not ideal, but there's no point in continuing with cacophony lurking around every bar. I'll get started with the *finale ultimo*. Go tell Ezra what we're doing."

Oliver hurried back up the aisle. As Hugh slung his long legs over the pit rail, he thought back to Oliver's response to his question about Geoff's discarded score. He had described the situation as "a bit complicated."

Hugh wondered what, exactly, that meant.

SIX

ISOBEL HANDED HUGH the trumpet part for the overture. "That's the last of them."

Hugh put his hands over his heart in gratitude. "I don't know what I'd have done without you two."

"I'm just glad we could help," Sunil said.

Distressed by the clams coming from the orchestra, Isobel had poked her head into the pit at her earliest opportunity. When the bassoon player told her about the mistakes in the parts, she had relayed the information to Sunil. Every break they had during the first act, they'd raced to the pit to help Hugh and Oliver make corrections. With four of them on the case, they'd been able to move quickly and had restored all the parts by intermission. As a result, they would be able to run all of act two with the orchestra, whose members had met the debacle with disinterested shrugs and returned to their reading material of choice.

Sunil darted toward the door. "We'd better change for act two."

"I'll catch up with you." Isobel came up behind Hugh and rubbed his shoulders. "You okay?"

He met her hand with his and turned to face her. "My pulse is still racing, but I'll manage. It was quite a shock when everything went to pieces."

"Took us by surprise onstage, that's for sure."

Oliver approached them from the other side of the pit. "Everything's back on the stands. We should be good to go."

"Thanks, Oliver. You were tremendous."

"No problem." He smiled. "That's the gig, isn't it? I'm getting a Coke. You want anything?"

"A Coke would be great, thanks."

"I'd better go," Isobel said.

"Before you do..." Hugh pulled her closer and waited for Oliver to clear the door. "I had a brief chat with Oliver."

"And?"

"He said the reason Geoff isn't musical director is that he got another job."

Isobel frowned. "What about the score?"

"Oliver said it was complicated, but Kelly called places before I could probe further." Hugh smiled weakly. "I guess I'm not a very good detective. It's harder than it looks."

"You didn't do too badly your first time out," Isobel said, trying to mask her disappointment. "There's obviously something there." She pointed to the corrected trumpet part in his hands. "Do you think Oliver did this?"

Hugh exhaled slowly. "As fond as I am of Oliver, I have to admit, the thought did cross my mind. Anyone with a pencil and a sense of mischief could have scribbled haphazardly over the parts. But they were carefully marked with the Latin *vide*. Whoever it was knew exactly what he was doing."

"See that?" Isobel beamed. "You're not so bad at this after all."

"It's more than that, though," Hugh said. "Oliver set the parts out last night. He had all evening to muck about with them before putting them on the stands. It's hard to imagine anyone else going to the trouble, and if his brother did get the shaft, he certainly has good reason to sabotage the musical end of things."

"Right, but what about all the other stuff? We've moved beyond any chance of coincidence." Isobel began to pace. "This seems like another move by the same person, and whoever it is not only has access and a motive, it's someone who knows his or her way around the theater." She pointed to the ceiling. "Whoever rigged the masking would have to know not just how to loosen the ties, but how to get up there. Does that sound like your average assistant musical director?"

"When you put it that way, no. So you don't think it was Oliver?" Hugh asked hopefully.

"Anybody who knows Geoff's history with the show is going to suspect Oliver instantly. If he were going to mess around, he'd do something where he wasn't the number one obvious suspect with motive, means, and opportunity. He's no dope." Isobel fiddled with the lace on her bodice. "You know, yesterday afternoon after the masking and the note in my book, I was sure this was all about Arden, but it's definitely about the show. The note was probably meant for me, the curtain could have fallen on anyone, and Arden doesn't drink coffee. If somebody was targeting her specifically, why do something that could—and did—miss her entirely and get five other people sick?"

"And the mucked-up orchestra parts affected everyone," Hugh pointed out. "You realize that if it wasn't Oliver, whoever tampered with them must have come back late last night or early this morning."

"That's it!" Isobel grabbed his arms excitedly. "I said you were brilliant, and you are. That's why the person wanted rehearsal to end early—not because he or she hates tech! Our saboteur spiked the coffee with a laxative in order to sneak back in and mess with the orchestra parts. The coffee was a means to an end."

"Which means we're looking for a classically-trained musician with a background in theater tech who didn't drink the coffee."

Isobel giggled in spite of herself. "This is starting to sound like *Airplane*."

"What you're saying makes sense, though. It must go beyond you and Arden," Hugh said. "Someone wants to keep this show from opening."

Isobel sobered again. "And there are any number of people who might prefer this piece of dreck never see the light of day. Like those of us singing these ridiculous lyrics."

"Places!" Kelly's voice echoed over the monitor.

Isobel glanced down at her dress. "I have to change. To be continued."

She turned and slammed straight into a staggeringly handsome man she'd never seen before, but who looked vaguely familiar.

"Oh, sorry, I didn't see you."

"So you think the show is a piece of dreck?" he said.

Isobel felt her face grow warm, but before she could stammer her way out of her predicament, he held out his hand.

"Don't sweat it. I'm Geoff Brown, Oliver's brother. And I couldn't agree more."

SEVEN

ISOBEL WOULD HAVE FORFEITED a week's salary to stay downstairs and quiz Geoff. Or at least be a fly on the wall to hear what passed between him and Hugh. But when the band struck up the entr'acte almost immediately, Isobel realized that any exchange between Geoff and Hugh must have been cursory at best. There was no time to change her costume. She'd have to wait until after the opening of act two. Fortunately, she was blocked toward the back of the stage, so she might get away without Thomas noticing.

She tried to concentrate on the words to "Semper Fidelis" ("So gather around and hear the Sousa Band / They have traveled so far and wide / Their appeal cannot be denied"), but she kept being pulled back to something she'd said to Hugh. If they thought tampering with the orchestra parts was one coincidence too many, surely stage management must think the same. Perhaps it was time to go to Kelly.

"May I present Miss Marjorie Moody," said Chris, as Sousa.

Why hadn't there been a company meeting? Some kind of warning issued?

"May I present Miss Marjorie Moody," Chris repeated, more deliberately.

Sunil elbowed Isobel, and she jumped.

"Marjorie Moody? I've never heard of her." The line flew from Isobel's mouth automatically.

"If Sousa's got her, she must be good," Sunil responded. Although he said the line in character, his eyes telegraphed a message to pay attention.

Talia swept forward in a beaded lilac gown and dropped a deep curtsy. The orchestra struck up the accompaniment to "Ah, fors'è lui" from *La Traviata*, which, to Isobel's ears, sounded bizarre without a string section. With one foot in the opera world herself, Isobel might have been jealous of Talia getting to sing the famous aria, except that it didn't suit Isobel's light lyric soprano.

She forced herself to stay focused until the aria ended. The ensemble dispersed, and Arden and Chris began their scene. In the wings, Isobel pulled Sunil over to a quiet spot next to the props table. Before he could question her about her lapse onstage, she told him about the surprise visitor in the pit.

"How long has Geoff been lurking around the theater?" Sunil asked.

"Good question."

"And what is he doing here at all?"

"Gloating over the failure of a property he was once deeply involved in?" Isobel suggested.

"If he's sure it's destined to fail, then why is he sabotaging it?"

"To be fair, we don't know for a fact that he is." Isobel tucked a stray wisp of hair under her wig.

Sunil twirled his straw boater in his hands. "Nothing so far has succeeded in stopping the show. The masking, the coffee, even the orchestra parts—minor setbacks at best."

"I'm not sure Hugh would agree that the problem with the parts was minor, but I take your point," she said.

Sunil made a sudden move toward the stairs.

"What? What is it?" she asked.

"I have to change into my Pawnee costume!"

She put a restraining hand on his arm. "That's after the end of the international touring medley."

"Didn't we just do that?"

"No, that was the seaside concert scene."

"Are you sure?"

"Positive. The touring medley is the one where Talia sings 'Je suis Titania.'"

Sunil let out a long, slow breath. "Jeez. Who can tell? It's the same friggin' scene over and over again."

"They are narratively redundant," Isobel agreed. "But most shows have second-act problems."

Sunil raised an eyebrow. "And first-act problems?"

"You're getting off the point."

"And the point was?"

"It was yours, actually. That these little things have been annoying, but none of them has succeeded in stopping the show. Which raises an interesting question."

"What?"

"How much mischief is the person trying to make? Just enough to make this an uphill battle, or does someone really want to keep the show from opening?"

"Does it matter?" Sunil asked.

"Of course it matters. Because if the person's mission is to stop the show, it remains unaccomplished."

Sunil shifted his weight nervously. "Meaning you think something more serious might happen?"

Isobel felt a sudden shiver. She wrapped her arms around herself. "I don't know. Maybe. But if someone wants to keep an audience from seeing the show, time is running out."

"We have to go to Kelly," Sunil declared. "As soon as rehearsal's over."

They made it through act two without a hitch, and the orchestra played Hugh's corrected arrangements beautifully. After staging the curtain call, the company was given ten minutes to change out of costume before they reconvened in the house for notes. Ezra went first, praising their performances and giving no adjustments, which Isobel took to mean he'd given up on them. He was followed by Hugh, whose comments were necessarily limited to act two.

"I apologize for not giving you my full attention in act one, due to difficulties with the orchestra parts. But it's all been straightened out."

Arden's hand shot into the air. "You mean we're going to do act one with the orchestrations for the first time tonight—in front of an audience? In front of Broadway producers?"

After a stunned silence, everyone began chattering at once. Some company members had obviously been given a heads-up and were nodding smugly at each other. Others, their faces a mix of excitement and terror, were clearly hearing this news for the first time. Isobel gave Sunil a told-you-so look.

Kelly clapped her hands. "Enough! There are no Broadway producers coming tonight. I don't know who started that rumor, but it isn't true."

Several heads swiveled toward Thomas, who shrugged innocently.

"Thank God," Sunil murmured under his breath as Isobel wilted.

Hugh smiled gratefully at Kelly and jumped back in. "I promise we will be as attentive to balance issues tonight in act one as we were this afternoon during act two. Oliver gave me a few notes, but mostly it was quite good."

"What was the problem anyway?" Arden pressed. "If you had an orchestra rehearsal yesterday, why did it sound like shit?"

All eyes turned to Hugh, who cleared his throat. "There was...erm..." He caught Isobel's eye, and she gave an encouraging nod. "Somebody decided to have some fun with the parts and mark in cuts that didn't exist."

The company immediately began to chatter again.

Chris's outraged tones rang out above the others. "What kind of jerk would do a thing like that?"

Isobel saw Hugh's eyes flick toward Oliver, who had turned to reassure Talia. A quick glance around the auditorium confirmed that Geoff was nowhere in sight. If he had stayed to watch the rehearsal, he had since disappeared.

"I don't know," Hugh answered. "Somebody having a bit of a lark, I suppose. But I'm keeping the parts with me this afternoon, so there's no chance of it happening tonight."

Jethro stood up. "Hugh, if you're done, I have a few notes."

A rustle of annoyance ran through the company.

Jethro turned eagerly to the principals, who were clustered in the same row. "Chris, I don't like that menacing tone you're getting when you and Marissa argue about the royalties."

Chris darted a sideways glance at Ezra. "Um, yesterday Ezra asked us to raise the stakes. He wanted me to be more assertive."

"You're John Philip Sousa, granddaddy of the march." Jethro spread his arms in an expansive gesture, nearly clocking Heather with his clipboard. "You're an upbeat personality and a gentleman."

"Even an upbeat gentleman is going to fight for his rights if they're challenged," Chris argued.

Jethro ran an agitated hand through his mop of ginger hair. "Sousa's our hero. The audience has to root for you. Nobody's going to root for a man who berates a woman the way you did."

"I didn't write the scene. You did."

"It's not supposed to be an out-and-out fight."

"You do know that *drama* in Greek means conflict," Chris said.

"Jethro, why don't you and I talk through any acting notes first, and I'll pass along what I think is necessary," Ezra said diplomatically. "Maybe you can stick to things that pertain directly to the material."

"This does pertain to the material," Jethro snapped. "I didn't write Sousa as an argumentative asshole."

"And Chris isn't playing him that way," Ezra said steadily. "He's merely pursuing his objective in the scene, which is to protect his royalty share."

"He comes off like an argumentative asshole," Jethro insisted.

"I don't suppose Ezra's going to employ the 'takes one to know one' defense," whispered Sunil.

"We've discussed this, Jethro," Ezra said. "It's not up to you to give the actors performance notes. That's my job."

"Which you have proven incapable of doing to my satisfaction."

Isobel sucked in her breath. "There's no way this ends well."

"We can discuss this with Chris after—"

"And another thing," Jethro interrupted him. "Isobel—"

She sat up, startled to hear her name.

"You need to be sweeter and not too forward. Emma isn't a sex kitten."

"But she and Sousa are flirting," Isobel protested. "That's the whole reason her stepfather wants to break them up. She's the soubrette."

"She isn't a hussy." Jethro's voice went up a few notches.

"Okay, folks, we have to break," Kelly intervened. "Equity rules."

Jethro waved his notebook. "I'm not done! I have more—"

"Great work this afternoon. Everyone back at half hour for opening night," Kelly steamrolled him. "Thank you!"

The company scrambled to their feet and fled as quickly as they could.

"Arden? Arden, wait! I've got quite a few notes for you." Jethro hurried out after her.

"This is bullshit!" Ezra exploded. He whirled on Kelly. "He is out of line. I don't want him approaching my actors. If you don't stop him, I will."

Kelly held up her hands defensively. "I don't have the authority to stop him."

"Then I'll go to the person who does." Ezra stormed off.

"Good luck with that," Kelly muttered.

Isobel glanced at Sunil. "Maybe this isn't the time..."

"There is no other time. We open in three hours." Sunil exited their row and marched over to the stage management table. Isobel followed, excusing herself as she squeezed past Marissa, who was chewing a strand of frizzy hair and staring at the floor.

"I've never seen him lose his temper like that," Heather was saying as Isobel and Sunil approached.

"Oh, there have been quite a few blowups between those two," Kelly replied. "Ezra's come close to quitting more than once."

"Why hasn't he?" Isobel asked.

"A job's a job," Kelly said. "What's up?"

"We were talking about what happened with the orchestra parts and wondering whether it might be connected to the other stuff," Sunil said.

"What other stuff?"

"Well, the masking that fell," Isobel said. "Then the fact that so many people got sick after drinking the same coffee last night. And this note." She saw Marissa looking over curiously, and she angled her body away. She handed the script page to Kelly.

"When did you find this?" Kelly asked.

"Yesterday, after the first break. I'd left my script in the house. The thing is, I don't know if it's intended for me or Arden."

Kelly rattled the paper thoughtfully. "To tell you the truth, it never occurred to me that the masking was anything but an accident, and I figured there was a stomach bug or something going around. But the orchestra parts, and now this. You might be right."

"Maybe you should make an announcement to the company to be on their guard?" Isobel suggested.

"Won't that freak everyone out?" Heather said timidly. "People are nervous about opening night as it is."

"I'll bring this to Felicity and let her figure out how to handle it. It's above my pay grade. But thanks for telling me.

You guys better go, or you won't get much of a break." Kelly slipped the note into her binder and turned to Heather. "Can we look at the cue into the banquet scene? It needs to go earlier."

Isobel and Sunil made their way out of the row, not speaking until they reached the aisle.

"I don't know about you, but I didn't find that particularly reassuring," she said.

"Me neither. But I don't see what else Kelly can do. If something's going to happen tonight, it's going to happen."

"You're right." Isobel's expression was grim. "And unless we're smart enough to figure out what it is in advance, we have no way of stopping it."

EIGHT

DELPHI KRAMER WAS STUCK in traffic and furious. It was the last straw in a twenty-four-hour period that had gone from bad to worse and was now careening headlong into disastrous.

"What the hell is going on?" she barked at the cab driver.

He caught her eye in the rearview mirror. "There was an accident on the exit ramp from the thruway. Everyone's detouring. It's a big mess."

Delphi gave an exasperated sigh. "You couldn't have told me before I got into your cab?"

"What're you gonna do, walk? It's two miles from the train station to downtown, almost three to Livingston Stage. At least you're sitting."

"I just spent two and a half hours sitting on a train—no, make that three hours, because we sat outside fucking Poughkeepsie for a half hour—and now I'm totally late!" She kicked the seat in front of her and fumed.

"Calm down. I see a coupla cops up ahead, and it looks like it thins out after that."

Delphi grumbled and sank lower in the backseat. This whole plan was harebrained. Isobel was the impulsive one. Unlike her roommate, Delphi preferred to stake out a situation and calculate the odds of a satisfactory outcome. But when Carlo Alessandrini, the maître d' at the restaurant where she waited tables, had unexpectedly—shockingly, in fact— fired her last night, she had been at a complete loss. Without Isobel there to absorb the blow, Delphi had found herself channeling her absent friend, stalking the small L-shaped studio apartment they shared and regaling the indifferent furniture with the kind of nonstop, stream-of-consciousness monologue Isobel was prone to delivering. Delphi finally wore herself out, drained what was left of their Bushmills, and fell into a heavy, self-pitying sleep. When she woke up, it had taken several minutes before she remembered what had prompted her to down a third of a bottle of whiskey, and then she burst into tears—a reaction even more uncharacteristic than indulging her wounded pride the night before.

As she soaked in the bathtub, her Botticellian blond curls piled high and secured on top of her head with a retro hot pink hair pick, she missed Isobel more than ever. Tonight was opening night of *Sousacal*, and Delphi knew their dress rehearsal was that afternoon, but she'd hoped she could at least get Isobel on the phone that morning. When her call went to voicemail, she realized Isobel was probably still asleep after their ten-out-of-twelve. She could have tried Sunil, but he was the last person she wanted lobbing questions at her. It was painfully obvious that he carried a torch for her, and the truth was she was on the fence about him. Delphi found talent attractive, and his smoldering good looks made him distinctly her type, but she wasn't certain enough to jeopardize their friendship. Delphi, who hailed from a family of similarly floral-named sisters (Delphi was short for Delphinium), placed special value on platonic male friendship.

Even so, she was feeling distinctly left out. While she had been trapped in the restaurant's wine cellar fighting off Carlo's aggressive advances (which Isobel had long predicted, but Delphi had never actually expected), her two best friends had been enjoying the exciting run-up to opening night of a new musical. Granted, Isobel said the show was terrible, but Isobel was a snob. Delphi was sure it couldn't be that bad.

She was about to find out for herself. Or would be, if the traffic from the Albany train station weren't impossible. She had leapt out of the bathtub that morning, propelled to her laptop by the inspired but obvious solution. Naked and dripping (a benefit of being alone in the apartment), she had navigated to Amtrak's website, done some quick calculating in her head, and found a train that wouldn't kill her whole day, but would get her there in plenty of time for the eight o'clock curtain. Then she'd indulged in some retail therapy, grabbed a quick lunch, and returned home with enough time to throw some necessaries into a bag and race out the door to Penn Station.

She needn't have raced, because after sitting on the train for an hour, it was announced that there was a mechanical failure and they would all need to take the next train. She waited another forty-five minutes for that one to depart, and then there was the inexplicable half-hour hiatus in Poughkeepsie. When she'd asked the conductor why they were stopped, he had returned the singularly unhelpful, "So we can have this conversation." Finally, they had started moving again. The train had pulled into Albany-Rensselaer at seven forty, and here she was, stuck in traffic.

It was only now that the true cost of her impulsiveness dawned on her. In the middle of everything else, she'd neglected to buy a ticket for the show.

"Son of a bitch!"

The cabbie scowled in the mirror. "Hey, lady, I'm doing everything I can!"

"I know, sorry." She let out a strangled groan and pulled out her cell phone. She quickly located the theater's phone number. After three tries, she got through.

"I'm sorry, we're totally sold out. It's opening night," the woman intoned disapprovingly in her flat, upstate New York accent.

Of course, thought Delphi. Because nothing was going right today.

"Please," she begged. "I have friends in the show. I decided to come up from the city last minute to surprise them. They don't know I'm coming. Don't you hold house seats?"

"They're all spoken for."

"Standing room?"

"Against fire regulations. But come anyway. We sometimes have subscribers who don't show. When you get here, come find me. My name is Miriam, and I'm the box office manager. I'll see what I can do."

"I'll be there in ten minutes!"

"Five," said the cabbie as a policeman waved them past, and the taxi picked up speed.

"Five," Delphi repeated into the phone. "Miriam, thank you so much."

"No promises. By the way, who are your friends?"

"Isobel Spice and Sunil Kapany. And Hugh Fremont."

"Oh, that Hugh." Miriam giggled. "He's such a charmer."

"How's the show?" Delphi asked.

Miriam paused. "You'll see."

NINE

ISOBEL HAD COMPLETED her traditional opening night rituals, but given the events of the past twenty-four hours, she decided it wouldn't hurt to devise a few new ones for good measure. Hugh had given her a box of Godiva chocolates, and after choosing the red foil-wrapped heart, she resolved to save the rest and eat one before each performance. She also sang the song she'd learned in sixth grade listing all fifty states in alphabetical order and followed that with the first fifty digits of pi, which her brother Percival, a math prodigy, had set to music when he was six.

She wished Percival were coming for opening night and Delphi too, for that matter, but Percival was deep into midterms at Columbia, and Delphi didn't want to give up any work hours, which Isobel understood. Percival, as was his wont, had written her a humorous light verse in praise of her achievements, but the opening night gift that was most unexpected and made her happiest was the bouquet of flowers from her friend James Cooke. She wondered if friend was the proper designation. He had started as her temp agent, when she sandblasted her way into his office a year ago and insisted he send her out despite her lack of office experience. Their relationship had progressed stormily, and he no longer worked at Temp Zone, but they had parted on good terms.

She had given James's flowers pride of place on her side of the dressing table she shared with Talia, and as she reread his note, "Knock 'em dead—figuratively speaking, of course," Isobel felt a rush of warmth and affection. James, who was not a theater person, had not only known the right thing to do, but had taken the trouble to do it.

Talia peered into the dressing room mirror, turning her head from side to side.

"What do you think?" she asked.

"You could use a touch more color in your cheeks. Those lights are bright, and you're still a little peaky from last night."

Talia reached for the blusher, and it flew out of her hands and into Isobel's lap. "Sorry. I don't know why I'm so nervous."

"It's opening night!"

Talia took the blusher from Isobel and applied it with a shaky hand. "It isn't only that. I thought everyone was acting a little strange this afternoon. What if you're right and someone is trying to sabotage the show?"

"Then only one person would be acting strange. If you ask me, it's because now they know there are Broadway producers coming."

"But Kelly said—"

"She's just trying to keep everyone calm."

Talia's face went pink under her reinforced rouge. "So it is true? I thought Arden was a little delusional."

"Well, Arden *is* a little delusional, but yes, it's true."

"You really don't like her, do you?"

Isobel shrugged at her reflection in the mirror. "It's more that she doesn't like me." She rose to take down her bonnet from the wig head on the shelf above the table. "Do *you* like her?"

Their eyes met in the mirror as Isobel tied a neat bow under her chin.

"I think it's wise to stay on her good side." Talia shuffled her feet in her white lace-up boots. "How do you know it's true about the producers?"

"I heard it from Thomas, and the costume people always know everything." Isobel bit her lip. "Sorry. That probably didn't help your nerves."

Talia positioned her own bonnet over her wig and tied it under her chin. "At this point it doesn't much matter."

"Break a leg," Isobel said.

"Thanks. You too."

Isobel left Talia in the dressing room and went off in search of Hugh. She found him pacing nervously in the pit.

"How's it going down here?"

"All the parts are on the stands, and I'm guarding them like Cerberus. What's the mood upstairs?"

"The usual jitters, magnified by the possibility of sabotage and Broadway producers." She was seized by a sudden suspicion. "Did you know?"

Hugh smiled sheepishly. "I did."

"And you didn't tell me?" she cried indignantly.

"I didn't want you to get your hopes up. I doubt it will come to anything. They probably won't even show. You've seen *Waiting for Guffman*."

She tugged his sleeve. "But what if they do? I know I don't have a big part, and it's all pretty sketchy anyway, but as long as I show some talent, even if they think the show is awful, which of course it is, they might like my performance and remember me, right?"

He took her in his arms. "Nobody who has ever seen you could forget you."

An ostentatious cough startled them apart.

"If you two lovebirds are finished, I'd like to find out what the orchestration is going to be for my first-act song, since I didn't get to hear it this afternoon," Arden said.

"Actually, we weren't finished." Isobel planted a long, lingering kiss on Hugh's mouth. She pulled away and smiled sweetly at Arden. "There. Now we are. Good luck tonight!"

Arden gasped and took a faltering step backward. "It's bad luck to wish someone good luck, you idiot! That's why you say break a leg or *merde*."

Isobel caught Hugh's eye and winked. "You don't believe in all that superstitious stuff, do you?"

Arden huffed and looked away, but Isobel divined from the tightness around Hugh's mouth that he believed in it. She hoped her irreverence hadn't just undone all her brand-new good luck charms.

DELPHI LET OUT A LONG, slow breath as the opening number finished and the cast held for applause. The clapping started slowly after an overlong pause during which the audience, despite the unmistakable cue to clap in the form of a giant cymbal crash, collectively tried to decide what to make of what they'd just seen.

"'Antonio is a happier pappy now'?" she muttered. "Please, God, tell me I did *not* just hear that."

"Sadly, you did," said a male voice next to her.

She glanced over and saw a slightly built man with round glasses, a boyish face, and receding ash-blond hair. He was scribbling in a notebook.

"Are you a critic?"

He raised an eyebrow. "Aren't we all?"

Delphi bit her lip to keep from laughing out loud. Onstage, the scene continued with a medley showing young Sousa, known to his family as Philip, morphing with astonishing speed from a pink plastic prop baby to a boy of around ten, who was charged with playing Philip from ages five through fifteen, when he disappeared behind a gazebo and reappeared as an adult actor.

And to think I nearly killed a cabbie over this, Delphi thought.

Finally, Isobel and Sunil came onstage together as Emma and Benjamin Swallow. Isobel looked particularly fetching in a blue and white dress and flower-trimmed bonnet, but it was Sunil who took her breath away. His burnished complexion shone against his pale seersucker suit, and she could feel the heat of his eyes from her seat in the fourth row. She had seen Sunil onstage before and knew he had a gorgeous voice, but she'd never seen him costumed quite so attractively. The slim, nineteenth-century suit clung to him in an appealingly suggestive way, and she gained a new and visceral appreciation for why clothes that hid the body were considered sexy.

Sousa came back onstage, and the three of them had a brief scene. Then there was a duet between Sousa and Emma, "Song of the Sea," based, according to the notes, on an actual poem of Emma Swallow's.

> *I stood by the cruel, crawling sea*
> *And this was the dole it brought to me.*
> *A song so strange came in with the tide,*
> *Mine eyes were blinded, my strong heart died.*

The song was sweet, but it ground the action to a halt. Delphi applauded enthusiastically for Isobel, but the critic groaned and flipped a page of his notebook.

"Hey, that's my friend!"

He continued to scribble without looking up. "Nothing against your friend—lovely voice—but you pays your money, you takes your chances."

He was right, of course. If Isobel and Sunil were watching this debacle with her instead of appearing in it, they would be engaged in an eye-rolling competition, which would culminate in a full-scale takedown at the bar afterward. Or during intermission, because she couldn't imagine they'd stick it out for the second act. But there were her two dearest friends, soldiering on in the face of material that was either intentionally sappy or unintentionally hilarious, and she had traveled the better part of a day to see them. If they could tough it out, so could she.

Oh, and here was Sunil again, putting the kibosh on the budding romance between Isobel and—Delphi glanced at her program—Chris. Somehow it was easier to process the actors as themselves, rather than their characters. And here was a stunning auburn-haired beauty in danger of being capsized by her anachronistically surgically-enhanced bosom. Delphi noted with some disgust that her seatmate was sitting bolt upright with a moony smile on his face. With a sharp intake of breath, she suddenly recognized him as the *New York Post*'s bitchy theater columnist, Roman Fried. What had brought him to the wilds of Albany—and how could she save Isobel from his poison pen?

The scene onstage continued, and Delphi realized that the beautiful redhead was the infamous Arden Claire—whose real last name, according to Isobel, was Horowitz—in the role of Sousa's wife. She wasn't a bad actress, but she seemed far too glamorous and contemporary for the role. Isobel's complaints weren't simply ego, Delphi conceded. The truth was, Isobel would have been much better as Jennie Sousa.

"The Washington Post" began—one of the few Sousa marches Delphi recognized—and she groaned inwardly as more embarrassing lyrics assaulted her ears. Next to her, Fried scribbled furiously on his notepad, while his eyes remained glued to Arden. Chris whirled Arden around and pulled her onto his knee. She sat for a moment, gazing at him with a look more of hatred than love, then jumped to her feet. Chris extended his arm, and Arden twirled into his chest, which reminded Delphi of the disco moves she and her sisters had spent their childhood perfecting. In a single, graceful gesture, Arden dipped backward and Chris caught her under the small of her back.

But then a strange look crossed Chris's face, and he buckled under Arden's weight and sank to the floor. He kept singing, but his eyes telegraphed panic. He looked toward the wings, shaking his head furiously, and as he gently set Arden down on the stage floor, the curtain fell.

TEN

ISOBEL STOOD ROOTED to the spot, distracted from her silent run-through of the lyrics by Chris and Arden's unrehearsed choreography. It wasn't until the curtain hit the floor and all hell broke loose around her that she realized Arden had passed out.

Heather, white-faced, rushed onstage screaming into her headset, "Call 911!"

Chris crawled backward away from Arden and pulled himself to his feet. He glanced around helplessly. "She was dead weight. One minute she was fine, and then she just dropped."

"That's what happens when you faint," snapped Marissa.

"Arden? Arden!" Heather shook her gently. When there was no response, she put her ear to Arden's mouth. "Her breathing is faint. I don't know what to do!" There was an edge of hysteria to her voice.

Felicity burst into the wings, followed by Jethro and Ezra.

"What's going on?" Felicity demanded.

"She passed out. Kelly is calling 911," Heather said in a trembling voice.

Ezra pushed forward and knelt by Arden. "Everybody back," he cried and immediately began chest compressions.

Cast and crew alike huddled in groups, spilling from the wings onto the stage behind the curtain, but nobody dared speak. The confused murmuring of the audience filtered over the backstage monitors until someone thought to turn them down. But as Ezra's compressions became more frantic, the company too began to whisper, and Isobel heard muffled sobbing from somewhere behind her.

Ezra was just starting to tire when the paramedics arrived, and he stood aside gratefully to let them take over. His body was shaking, and he sank into Heather's chair. Kelly and Heather hovered nearby, clutching each other guiltily like babysitters whose child has fallen off the jungle gym on their watch. Jethro and Felicity retreated to the rigging, their concerned voices rising and falling. Isobel sidled over to Marissa.

"Do you know if Arden had some condition that might make her pass out? Did she take any medications?"

Marissa shook her head. "No idea."

"I thought you guys were good friends."

Marissa gasped. "Oh my God, you talk about her like she's dead!"

"I didn't mean it like that. I—" Isobel flailed.

Marissa stalked over to Talia and whispered something to her. They turned cold stares on Isobel.

Sunil joined Isobel. "What was that about?"

"Came out wrong," Isobel mumbled.

Felicity was speaking to one of the paramedics. Her voice rose. "But is she going to be all right?"

"We have to get her to the hospital. Someone needs to come with her."

"Heather, you go," Kelly instructed.

"Stand back, please."

The company parted, and the paramedics rolled Arden through on a stretcher with Heather trailing them, looking terrified. Felicity jumped aside as they cut past her.

A hush fell, and Felicity turned, her lips set in a thin line. "I'll go out front and make an announcement. Isobel!"

She started. "Yes?"

"Can you finish the show for Arden? Even if you have to hold the script."

Isobel felt every eye on her. She swallowed. "I can do it without the script."

Immediately, everyone started murmuring. Felicity quieted them. "How long do you need?"

"Not much. Maybe five or ten minutes, just to get my head together." She glanced down. "I'll have to wear my own costume."

"That's fine," Kelly said. "I'll need someone on headset back here."

"I'll do it," Ezra said.

"What do you do in act two?" Felicity asked Isobel.

"Only the maid."

"I can cover it," Marissa volunteered. "Once I'm done as Mrs. Blakely, I'm ensemble."

"Thank you, everyone, for being flexible, and thank you, Isobel, for being prepared."

With that, Felicity pushed through the break in the curtains, and the chattering in the house trailed into silence at her appearance. Suddenly, Isobel found herself shaking uncontrollably. Sunil and Hugh rushed to her side.

"What is it?"

"What's the matter?"

"How can I go out there? I mean, I *think* I know it, but I've never had an understudy rehearsal. Maybe I should bring my script. I don't know what any of the movements feel like!"

Before either of them could respond, Chris came up behind her.

"There's not much left in act one. Let's walk through the rest of 'The Washington Post,' and I can rough you through the finale. Then we can talk through act two during intermission. You'll be great. Everyone knows you've been preparing your ass off."

Isobel searched his eyes for any hint of accusation, but his expression was sincere. He leaned in closer. "Even with no rehearsal, you're going to be better than Arden." He took her arm and led her onstage to the gazebo. She glanced over her shoulder at Sunil and Hugh, who nodded encouragingly.

Ten minutes flew past, and Isobel found that putting her body through the motions with Chris calmed her. When the curtain rose again, Isobel and Chris were greeted by loud cheering and applause. They began at the top of the scene and got another big hand after the duet. Isobel glanced down at the pit, where Hugh was beaming at her. He blew her a kiss, which she acknowledged with a flutter of her eyelids. Before she knew it, they were up to the act one finale, and when the curtain came down for intermission, the cast flocked to congratulate her, any residual suspicion eclipsed by relief that the show was going on.

Isobel returned to her dressing room and found her phone buzzing with a string of text messages from Delphi. She picked it up, scrolled through, and shrieked.

"What is it?" Talia asked, alarmed.

"My best friend is here! She came up from the city to surprise me."

Talia eyed her curiously. "You really didn't know she was coming?"

"What?" Isobel looked up. "No! I had no idea. She told me she couldn't get off work, but now she says it's a long story." She scrolled further and gasped. "She's sitting next to that theater columnist from the *New York Post*. The obnoxious one, you know who I mean."

"No, I don't," said Talia coolly. "I'm an opera singer."

"Yes, you do. Roman Fried." Isobel stared at the ceiling. "I wonder what brought him up here?"

"Hmmm."

"What?"

"I just think it's funny, that's all."

A warning bell went off in Isobel's brain. "What's funny?"

Talia looked squarely at her. "Arden gets sick, you're totally ready to jump in, and your best friend and some theater critic from New York are here. Oh, and the Donnelly Group. With all the stuff that's been going on, it starts to look a little fishy, you know?"

"No, I don't know." Isobel felt her neck burn with anger. "I can't believe you would suggest that I hurt Arden so I could, what…play a slightly less shitty part in a shitty show?"

There was a knock on the door, and Thomas poked his head in, holding Arden's second-act costume, an emerald green off-the-shoulder evening gown.

"It's going to be big on you, but I took it up a few inches so at least you won't trip." He looked from Isobel to Talia. "Did I interrupt something?"

Isobel found her voice first. "No, it's all right. Come in."

She started to unbutton her bodice but found her fingers were trembling.

"Here, let me do that. You must be a bundle of nerves."

Talia let out a disgusted snort and pushed past Thomas out of the dressing room.

"What's up her ass?" Thomas asked.

Isobel held out her arms and let Thomas's quick fingers fly over the restricting buttons.

"She thinks I engineered Arden fainting so I could go on for her."

Thomas pulled back and locked eyes with Isobel. "Did you?"

"Why does everyone think I'm responsible for what happened to Arden, just because I'm doing the job I was hired for?"

"You pulled the masking down on her," Thomas reminded her.

"It was an accident! Besides, I'm scared of heights. No way could I ever go up to the flies to mess with it, if I even knew how."

"And I heard someone put Ex-Lax in the coffee."

"Which Arden didn't drink. And the problem with the orchestra parts didn't affect her any more than the rest of us."

"If you didn't do anything, then you have nothing to worry about," Thomas placated her.

She wriggled out of her bodice and turned so Thomas could undo her skirt. "I can't believe anyone would think I would hurt Arden."

"Girls are jealous bitches. You don't need me to tell you that."

"I hope Arden is going to be okay. Honestly," Isobel said.

He patted her shoulder. "Of course you do, honey."

Isobel stepped into the gown. Thomas pulled it up and fastened it.

"It's beautiful."

"Nothing but the best for the leading lady. Whoever she may be. Ready for act two?"

Isobel exhaled. "Bring it."

Thomas pulled open the door, startling Felicity and Kelly, who were standing there about to knock, faces ashen.

Isobel's stomach dropped. "I was nervous! I promise it'll get better the more I do it."

"You'll have plenty of chances," Felicity said in a tight voice. "Heather called from the hospital. Arden is dead."

ELEVEN

IT TOOK EVERY OUNCE of Isobel's concentration to get through the second act. She hadn't put nearly as much preparation into it as the first, and Ezra had to throw her a few lines from the wings. But every time Isobel started to relax into the role, the image of Kelly's stricken face and the tone of Felicity's clipped announcement outside her dressing room door intruded, reminding her of the awful turn of events that made her both leading lady and prime suspect, should Arden's death prove to be from anything other than natural causes.

She also wasn't sure who else knew yet, and she floated through the rest of the show in a surreal haze, hoping she would wake to find it was all a bizarre dream caused by too many pizza-flavored Goldfish before bed. On the other hand, Thomas had been with her when the news was delivered, which meant by the finale, everybody would know. But Isobel decided, as she watched Marissa overact her scream upon finding Sousa dead in his hotel room, that she wouldn't believe Arden's death was real until she heard it from someone else.

"I've been waiting to tell you until you finished your last scene," Sunil whispered in her ear, "but Thomas just told me...Arden is dead."

So much for that.

Isobel clutched his hand. "Felicity told me at intermission. I was trying to put it out of my mind."

"She told you at intermission?" Sunil asked. "That's terrible. It's not like you didn't have enough on your mind. She's lucky it didn't throw you off your game."

"It almost did. But in some ways it made me focus more. Of course I'll probably totally fall apart as soon as the curtain comes down."

Sunil managed a wry smile. "Just the fact that you're able to say that means you won't. And besides, you still have to go out there and greet your adoring public. Come on."

She followed him onstage, reminding herself to take Arden's position rather than her own for the "Stars and Stripes" finale.

> We loved you, but now you are gone.
> How we'll miss you, dear John Philip Sousa!
> In your marches your legend lives on,
> That conclusion is now foregone.
>
> You may think that this is the end,
> Of this red, white, and blue lollapalooza.
> To this country, you've been a great friend—
> Raise a baton and carry on for JP Sousa!

Chris bounded onstage from the wings and took Isobel's hand, and together they led the cast in a company bow. As they came up, he leaned over and kissed her cheek. He lingered for a moment and whispered, "I wish you were playing Jennie for real."

"I am now," Isobel said as they stepped back to make way for the curtain to come down.

"What do you mean?"

"Arden is dead."

The curtain went up to polite applause, and they stepped forward again. Isobel bowed, but Chris stayed upright. As soon as the curtain came down again, he wrenched his hand free and ran offstage left. Isobel took Arden's spot in the wings stage right and watched as the ensemble came together and took their bow in a line. She tried to catch Chris's eye across the stage, but he was pacing in a tight circle, running his hand over his pomaded hair. Sunil went out without her, and then Talia took her bow, laying her hand across her heart with a level of false modesty rarely seen even at the Metropolitan Opera. Then Isobel stepped out for her curtain call.

She was greeted by a thunderous ovation, and several people in the audience jumped to their feet. For a sublime moment, all her worries vanished, and she soaked up the adulation knowing she had delivered a better performance than anyone would expect from an understudy who'd had no rehearsal, especially given the unfortunate circumstances. Chris joined her and bowed mechanically, evidencing no enjoyment of the applause. She remembered to gesture to Hugh in the pit, and she blew him a kiss for good measure. Then one more company bow, and the final curtain came down.

Everyone was hugging and congratulating each other. Sunil picked Isobel up and spun her around.

"You sure showed me! I guess I'd better start studying up."

He set her down and met Chris's stormy eyes.

"Are you planning to get rid of me, too?" Chris spat.

"What?"

"Arden is dead. Am I next?"

"God, no! I didn't mean that at all." Sunil held his arms out helplessly. "Nothing better happen to you, because I haven't learned your part!"

"Yet." Chris stalked off.

Isobel bit her lip. "I shouldn't have been the one to tell him."

Suddenly, Felicity was there, with Jethro, Ezra, Kelly, and a tall, stooped balding man in a suit whom Isobel had never seen before.

"May I have your attention." Felicity raised her hands and voice simultaneously. "I'd like the entire company onstage, please."

The stage crowded with people. Isobel saw Hugh waving to her from the wings, but she had no path to him.

"As you are all aware, Arden collapsed onstage tonight," Felicity continued when everyone had assembled. "Paramedics took her to Albany Medical Center, but they were not able to revive her. I'm sorry to report that she has died."

Witnessing the shrieks and gasps of her fellow actors, Isobel realized that except for telling Sunil, Thomas had been the soul of discretion. She glanced apologetically at Chris, but his gaze remained fixed on the floor.

"We don't yet know the cause of death, but as soon as Arden's family is notified and I have that information, I will tell you what I can. I want to introduce Magnus Carlsson, president of the board of directors of Livingston Stage, who would like to say a few words."

The tall, balding man stepped forward and cleared his throat.

"I realize this is an unspeakable tragedy and a shock for everyone," he said, "and I want you all to know that we will provide whatever support you need to get through this difficult time."

"Which means what, exactly?" Sunil whispered to Isobel. "Counseling?"

"But I also want to remind everybody of that old theatrical saw: the show must go on. Livingston Stage has invested a significant amount of time and money into this project, and we believe strongly in its future. Tonight's performance was outstanding. You all pulled together, and Isobel Spice in particular came through. Let's give her a round of applause."

As much as Isobel relished praise, this was the worst possible thing the interloper could have done. She looked down at her boots rather than face her fellow actors, knowing she would see only resentment and suspicion. After the awkward moment passed, she dared look up again. Chris was watching her, and when she caught his eye, he shook his head and turned away.

"So we will forge ahead, honoring Arden's memory with our humble offering to the theater gods, which, if tonight's performance is any indication, will be received with affection and open arms. Thank you, all."

"And no more sacrifices, we hope," Sunil said under his breath. "Who is this doofus?"

"I don't know, but I wish he hadn't done that. The collective consciousness doesn't need any more ammunition against me," Isobel said.

They made their way toward Hugh, who hung to the side to wait for them while the others passed. He swept Isobel into a fierce embrace.

"What a night. Are you all right?"

"I think so. It's terrible about Arden. I don't know what to say."

"I know. It's unthinkable. But you were a champ."

"You were, too." She kissed him. "Thanks for getting me through the show."

"Nonsense, it was entirely your doing. All I did was wave my arms like I always do."

"Hugh?" Kelly called. "Can you come here?"

"Go on," Isobel said. "We'll find you after."

Hugh joined Kelly and Ezra, while Isobel and Sunil regarded each other in silence.

"What do you really think happened to Arden?" Sunil asked.

"I have no idea," Isobel said. "I was watching from the wings, but I didn't notice anything strange. She just collapsed."

"I wonder what it looked like from the house," Sunil said. "If only there were someone we could ask."

Isobel gasped and grabbed his arm. "There is! Meet me in the lobby after you change. I have a little surprise for you."

TWELVE

"YOU WERE AMAZING!" Delphi threw her arms around Isobel. "But oh my God, this is terrible."

"I know," Isobel said. "Poor Arden."

Delphi released her. "I mean the show. It's an absolute piece of shit."

For a moment, Delphi was afraid she'd said the wrong thing, but then Isobel's expression changed.

"I did warn you," Isobel said.

"Do you think Arden will recover?"

Isobel's eyes widened. "You haven't heard? She's dead."

"Well, aren't you a sight for sore eyes!" Sunil caught Delphi in a strong hug.

"What?" Delphi screeched.

"And a sound for sore ears." He thrust a knuckle into his ear. "Thanks for that."

Still reeling from Isobel's bombshell, Delphi held him more tightly than she normally would have. When she pulled away, she saw surprise register on his face.

"Isobel just told me about Arden," she said, explaining the screech and the hug, both fairly out of character for her.

"Did she tell you about the other stuff?" Sunil asked.

"What other stuff?" Delphi groaned. "Why is there always 'other stuff'?"

"There's time for that later," Isobel said. "But what made you decide to come? I can't tell you how much better I felt about everything when I saw your texts."

"Oh, well, I...I lost my job."

"What?" Isobel cried. "But I thought Carlo adored you!"

"Um, yeah, that was the problem. I'll tell you more later." Delphi snuck a sideways glance at Sunil. Isobel, hoping to deter Carlo's outrageous flirtations, had once told him Sunil was Delphi's boyfriend. Even after Delphi reassured Carlo countless times, he never quite believed her, and the whole thing had remained a sore subject between her and Isobel. She really did not want to discuss the matter in front of Sunil.

"Can I crash with you tonight?" Delphi asked.

"There's a couch in the living room, or we can throw some pillows on the floor of my room. How long are you staying?"

"Hadn't thought about it," Delphi said. "This whole trip was a bit of an impulse purchase."

"There you are! I went upstairs, but—" Hugh stopped short. "Hail, hail, the gang's all here! Hello, Delphi."

Delphi gave Hugh a nice long hug with no qualms. The more time she spent with Hugh, the more she liked him. She sometimes wondered whether Isobel fully appreciated the quality of the catch she'd landed.

"I hate to interrupt this happy reunion, but Felicity asked me to fetch you, Isobel."

"Stay here, you two. I won't be long."

Isobel returned to the theater through the main doors, Hugh's arm slung protectively around her shoulders. As soon as they were out of sight, Delphi whirled on Sunil.

"I'm counting on you to tell me what's going on around here. Other stuff. And...go."

Sunil tsked. "All business. No 'It's great to see you' or even, God forbid, 'You were really good in the show.'"

Delphi bit her lip, mortified. "Sorry. There's such a swirl of information, I can't keep up. You were terrific." She smiled mischievously. "I particularly liked your Pawnee chief."

"Argh, never mind. I'm going back to your original question." He led Delphi over to one of the upholstered benches. "There's been a series of pranks leading up to tonight. We think someone is trying to sabotage the show."

"I'd have thought the show was doing a fine job of that all by itself," Delphi responded. "But go on. What happened?"

"First some masking fell on Arden, and unfortunately, Isobel was moving it aside for her when it came down."

"Ouch."

"And then half the company got an incapacitating case of the runs during tech after drinking from the same pot of coffee in the green room. At least we're pretty sure that's what did it."

"Sousa's revenge?"

"Considering the mess we're making of his life story, he's well within his rights," Sunil concurred. "Anyway, the first thing could have been accidental and the second coincidental. But not the third thing."

"What was that?"

His tone grew more serious. "Someone tampered with the orchestra parts before the dress rehearsal. Adding new cuts, erasing old ones, something different in each part. It was a complete mess. Hugh had to spend the whole rehearsal fixing them, so tonight was our first time doing the whole show with the orchestra."

Delphi took this in. "Definitely not accidental. Though I have to give the person props for creativity."

"And now Arden. If her death wasn't from natural causes, this all becomes sinister in a whole new way."

"Not to mention dangerous."

"When Arden collapsed, what did it look like from the house?"

Delphi tried to recall the scene. "They were singing that insipid duet, and Sousa whirled her around and dipped her backward. Then she kind of kept going down, and he went with her and set her on the ground. Thinking back, it's obvious she lost consciousness, but it happened so fast I'm not sure we realized it at the time."

"Did Arden break character at all? Did she look like something might have taken her by surprise? Or did she just go limp?"

"Now that you mention it, she gave Sousa—what's his name again?"

"Chris."

"She gave Chris a dirty look at one point. It was quick, a flash of disgust, but it seemed out of character. I'm not sure I'd have noticed, except I was staring at her, trying to decide what about her was enough to make Roman Fried drool all over his notebook."

"Roman Fried? You mean the *New York Post* theater columnist?"

"Yeah. I was his plus one."

"Why would he come all the way up here—and for this?"

"Never got a chance to ask him," Delphi said. "He ran out as soon as the show was over."

"To file his copy, no doubt. What a scoop."

"Until Arden appeared, he most definitely was not a fan of the show." Delphi frowned. "I hope he's kind to Isobel. At this point, she's the main event. He'll have to mention her."

Sunil put his arm around her. "You have no idea how glad I am that you're here. You ground her better than anyone. Even Hugh."

"That's why you're glad I'm here? For Isobel?"

He laid a hand on his heart. "I didn't know you cared." His expression shifted slightly. "Actually, I really didn't know you cared."

Delphi smiled wanly. She'd meant it as a joke, but obviously Sunil was hoping it might be an opening to a conversation she had assiduously avoided.

"You know I'm always happy to see you," she said lamely.

His eyes searched hers for a moment, and to her relief, he let the matter drop.

"I'm sorry about your job," he said.

She tugged at the zipper on her backpack. "I'll find another. No shortage of restaurants in New York City." She sighed. "Although there's no shortage of waiters, either."

"You mean actors," he said.

"You've never had to hold down a survival job, so you don't get to mock. And don't launch into your spiel about minority typecasting. You're playing a nineteenth-century Philadelphia gentleman."

He cocked his head. "And an Indian chief."

She was too tired to point out that she felt equally objectified by Carlo grabbing her ass and trying to kiss her, and at least Sunil was being paid to act. Even though he hated being pigeonholed, Sunil worked more often than Isobel and Delphi combined, and it was sometimes hard to be sympathetic.

"Let's just sit quietly until they get back, okay?" she said.

"That's something Isobel would never suggest." He pulled her close. "That's what I mean. It's a really good thing you're here."

THIRTEEN

FELICITY GESTURED FOR ISOBEL and Hugh to take a seat in the back of the house, where she, Jethro, Ezra, and Kelly were gathered.

"First of all, I want to thank you for being prepared," Felicity said. "You did an excellent job tonight."

Isobel felt her chest swell with pride. "Thank you."

"As I mentioned briefly at intermission, we'd like you to take over the role, but there is one issue we need to address," Felicity continued. "Arden is—er, was a member of Actors' Equity. That means we have to replace her with an Equity performer. If you want to continue in the role, you'll have to join the union."

Isobel's mouth dropped open. In all her fantasies about going on for Arden, the possibility of joining the union had never occurred to her. This was an incredible opportunity. The jobs that would open up for her, the auditions she could get into! Most actors knocked around for years before they were able to vanquish the notorious catch-22 that was joining the actors' union. You had to be cast in an Equity production in order to join the union, but you couldn't audition for an Equity production unless you were already a union member. Isobel had apparently stumbled onto a top-secret loophole: taking over a union role as a non-union understudy.

"Yes, of course," Isobel said. "That's no problem. That's— great!"

"Wonderful!" Jethro beamed at her.

Hugh tapped her shoulder. "Can I talk to you privately for a moment?"

Isobel whipped her head around, startled. "What?"

He guided her to her feet. "Can you give us a sec?"

Hugh led Isobel down the aisle toward the stage. When they were out of earshot, he spoke softly.

"I know this is exciting for you, but think about it first. Taking an Equity contract gets them out of a tight spot, but it isn't necessarily the smartest career move for you."

"How could it be bad?"

"First of all, there's the initiation fee. It's over a thousand dollars. Felicity will be paying you a higher salary on an Equity contract, but not that much higher. That's a considerable expense."

Isobel swallowed. "I can ask my parents for a loan."

"But this is the main thing: you'll be less employable once you join the union."

Isobel opened her mouth, outraged, but Hugh steamrolled right over her, which was quite unlike him.

"This isn't about talent. Think about how and why you're here. Your role was designated non-union in advance. Most regional theaters—summer stock, too—have a limited number of union contracts. The last category they're going to use them on is young women. There are simply too many of you to choose from. This show is your first solid regional credit. If you jump now and get your card, you're skipping an important step. You have to build your resume."

"But think of all the things I can get seen for! That *Phantom of the Opera* audition where I met you? I wouldn't have to sit outside the Equity lounge all day on a folding chair hoping for a chance to sing sixteen bars for the casting director while he's packing up for the day."

"And the result would be the same. You'd still not get hired," Hugh said. "As I told you that day, it was a required call. They weren't really looking. Without an agent getting you appointments, those are the kinds of auditions you'll be going to. And no agent is going to take you on with only one decent credit."

Isobel's temples throbbed. "I can't believe you, of all people, would try to hold me back. You don't think I can compete?"

"Darling, you know I think the world of you. I just want you to give this some thought. I know it sounds good—"

"Better than good. It's the lead in a new musical the Donnelly Group is looking at, and besides"—a triumphant smile crossed her face—"I *have* to do it. I'm contracted as the understudy."

"You can step in for three days in an emergency without having to join the union."

"You mean, let them bring in someone else and go back to playing Emma?"

"Right."

"But they want *me*."

"Of course they do. It's easier and cheaper for them to keep you in the role. They'd have to find someone else who could learn the show in three days, and that would cost them. I'm telling you, they need you more than you need your Equity card right now."

She narrowed her eyes. "How do you know so much about Equity regulations?"

"I overheard Kelly and Heather discussing it." He took Isobel's hand. "My mum always says never make a big decision without sleeping on it first."

"But—"

"Do that for me? Take the night. The offer will still be there in the morning. Run it past Delphi and Sunil. See what they think. For once, don't rush in. Okay?"

His arguments, valid or not, felt like a betrayal. On the other hand, it was tempting to make Felicity sweat a little. And Isobel had never seen Hugh so insistent. She supposed sleeping on it couldn't hurt, although she was pretty sure she knew what her answer would be.

"All right."

He gave her a quick kiss and they rejoined the others, who were arguing heatedly about who should take over as Emma.

"I don't care, just pick one," Felicity said.

Ezra scrabbled at his beard. "I can't pick any of them. Marissa is playing Sousa's mother and Talia is his sister. They can't show up in the next scene as his girlfriend."

"Then grab someone from the ensemble," Felicity said.

"Who?" Ezra asked. "Remember, we were trying to assemble a believable town? That's why our ensemble looks like the first ten people we picked up at the DMV."

Jethro's voice broke through. "We'll have to hire someone."

Felicity shook her head impatiently. "Where are we going to find someone who is available and can learn the show overnight?"

"Delphi!" They all turned to look at Isobel. "My roommate from New York. She looks like a Botticelli, and she's a phenomenal actress. She does a lot of Shakespeare, so she can memorize complicated text quickly, and this isn't even complicated." She darted a look at Jethro. "I mean, it isn't Shakespeare. It's only the scenes with Swallow and Sousa and then the maid in act two. I'm sure she could learn those lickety-split, and then you could work her into the ensemble scenes once she's got those down."

Hugh let out a nervous chuckle. "It's a creative idea, but Delphi's an alto, and from what you've told me not a very good one. What about the Emma/Sousa duet?"

His words chilled the air.

Ezra folded his arms. "I've made it clear what I think about the duet."

"I'm not cutting 'Song of the Sea,'" Jethro said through clenched teeth.

"It slows down the action," Ezra said. "We don't spend enough time with Emma to warrant a song."

Jethro jutted out his chin defensively. "It's an actual song that Sousa composed to lyrics Emma wrote. It demonstrates their love and helps us understand why he's crushed when her stepfather blocks the marriage."

"What if you gave the whole song to Sousa?" Isobel suggested. "She sends him the poem, and he returns it with a melody. It's his musical love letter to her. It could be just one verse and it wouldn't slow things down." She glanced at Ezra. "As much."

"That's exactly why it has to be a duet," Jethro insisted. "It starts as a love letter to her, and she joins in and that's what makes us think they're going to wind up together."

"But they *don't* wind up together," Ezra said, bringing his fist down on the seatback in front of him.

"We're leading the audience on," Jethro said. "We're creating an expectation and then bam—we're disappointing them."

"No, you're boring them," Ezra returned.

Jethro's face darkened to a dangerous plum.

Felicity cut in. "How soon could your friend get here?"

"She *is* here," Isobel said. "In the lobby. She came up to see the show."

Felicity stood up. "That settles it. There's no time to call down a list. We need an actor in place by tomorrow morning."

"But my duet," Jethro protested.

Felicity put a staying hand on Jethro's arm. "We are all going to have to compromise, and if that means a change in the duet, so be it. Perhaps it will turn out to be temporary. But I'm convinced this is the best way. Ezra, I know you were planning to go back to the city tomorrow, but—"

"I'll stay to put in Isobel and her friend."

"Thank you."

"That's the stage manager's job once the show is open and frozen." Jethro glared at Ezra.

"Frozen? This isn't Broadway, Jethro," Ezra said. "We'll adjust as needed to continue to improve *your* show and make it work. And if we're putting in not one but two actors, I will stay in Albany and see to it myself."

"There's one other thing," Isobel said. "I haven't decided yet whether I want to join Equity. I might want to fill in for three days until you can find someone else."

All eyes turned to Isobel.

"Why on earth would you want to do that?" Felicity asked icily.

"I don't necessarily." Isobel shifted her weight uncomfortably. "I want to sleep on it. That's all."

Felicity's sculpted eyebrows shot up. "Chances to join the union don't come along every day. Most actors in your position wouldn't dream of passing this up."

Isobel gave Hugh a look. "Yes, I know."

"I expect your answer first thing tomorrow morning," Felicity said. "Either way, we'd better go hire your friend."

FOURTEEN

ISOBEL SHOOK A PILLOW into a case and tossed it to Delphi. "You're sure this is all right?"

"Will you stop? This is fine." Delphi added the pillow to the pile of sofa cushions on the floor of Isobel's room and flopped on them. "Why aren't you and Hugh sharing a room?"

"We talked about it, but he was afraid it would look unprofessional. And to tell you the truth, I wanted my own space. I don't exactly get that at home. No offense."

"None taken. But you didn't argue with him, which is probably what he wanted you to do," Delphi said shrewdly.

"As you can see, the rooms are only big enough for a twin bed. And a friend on the floor."

"That's not the point," Delphi said.

"You're barking up the wrong tree. It was mutual. Anyway, if you get too uncomfortable, you can put the cushions back on the sofa and sleep in the living room."

"Or I could kick you out of your bed and make you sleep on the floor."

Isobel wagged a finger at her. "You have to be nice to me. I just got you a job."

Delphi pulled a knobbly crocheted blanket to her chin. "I know I'm going to live to regret this. I'll be in your debt until I cash in my Equity pension. If I ever manage to join the union, that is."

Isobel had hoped to broach her Equity dilemma at the opening-night party in the café, which went on despite Arden's death, albeit somewhat subdued. But Hugh had stayed by her side all evening, and she didn't want his opinion influencing Delphi and Sunil. She'd resigned herself to trying to catch Sunil in the morning, but Delphi had just given her the perfect opening. Before she could frame her question, however, Delphi interrupted her thoughts.

"Say it: you think somebody killed Arden."

Isobel perched on the edge of the bed. "Yes, I do. And if that's the case, we'd have to be looking at some kind of poison. There was no obvious wound of any kind."

Delphi lay back and gazed at the ceiling. "Poison's tricky. Not always traceable. We may never know for sure."

"That would make me very nervous."

"All of this should make everyone very nervous."

"Unfortunately, it should also make everyone suspect me," Isobel said. "Between the masking and the note—"

Delphi rolled onto her side and propped herself up on her elbow. "What note?"

"Sunil didn't mention the note?"

"He did not."

Isobel hopped off the bed and grabbed her jeans from the floor. "I'll show you—" She stopped, the jeans dangling from her hand. "No, wait, I gave it to Kelly."

"What did it say?"

"I'd left my script in the house during tech, and somebody drew an arrow pointing to one of Jennie's highlighted lines and wrote 'Die, bitch.'" Isobel gave a little hiccup. "And she did."

"But if it was in your script, it was probably meant for you. Because if you're covering, you're Jennie also. In a way."

"Yeah, but I'm not dead." She shuddered. "Yet."

"I think the police need to know about that note. Do you know what Kelly did with it?"

"She was going to show it to Felicity, but I don't know if she ever did, given everything."

"Did Arden have enemies?"

"She was a diva, but what show doesn't have one of those? Even if she drove us all nuts, I can't imagine anyone had a reason to kill her."

Delphi gave her an appraising look. "Except you."

"*Et tu*, Delphi?"

Delphi sat up. "Come on, you're the only one who benefits in an obvious way from her death. You stepped in and saved the day in front of Roman Fried, and now you get to take over her role. Your name will be all over the *New York Post* tomorrow."

"But I had no idea he would be here!"

"No, but you knew there were going to be producers in the audience."

Isobel threw up her hands. "Whose side are you on anyway?"

"Yours, of course. But objectively speaking, it doesn't look so good."

"It's even worse than you think." Isobel plopped back down moodily on her bed, which responded with an extended creak of disapproval. "Arden's on an Equity contract, which means her role has to go to an Equity actor."

"Does that mean you don't get the part?"

"It means I have to join Equity."

"What?" Delphi clapped excitedly. "That's amazing. Oh my God, I'm so jealous!"

"Now that's the reaction I was looking for."

"What do you mean?"

"Hugh doesn't think I should do it. I can fill in for three days without joining while they find someone else. He thinks I need to keep building my resume. He says I don't have enough credits yet to be competitive." She felt a tear form in the corner of her eye.

Delphi pulled a wayward curl and let it spring back into place. "He's not wrong. But if it were me, I'd take it and hope for the best. What does Sunil think?"

"Haven't told him yet."

"You're right, though. If it turns out Arden was murdered, it'll totally look like you killed her to get your Equity card."

Isobel erupted with a sound that was somewhere between a gasp and a snort. "Who on earth would do a thing like that?"

"The same kind of people who kill elderly relatives for their rent-controlled apartments," Delphi said darkly. "Okay, I gotta sleep. I have to learn your track tomorrow, and you know I'm not the quickest musical study. I need every brain cell I can spare."

"So you think I should do it?"

Delphi yawned. "It's in my best interest, isn't it? Then I'd get to play Emma for more than three performances. But yeah, take the contract. Live dangerously. Good night."

Isobel switched off the lamp and hunkered under her covers. She lay awake for a long time, staring at the ceiling. She had gone on for the lead at the last minute and saved the day in front of an influential theater critic and probably a producer, and now she was being handed her union card—all in one night. But the fact that her good fortune had come at the expense of someone else's life made it impossible to relish her triumph.

FIFTEEN

WHEN ISOBEL WOKE and saw the pile of cushions on the floor, it took a moment before she remembered why they were there. Delphi was up and out early to learn her role, working first with Hugh on the ensemble music. Depending on how she fared, he would try her on the duet, although nobody but Jethro wanted him to succeed. Then Ezra would spend a few hours working her into the two Emma scenes with Chris and Sunil and blocking her into the group numbers. It wasn't much in the way of rehearsal. Isobel didn't envy Delphi going on pretty much cold in front of the second-night audience.

Isobel found the kitchen empty. She opened the fridge and removed her last yogurt. It was time for another trip to Price Chopper. The *New York Post* sat atop a pile of newspapers on the table, opened to Roman Fried's column. She parked her spoon upright in the yogurt and scanned for her name, which, to her mild annoyance, didn't appear until the end.

> *The proverbial day was saved by a game young actress named Isobel Spice. Though no improvement over Ms. Claire in looks, Ms. Spice offered an attractive singing voice and managed to discharge her duties without the manic edge that typically plagues understudies released from their cages for the first time.*

"I believe that sentence appears in the dictionary as an example of the word *backhanded*," Sunil said, entering the kitchen. "The way 'For God, for country, and for Yale' is the dictionary's example of anticlimax."

Isobel looked up. "How do you happen to know that?"

"My brother went there. He made the mistake of bragging about it to me once, and I taunt him with it at every opportunity." Sunil pointed to the newspaper. "No such thing as—"

"Don't you dare finish that sentence." Isobel tossed the paper aside. "At least he liked my voice."

"Good for you." Sunil opened the refrigerator and removed a carton of eggs. "I'd have thought you'd focus on the negative. Did you read the whole thing or just your part?"

Isobel bristled. "I like to read up from the bottom."

"Mhm."

She returned to the column and started at the beginning.

> *An anonymous tip led me up the Hudson to Albany's fabled Livingston Stage Company for "Sousacal," a new tuner depicting the life of John Philip Sousa. The riotously ridiculous title alone promised a gut-buster on the order of "Elephant! The Musical," winner and still champion of the Best Worst Musical Award (selections on display in the wonderful movie "The Tall Guy" with Jeff Goldblum and Emma Thompson). With a Fried rating of 5 Elephants (so bad it's brilliant), this excerpted masterpiece remains the benchmark for unintentionally hilarious musicalizations of unsuitable subject matter.*

> *I am obliged to report that "Sousacal" falls short of a perfect score with 4.5 Elephants. The plodding story rises above a 4 (just plain bad) thanks to some of the most laughable lyrics ever dashed off to a Sousa march. Oh yes, the entire*

misguided score is comprised of Sousa marches.
Let's just say it must have looked good on paper.
Even more unfortunately, the show was brought
to a screeching halt toward the end of act one
when former Miss New York Arden Claire, in the
role of Sousa's wife Jennie, collapsed onstage,
necessitating a change in personnel.

Isobel skimmed past the part that mentioned her
and read the conclusion.

We wish the comely Ms. Claire a speedy recovery
from whatever ails her. (Although if she's smart,
she'll continue to call in sick until the final
fanfare.)

She set the paper down again. "Well, that's quite a
bombshell."

"Seriously. Who knew Roman Fried was straight?"

Isobel made a face. "I don't mean that, although I grant
you that is a bit of a surprise. No, how about the fact that he
was there on an anonymous tip?"

"I guess I glossed over that." Sunil cracked two eggs into a
pan. "I wonder who tipped him off."

"And why? And what did they say to him?" She picked up
the *Albany Times Union*, which lay underneath. "He didn't
come expecting a winner. He obviously came to trash it."

"That's his stock-in-trade. But I get what you're saying.
Did his source say, 'You've gotta come see this piece of crap,'
or did they say, 'You've gotta come see this amazing new
show' and he immediately recognized the clucking of a
turkey?"

"Turkeys don't cluck—they gobble. And I'm guessing the
former, since it was anonymous." Isobel opened the Arts
section and started thumbing through. "Anyone who was
bullish on the show would have identified himself."

"He might not have been anonymous to Fried. Fried could just be protecting his source." He glanced over his shoulder. "Don't bother. Nothing yet."

Isobel tossed the *Times Union* aside. "Fried doesn't know Arden is dead."

"He'll find out soon enough." Sunil finished scrambling and switched off the burner.

"If you had a chance to get your Equity card now, would you?" Isobel asked.

"Where did that come from?" His eyes widened. "Oh, I see. You'll get yours taking over Arden's part. Congratulations!"

"Hugh thinks I should cover the role up to the Equity limit while they find someone else, and Delphi thinks I should take the money and run. You're the tiebreaker."

Sunil brought his eggs to the table. "That's a tough one. Either way it's a gamble. If you take it, you might not work again for a while, it's true. Then again, it could be years before you get another opportunity to join the union."

"Thanks a lot."

"That's not a comment on you, by the way. It's how the business works. It probably won't be *years*, but you never know."

She spooned up some yogurt and let it drip back into the cup. "What about how it will look to the others?"

"What do you mean?"

"Will it look like I killed Arden to get my Equity card?"

"First of all, we'll probably find out that Arden had an aneurysm—that's my educated guess from having played Dr. Singh on one episode of *CSI*—and second of all, that's got to be the world's worst motive for murder." Sunil took a bite of egg. "Oh, and third of all, anyone who knows you at all knows that the role of murderer is not in your repertoire."

"Do you think I should take my card?"

Sunil waved his fork in her direction. "I think you should do whatever you want."

She stacked the newspapers neatly at the side of the table with a sigh. "Yeah. I have about two hours to decide what that is."

OH, GOD, SHE REALLY can't sing, Hugh thought.

He forced a smile. "That's great!"

"It is?" Delphi asked hopefully. "It feels a little rocky."

"You'll be standing next to Marissa for this number. She's on the alto line as well, so listen to her and you'll be fine."

"Yes, fine, fine." Jethro's voice boomed across the rehearsal studio. "Can we look at the duet?"

"Just a moment." Hugh excused himself to Delphi and crossed the room to the table where Heather and Jethro were sitting with an empty chair between them.

Hugh leaned down and said in a low voice, "This is a waste of time, of which we have precious little. I'm sure you can hear that Delphi has a character voice, not a lyric voice."

"She has to try," Jethro insisted.

"I know what you want it to sound like, and it won't be that. She won't sound like Isobel," Hugh argued.

Jethro folded his arms. "Humor me. And then we'll know for sure."

"Right," Hugh said with false cheerfulness. He returned to Delphi. "We're going to give it the old college try."

"Drop the key," Jethro called.

Hugh transposed the song down a step on sight and taught Delphi the melody. It sounded about like he expected.

"Another," Jethro called.

Delphi raised a questioning eyebrow at Hugh, who shifted his hands farther down the keyboard, and then farther. When they were a third lower than the written key, he stopped.

"This is way too low for Chris. Even if we modulate back up for him, you can't have Emma singing lower than Sousa. And how will we find a key that works for both of them when they sing together?"

Jethro stared stonily at Hugh. Then he sprang up from the table, making Heather jump, and left the room without another word.

"Does this mean the song is out?" Delphi asked, her eyes glistening.

Hugh reached for her hand over the top of the upright piano. "Ezra has been fighting to cut this damn song since the first read-through. Although she'll never say it in front of Jethro, Felicity agrees. It has nothing to do with you."

"You're very kind, but full of shit. I sound like a rhino in heat." A tear rolled down Delphi's cheek. "This is why I don't do musicals anymore. I don't know what I'm doing here."

"Saving the day, that's what. Hang on a moment."

He crossed the room to Heather, who was making notes in her binder.

"I think we need a five."

"Sure." Heather peered around him. "Is she okay?"

"A little upset, understandably."

"I hope she's a better actor than she is a singer," she whispered.

"I can absolutely vouch for that." He followed Heather's gaze and took in Delphi's tight black jeans, Nine Inch Nails T-shirt, and nose ring. "Lose the silver and black, put some rosy makeup on her, and she looks like a Dresden doll."

"Yeah, I can sort of see it. And it's not like we have much choice at this point." Heather examined the eraser on her pencil. "Ezra is right about the song. It's just too bad that…"

"What?" Hugh asked.

She looked up at him. "What do you think of the show?"

"Oh, well, I…" He took his glasses off and wiped them on his shirttail. "I could have done without quite so many marches."

"Ha," she snorted.

"And honestly, that's the one thing 'Song of the Sea' has going for it. It's not a march. But don't tell Jethro. He doesn't need any more ammunition."

Heather gave him an enigmatic smile, and Hugh returned to the piano, where Delphi was folding the sheet music to the duet in half. But he couldn't shake the feeling that Heather was getting at something, and he'd missed it.

SIXTEEN

"I DON'T THINK Arden smoked," Felicity said.

Isobel paused outside the door to Felicity's office, which was open a crack. She waited for a response, but when Felicity spoke again, Isobel realized she was on the phone.

"I see. No, of course. I understand. Please let me know when you have more information. Thank you."

Isobel lurked for a moment, waiting to see if Felicity was the sort of person who talked to herself and might repeat whatever had just been said on the other end of the line, but all she heard was the desk drawer open and shut and the clacking of computer keys. She rapped lightly on the door.

"Come in," Felicity bade her. "Are you here to sign your Equity contract?"

"Yes."

"Good. Makes things easier all around."

Isobel had a flash that Hugh was right and she was somehow getting the short end of the stick, but she'd made up her mind decisively after speaking to her brother Percival, whose opinion she valued more than any of her friends'. He'd encouraged her to take the risk and had given her an idea.

"On one condition," she said.

"Oh? And what's that?" Felicity said with a touch of amusement.

"I'm helping you out of a difficult situation by saving you the time and expense of finding someone to replace Arden, but it's costing me money. I think it's only fair that the theater split the Equity initiation fee with me."

Felicity stared at her, and for a moment Isobel feared that she'd miscalculated. But to her surprise, Felicity's mouth widened into the first true smile Isobel had seen since her false friendliness at the auditions. A chuckle welled up from deep within her.

"Why not? Kelly has your contract ready to go," Felicity said. "She'll be in at one."

Isobel had prepared herself for a flat no or at least an indignant outburst. Before she could recover and express her thanks, voices raised in argument distracted them both. Isobel heard footsteps in the hallway before Jethro and Ezra burst in.

"There's nothing to discuss," Ezra said.

"We are not cutting the duet," Jethro insisted.

"But you said yourself she can't sing it."

"Stop!" Felicity put up her hands.

Isobel backed out of the room but didn't leave entirely, positioning herself behind the two men, whose double girth made a convenient screen.

"Delphi stays. If she can't sing the duet, it's out," Felicity said firmly. "I've made that clear."

"But—"

"Jethro!" Felicity's bark was so unexpected that Jethro took a step backward and almost trampled on Isobel, who skittered out of the way just in time. "With everything else that's going on, you're being maddeningly shortsighted. Hugh will work on a solo version with Chris. From there, we'll have to see."

"I want to audition new actresses for the part," Jethro said.

"This is ridiculous!" Ezra exploded.

Jethro wheeled on him, forcing Isobel to dart around the corner. "You are trying to sabotage my show!"

Ezra's whole body shook with rage. "Are you fucking kidding me? I'm trying to save your show, you—you ape!"

"You rigged the masking to fall, you poisoned the coffee, you tampered with the orchestra parts..." Jethro took a deep breath and geared up for the final accusation. "And you tipped off Roman Fried, who trashed the show!"

Ezra shook his head in disbelief. "Why would I do anything to sabotage a show that has my name—my good name—attached to it?"

"Because I threw out your boyfriend's score."

Isobel gave a tiny squeak of surprise and clapped her hand over her mouth.

"How...dare...you," Ezra seethed.

"Do you deny it?"

"Geoff brought me in on the project, yes, but he is absolutely not, nor has he ever been, my boyfriend. Not my team. I have no idea what put that in your head."

"Fine, play dumb."

"I'm not the one who's dumb. No matter how much I might have preferred Geoff's score, I would never—*ever*—sabotage my own work. Nobody in their right mind would do such a thing. So stop talking out your ass and making excuses for your own failures."

"That's enough," Felicity said sternly.

"I suppose next you're going to accuse me of killing Arden," Ezra bellowed.

"Will you two stop—"

"Of course not," Jethro said. "I know who killed Arden."

A pregnant silence filled the air. Isobel held as still as possible.

Finally, Felicity spoke. "What are you talking about? We don't have any reason to believe her death was a result of foul play."

"Oh, but it was." A cryptic smile overtook Jethro's doughy features.

"Then who killed her?" Ezra asked, rising to the bait.

"The ghost of Robert Livingston," Jethro said somberly. "He haunts the theater, you know. I've seen him."

"OH, MAN," SUNIL SAID. "And what did Ezra say to that?"

Isobel followed him as he turned his grocery cart down the frozen food aisle. "He was more or less speechless," she said. "And then Jethro launched into this whole song and dance about how the ghost of Robert Livingston appears from time to time in full Revolutionary regalia, but only when he doesn't like someone's performance." She pulled a box of frozen spanakopita out of Sunil's hands and tossed it back in the bin. "Did you read the fat content on that?"

Sunil retrieved the spinach pie and dropped it in his cart. "Take it up with Hugh. Since he's stuck in rehearsal with Delphi, he asked me to pick up some stuff for him." Sunil waved a ripped sheet of music paper covered in Hugh's careful English schoolboy penmanship.

"I should probably pick up some stuff for Delphi, now that you mention it."

"Who was Robert Livingston anyway?"

"One of the Founding Fathers. Haven't you ever seen *1776*?"

"The movie, yeah. Wait, is he the guy from New York who keeps abstaining courteously?"

"No. That's Lewis Morris. Livingston gets a verse in the quintet. The one about popping the cork."

"In old New York. Right."

"Anyway, Felicity declared the duet down for the count, and kicked them both out. But this was interesting. Jethro accused Ezra of tipping off Fried in order to sabotage the show."

"Why would Ezra do that?"

Isobel stopped her cart and examined the nutritional information on a box of frozen pizza. "Jethro claimed Ezra was Geoff's boyfriend and he was getting revenge."

"Ezra? Totally struck me as straight."

"Me, too. So did Geoff, for that matter, although I only spoke to him for a second. But my gaydar is pretty dependable."

"By the way, did you ever find out what Geoff said to Hugh?"

"It was only a brief exchange of pleasantries, and I don't think he's seen Geoff since." She replaced the pizza and selected a different brand. "Boyfriend or not, I suppose Ezra could be trying to tank the show before it tarnishes his reputation."

"But what about the other pranks?"

Isobel tossed the second box in her cart and pushed on. "Ezra has full access to the theater, so that's not a stretch. The only thing is now he's stuck up here after his contract is over, when he could be on to the next thing."

"I'm sure Felicity will pay him."

"That's not the point. Why would he have done all that stuff if the result meant he had to associate himself with this show longer than necessary?"

"Because he thought the pranks would shut it down, not extend his job."

"He volunteered to stay. I heard him. He didn't have to." They turned the corner into the soda aisle, where she added two bottles of Adirondack seltzer to her cart. "Are you almost done?"

He snatched a bag of lime Tostitos from a column of chips. "I don't suppose you're going to let me get these?"

"Damn you. My kryptonite!" Isobel moaned. "Fine, throw 'em in. We need something to snack on when we play Celebrity."

"I wonder when we'll know more about Arden," Sunil mused.

"Felicity was talking to someone on the phone about her when I got there."

"You have an uncanny knack for being well hidden in the right place at the right time."

"The door was ajar," Isobel said innocently. "She seemed to be answering basic health questions about Arden. Didn't get much."

They turned into the cereal aisle, where Sunil grabbed a box of Rice Krispies and Isobel selected Kashi Crunch.

"It could have been natural causes if she had an underlying health condition of some kind. Or maybe she OD'd on beta-blockers," he said.

Isobel held up a box of fudge Pop-Tarts. "I wonder. I mean, we don't know much about her personal life, except her pageant career."

"And there's no reason to go digging. Not yet, anyway." He pointed to the Pop-Tarts. "Hypocrite."

"A treat for Delphi. They're *her* kryptonite." She dropped the box in her cart.

"Ice cream and then we're out." He leaned in suggestively. "You know you want it."

They returned to the frozen food section, and Isobel stopped short, causing Sunil to bump into her. Geoff and Talia were standing halfway down the aisle, engaged in heated conversation.

Isobel abandoned her cart and pulled Sunil behind a tower display of two-liter Sprite on sale.

Talia's clear soprano carried down the aisle. "I'm not playing games anymore."

Isobel's eyes widened, and Sunil put his finger to his lips.

"All right, I'll do it," Geoff said in a tight voice.

"Do you promise?" Talia asked.

"Sealed with a kiss. Can't do better than that," Geoff said.

"Then the answer is yes," Talia said.

Geoff didn't respond, and a few moments later, Sunil peeked around the side of the Sprite tower.

"Gone," he said. "That was certainly unexpected."

"It sure was." Isobel followed him to the ice cream compartment. "But it couldn't be more obvious what they were talking about. She's been doing his dirty work and she wants to stop. She's a musician, so she could easily have marked up the parts."

"What did he promise? And what did she agree to?"

"I don't know." Isobel grabbed his carton of Pralines and Cream and slammed it back in the freezer case.

"Hey, you okayed the ice cream!" Sunil protested.

"We've got to get out of here and go tell someone."

He stopped her cart with his foot. "Tell someone what? You have no evidence. They could have been talking about anything."

"Like what?"

Sunil threw up his hands. "How should I know? But running around spreading hearsay is not going to do much for your reputation around the theater. Now give me my ice cream back."

She sighed and retrieved the ice cream. "You're right. But we did learn one thing."

"What's that?"

"Sealed with a kiss? Obviously when Talia was telling us about Geoff, she left a few things out."

SEVENTEEN

BY THE TIME ISOBEL and Sunil returned to the condo, put away their groceries, and got to the theater, Delphi had finished her music rehearsal and was waiting to block her scenes on the stage. Kelly met them at the back of the house, waving a packet of papers.

"Ready to sign your first Equity contract?"

"Ooh, I just got a chill down the back of my neck," Isobel said with a shiver.

"It was probably Robert Livingston's ghost," Sunil quipped.

Kelly drew back, clutching the contract to her chest. "Did you see him?"

"What? Who?"

"The ghost." Kelly's eyes searched the air over Isobel's left shoulder.

"I was kidding." Sunil laughed. "I'm making fun of Jethro."

"Don't joke," Kelly said sternly. "The ghost is real."

"Ignore the nonbeliever," Isobel said, elbowing Sunil. "Have you seen it?"

"Yeah." Kelly nodded. "During the last show in the old theater, *Baristas: The Musical.* I was assistant stage manager, and I saw this glowing white blob on the monitor during the scene where Brianna is singing about how working at Starbucks is better than being a pole dancer. When I looked onstage, I saw him. It was hazy, more of an outline, but I definitely made out a tricorn hat and a cape." Kelly's normally firm voice began to tremble. "He had put himself on the end of the customer line. I called the cue early, because the button of the song is Brianna turning to help the last person, and the joke is there's nobody there."

"Wow," Isobel breathed. "We did a production of *Ruddigore* at Galaxy Playhouse in Vermont last summer, and I saw their ghost."

Sunil gave a skeptical cough, and Isobel stomped on his foot.

"Anyway, here's your contract." Kelly handed Isobel the papers. "Read it over carefully, and let me know if you have any questions." She moved away to confer with Ezra.

Sunil looked over Isobel's shoulder, and they read the contract in awed silence.

"Wait for me!" Delphi came jogging up the aisle. "This is historic. Whatever else happens, you'll always be the first of us to join the union."

"At the expense of someone else's life," Isobel said soberly.

"One has nothing to do with the other," Delphi said firmly. "I mean, it does, but not in the way you mean."

"At least now I can settle for a better class of rejection." Isobel scrawled her signature on each of the four copies. "I hope this isn't a mistake. Hugh thinks it is."

"Hugh, schmugh." Delphi snickered. "I never realized how much I've wanted to say that."

"Speaking of which, how did your music rehearsal go?" Sunil asked.

Delphi grimaced. "It was a painful reminder of why I don't sing in public anymore. The duet is now a solo."

"I got you fudge Pop-Tarts," Isobel said.

"Balm for the soul."

"What are you planning to do about clothes?" Isobel asked.

"I figure we can pop back to the city on our day off. Until then, I can borrow yours."

"You know my T-shirts are a lot blander than yours."

"I'll cope."

"I wonder if they'll move you into Arden's room in the other condo."

"They'll need some time to clear out her things," Sunil said. "And they may not rush to do that. Respect for the dead, you know."

"Who lives there?" Delphi asked.

The door swung open and Chris sauntered in.

"Chris, for one. And Ezra and Marissa." Isobel waved Chris over with a smile. "You haven't met Delphi, my roommate from New York. She was in the audience last night when everything went south, and she's a fantastic actress, and she's going to play Emma since I'm taking over as Jennie. Look, I just signed my first Equity contract!"

Now it was Sunil's turn to tread on her foot, which he did, more gently but still getting his point across. Isobel knew she was rattling and that boasting about her contract wasn't the most sensitive thing to do under the circumstances, but whenever her mouth took off like that, she found it impossible to stem the flow.

Fortunately, Chris had stopped paying attention and was eyeing Delphi, clearly pleased with what he saw.

"Our lucky day," Chris said, thrusting out a hand. "You're brave, aren't you?"

Delphi tugged her T-shirt down, pulling it tighter. "Hard to pass up a chance to work with my friends."

"Even with all the shenanigans?" Chris said. "I'm sure they've told you what's been going on. Things have been a little strange around here lately."

"So I gather. And here I am to make them stranger," Delphi said.

Kelly returned and held out her hand for Isobel's contract. "Signed?"

Isobel nodded and handed three of the copies to her. "I don't feel any different."

"Wait until you've spent three years unemployed," Hugh said, coming up behind her.

Isobel whirled around, surprised and hurt, but Delphi came to her rescue.

"Your job is to be supportive of Isobel's decision," she said disapprovingly.

Hugh held up his hands in self-defense. "I'm trying to protect her from disappointment."

"I don't need protection. What I need is rehearsal." Isobel turned to Kelly. "Is there any way Chris and I could run our scenes when Delphi is done? I'm afraid last night was beginner's luck."

"Yes. Ezra has added an hour for you two at the end. But Thomas wants to see you and Delphi in costumes first." She smiled apologetically at Chris. "Sorry about that. You're going to have a little time to kill, but Thomas needs to get started on alterations."

"No problem. I can chill in the café."

Chris flashed his handsome smile and left.

Sunil stared after him moodily. "You could have made it at least a little hard for him."

Delphi rolled her eyes. "Would you stop?"

"If I were smarter, I'd have stopped a long time ago," he said.

Isobel motioned Kelly a few steps away. "What happened to that script page I gave you with the note on it?"

"Oh! I was going to show it to Felicity, but with everything else last night, it slipped my mind."

"But you still have it, right?"

"It's in the front pocket of my book. Though I don't suppose it matters now."

"It matters now more than ever," Isobel said. "If it turns out Arden's death was unnatural, the note becomes evidence."

"Unnatural?" Kelly narrowed her eyes. "You have a suspicious mind."

"It said, 'Die, bitch!' I don't think I'm reading more into it than what's there, given what happened."

"I guess," Kelly said uncertainly. "Let's wait and see what we find out about Arden. I'll hang onto it just in case."

Sunil and Delphi had disappeared, but Hugh was waiting for her.

"Isobel."

"What."

He sighed and took her hands. She turned her head away.

"I'm your number one fan, you know that," he began.

"You're not acting like it," she said.

"Let's not bicker and argue about who killed whom…"

She kept her head averted, stone-faced.

"Wow. This is serious if even Monty Python won't make you laugh."

She looked squarely at him. "I don't understand why you don't want me to move forward in my career."

"I mean it, let's not argue for real," he said, chagrined. "What is it they say? Leap and the net will appear? I think you're brave. You leaped. This will all work out. I'm proud of you." He smoothed a wisp of hair that had come loose from her ponytail and tucked it behind her ear. "And I respect you even more for having the gumption to follow your heart and not listen to a fool like me."

"You mean it?"

"I do. Truce?"

"Truce."

Delphi and Sunil burst through the door, interrupting their kiss.

"Way to ruin a moment, guys," Hugh said.

"We've been sleuthing," Sunil said.

"Oh? Where, exactly?" Isobel asked.

"The box office," Delphi said. "And guess what we found out?"

"Last night's audience demanded a refund en masse?"

"Nope." Delphi smiled broadly. "My seatmate Roman Fried has a ticket again for tonight."

"Not only that—he's booked a seat for every performance this week," Sunil added. "It's as if—"

"He's expecting something to happen," Delphi broke in.

"And Arden collapsing last night wasn't it," Sunil finished.

Hugh glanced nervously at Isobel. "What does Roman Fried know that we don't?"

"I have no idea. But I bet I know who does." Isobel turned to Delphi. "I believe we're wanted in costumes."

EIGHTEEN

"OH MY GOD, YES!" Thomas held Delphi at arm's length and drank in the sight of her. "You look like a Sargent. No, a Renoir!"

"She hates hearing that," Isobel said. "That's why she has more piercings than a confused teenager."

"Some women take a lot of work to look good in period dress." Thomas glanced over his shoulder. "You know what I'm saying?"

"I know who you mean," Isobel said.

Thomas pursed his lips. "Saucer of cream for the kitty?"

"That came out wrong," Isobel protested. "I like Marissa. She's just full-figured."

Thomas picked up Arden's second-act dress. "There's nothing wrong with Marissa's figure. Victorian dress is particularly well suited to voluptuousness as long as it's proportional. Not to speak ill of the dead, but Arden was the challenge. A stick with boobs. No matter what I put her in, she looked like the cover model from *Sports Illustrated* dressed up for Halloween."

Delphi smirked in Isobel's direction. "Looks like you're going to have to share your cream."

Thomas waved his hand up and down the length of Isobel's body. "It's going to take some doing to make her clothes work for you. It's a four-incher."

"What's that?"

"I have to take in her costumes four inches in every direction. You're petite." He whipped a tape measure around Isobel's chest and made some quick notes. "You'll keep your own first-act costume. The blue muslin is sweet on you, and Emma and Jennie are both upper class, so that's fine. Besides, Arden's first-act costume is still at the hospital. No idea when, if ever, we'll see it again."

"And I'll wear this?" Delphi said, gesturing down at the mint and cream dress draped elegantly on her body.

"Yes. That was Talia's townsperson costume. She'll have to keep the Marjorie Moody gown on throughout, but we'll throw on a shawl or a cape for the first act. I've got some other pieces I can use." He knelt down behind Delphi and gathered up the excess fabric in the back. "This is a bit of a problem, though. I don't have a bustle for you. I'll have to stuff up some rolls and pin you. Won't be the most comfortable thing, but it'll do in a pinch. I might be able to borrow something from Capital Rep."

He unzipped Delphi, and she stepped out of the dress. "It'll all be altered and ready to go by tonight."

Isobel rubbed some yellow grosgrain ribbon between her fingers. "Did the people from the Donnelly Group show last night?"

"They did not."

Isobel's face fell. "That's disappointing."

"But you know who was here?" Thomas asked, his eyes glinting.

"Roman Fried from the *Post*," Delphi said.

Thomas jerked a thumb at Delphi. "I don't like her. She ruins my punch lines."

"I know because I was seated next to him."

Thomas gave a knowing smile. "You were in Irv Donnelly's seat."

Delphi and Isobel exchanged confused glances. "What do you mean?"

"I'm not sure exactly what it signifies, but I know that those two seats were originally meant for Irv and guest. And instead they were taken by Fried and…you."

Isobel frowned. "Do you think Donnelly is still going to come?"

Thomas pulled a black cape off a hanger and swirled it around his shoulders. "Who knows? It depends why he canceled and what his interest level was to begin with."

"And I suppose it depends on what else Fried writes this week," Isobel said.

Thomas stopped mid-swirl. "What are you talking about?

She affected a lofty smile. "He has tickets through the weekend."

"Reeeeally." Thomas turned abruptly and draped the cape over Talia's ball gown.

"We're wondering why he'd come back for more. Seems a bit masochistic," Delphi said.

"Indeed," said Thomas, his voice muffled by the rack of costumes.

"And also, who tipped him off in the first place," Isobel said. "Any ideas?"

Thomas emerged from the costumes, a thoughtful expression on his face. "Don't you think this is but one more example of sabotage? Add it to the masking, the laxative, the orchestra parts… Obviously, somebody wishes ill on this production."

"Yes, but who?" Isobel asked.

Thomas examined a pincushion shaped like a tomato. "There are candidates. The most obvious is Geoff Brown, of course." He appealed to the ceiling. "Why are the cute ones always straight?"

"Aha!" Isobel cried.

"Oh, my pearls!" Thomas gasped, clutching his chest. "Pleeease don't tell me you're shocked by my admission of homosexuality."

"Hardly," Isobel said. "But Jethro seems to think there's something going on between Geoff and Ezra."

"Why would Jethro think that?" Thomas sighed dramatically. "Ezra. There's another one. So manly. But, alas, also not for the likes of me."

"But seriously," Delphi broke in, "why would Jethro say Geoff and Ezra were a couple?"

"To make it look like they're somehow in cahoots," Isobel said. "Because if Geoff is responsible for any of this, the only things he could have done himself are tip off Roman Fried and mess up the orchestra parts. He wasn't around for the other stuff. As far as we know."

"Geoff may not have a boyfriend, but he does have a girlfriend." Thomas paused for effect. "Or three."

"I think he's dating Talia," Isobel said. "Sunil and I saw them in Price Chopper."

"But is he *just* dating Talia?" Thomas asked.

Isobel cast her mind back to the conversation. "She said, 'I'm not playing games anymore,' and then Geoff promised to do something. I don't know what. I thought she might be referring to doing his dirty work backstage, but maybe she meant being two-timed."

"Or three-timed," Delphi remarked.

"So who are the others?" Isobel asked.

Thomas pretended to think, but Isobel knew the names were on the tip of his tongue. "Heather, and there were rumors about Kelly. You know, it's a small theater community up here."

"So, basically, Geoff has slept his way through half the women in the company," Delphi said.

"That doesn't explain Talia. She's up from New York and she mostly does opera," Isobel pointed out.

"What about Arden?" Delphi asked. "Did Geoff date her?"

"Not that I know of, although that doesn't mean he didn't. There are only ten people in theater, you know. We all just change costumes."

"And three of us are in this room," Isobel quipped.

Thomas touched the side of his nose knowingly. "That's what I'm saying. It's a small world. It's certainly possible Geoff and Arden knew each other."

"It still doesn't answer the question we came in with," Delphi said to Isobel.

"My head is so turned around, I've forgotten what it was."

"Why is Roman Fried coming back to see the show six more times? Or are you too miffed that we found out before you did to investigate why?" Delphi jammed a loose pin into the tomato pincushion and tossed it to Thomas, who caught it deftly.

"*Au contraire.* I'm more motivated than ever to find out. After all, I have a reputation to uphold."

NINETEEN

PARADOXICALLY, ISOBEL WAS more nervous for her second performance as Jennie. She hovered by the entrance to the orchestra pit, chattering at Hugh.

"It's completely understandable," he said calmly. "Last night you were a hero. You could have botched everything, but it still would have been a triumph simply because you got through it. Tonight's audience is expecting a performance. And you're doing the whole show."

She tugged at her bodice. "Is that supposed to make me feel better?"

"I'm just saying you should cut yourself some slack. You haven't had the benefit of a rehearsal period." He tapped his baton against his palm. "Accept that tonight is not going to be perfect, and use the performance as an opportunity to get more comfortable. How's Delphi holding up?"

"Girl's got nerves of steel."

"Isobel! Can I talk to you for a moment?" Jethro lumbered toward her.

"Um, sure, I guess."

"You were magnificent last night," he panted. "I have to tell you—"

"If you have notes for Isobel, they'll have to wait until tomorrow. No notes after half hour, and we're at five," Hugh reminded him.

Jethro glared at him. "It's not a note!" He turned to Isobel. "I wanted to say you *were* Jennie. Absolutely uncanny."

"Oh! Thank you," Isobel said, flustered. "I don't know if my performance will be as good tonight. I'm kind of nervous. But I'll try my best."

"The sweetness that was missing in your Emma was right there with Jennie." To her surprise, Jethro took her hand and kissed it, and when he raised his head again, there were tears in his eyes. "Breathtaking. I'm deeply grateful."

"I told you," Hugh said as they watched him leave. "We all wanted you, but Felicity insisted the role be cast Equity. The Miss New York angle didn't hurt, either."

"Sunil said he thought Emma was better for me because she's feistier."

"She isn't really," Hugh said. "I think you were hitting her hard because you had so little to do."

She gave him a pained look. "You never said!"

"You never asked." He kissed her forehead. "But Delphi is Emma now, and you're Jennie, so go out there and enjoy being the star."

If Isobel hoped seeing Hugh before the show would settle her, it had the opposite effect. Feeling even more off-kilter than before, she went in search of Delphi and found her in the dressing room with Marissa. Thomas's head was up her skirt, while Marissa looked on, amused.

"If I didn't know better, I'd say you were being harassed," Isobel said.

"Just fixing the bustle roll," Thomas said, muffled.

"It came undone," Delphi explained.

Thomas reappeared, his blond hair tousled, and smoothed down Delphi's skirt. "You should be good to go. *Toi, toi!*"

He blew them all kisses and swanned out of the dressing room.

Isobel's stomach dropped. "Did Kelly call places?"

"Not that I heard," Marissa said.

"Whew! I thought I'd missed it. But what time is it?" Isobel asked. "I could have sworn five was about ten minutes ago."

"I wasn't paying attention." Delphi looked over her shoulder in the mirror. "Does this bustle make my butt look big?"

"That's kind of the point," Marissa said.

"What were they thinking back then?" Delphi wondered.

Isobel shifted her weight impatiently. "What time is it?"

Marissa picked up her watch from her dressing table. "Ten after eight."

"Kelly should have called places by now."

Marissa shrugged. "Second night. Probably still some kinks being worked out. I'm sure she'll call it any minute."

There was a knock on the door. Heather opened it and stuck her head in.

"See?" Marissa said. "What did I tell you? Places."

"Um, not exactly," Heather said. "We've got a little situation, so we're going up late."

"Situation?" Isobel's senses prickled.

"Nothing serious. I mean...it's serious as far as the show is concerned, but nobody's hurt. The stage manager's book is missing. Kelly can't call the show without it."

"What?" Delphi cried.

Marissa, unaccountably, burst into tears.

"I'm sure it'll turn up," Heather said, although she didn't sound like she believed it. "It's got to be somewhere."

"Like at the bottom of the Hudson," Isobel muttered.

"Dan is on his way in with his copy. It should only be a few more minutes."

Heather left to knock on more doors. Isobel turned to Marissa. "Are you okay?"

Marissa dabbed at her eyes with a tissue. "Yeah, sorry. I don't know what came over me. I guess it's all the tension, and Arden, and..." Tears trickled anew as Isobel and Delphi stood by awkwardly.

"We'll leave you alone for a bit."

Delphi followed Isobel into the hall. "The stage manager's book?" She whistled. "Someone is definitely trying to shut this thing down."

Isobel scuffed her boot against the baseboard molding and jumped when a piece of plaster fell off. "I'm not so sure. Is the person trying to shut it down or just hobble it? And if it's the latter, is he or she pranking it so Fried will write about the shenanigans? Because even if they don't succeed in shutting down the production, it's a great way to tarnish a new property."

"But shows go up late all the time for all kinds of reasons," Delphi said. "That alone isn't newsworthy."

Isobel spotted Sunil and beckoned to him. "There's also you going on cold for the first time. And who knows? Maybe something else will go wrong tonight."

Delphi chewed her lip. "You know, sometimes I hate the way your mind works."

"I'm troubleshooting. I think we should all be on our guard, that's all."

"Arden dying wasn't enough?" Sunil asked.

"That still could have been coincidental," Isobel said. "I mean, if somebody did murder her, why keep going with a prank like taking Kelly's book?"

Sunil put a finger to his lips. "We should keep our voices down," he warned.

"It goes back to the question of what the person is trying to accomplish," Isobel whispered. "Someone may have killed Arden, but that hasn't managed to kill the show."

Suddenly, she froze.

Delphi grabbed her arm. "What?"

Isobel shook her head slowly. "It's not a prank."

"What isn't?" Sunil asked.

"Hiding the book. It isn't a prank," Isobel said. "It's hiding evidence. Kelly had the script page with 'Die, bitch' in the front pocket of her binder. Bet you anything if and when the stage manager's book turns up again, the note will be gone."

TWENTY

IF ISOBEL AND DELPHI found the delayed curtain an additional source of agitation, Sunil was relieved, because it gave him more time to think. Loyalty demanded he tell them what he'd witnessed the night before, but he didn't want Isobel to go off half-cocked. Although she had gotten through opening night like a pro, finding out what Chris had been up to right before curtain couldn't fail to unnerve her, especially now that she was playing opposite him. It had unnerved Sunil when their discussion about Arden, the pranks, and the stage manager's book had cast a new light on what he'd seen.

Opening night, after Kelly had called five, he had gone outside despite the cold to clear his head and say the little prayer he always said before a first performance. Chris was standing behind a dumpster, and at first Sunil hadn't noticed him. But as Sunil paced back and forth, he caught sight of a tiny flame and called out, startling Chris, who jumped into view.

"Sorry, I thought something was on fire," Sunil apologized.

"My lighter." Chris fumbled in the dark. "I was saying the rosary. Always do before opening night. Just wanted to see what I was doing."

"That's why I came outside. To say a prayer."

"Is there a Hindu god of actors?"

"I'm Jewish. And while you'd think there would be, there isn't."

Chris walked over to him. "Are you adopted?"

"No, I'm an Indian Jew."

"Is there such a thing?" Chris gave an exaggerated Borscht Belt shrug. "Who knew?"

"Most people don't. Some say we're the lost tribe."

"You must—"

"Eat well, yeah. We do."

They stood in silence a moment. Then Chris said, "We should probably go in. It'll be places soon."

"I'll come in a sec. I need another moment."

It was Chris's hesitation following through on his move to go inside that made Sunil suspicious. That and the fact that Chris had held up the lighter, but not a rosary. He walked over to where Chris had been standing. An LED on the side of the building cast a shaded glow on the far side of the dumpster. Chris wouldn't have needed a lighter to see. What was he doing, and why did he react so guiltily?

Look at me. I'm turning into Isobel, Sunil thought.

He squatted on the ground. He wasn't sure what he was looking for, but figured he'd know when he found it. It didn't take long. A charred piece of paper was nestled by the corner of the dumpster. When he picked it up, he saw it was a string of nearly identical photographs, the kind from a five-dollar photo booth. Chris hadn't succeeded in burning it all the way, and enough of the woman's face remained in the top photo that Sunil recognized it immediately as Arden's.

His first instinct was to pocket the damaged photo, but he thought better of it and replaced it on the ground. No doubt Chris would come back to finish the job, and if the photo was gone, Chris would know Sunil had taken it. At that point, Arden was still alive, and Sunil had put it out of his mind in order to concentrate on the show. Even now with Arden dead, the fact that Chris burned a photo of her didn't make him guilty of—well, anything, except littering. But Sunil had forgotten about the note in Isobel's script, and suddenly it was impossible to deny that Chris's behavior seemed distinctly ominous.

By the time Kelly called places at twenty after the hour, Sunil still hadn't decided whether it was wise to tell Isobel what her costar had been up to opening night. Delphi's hand slid into his as they waited in the wings for their first entrance. He squeezed it affectionately.

"You okay?" he asked.

"More or less. I'm glad it's you out there with me."

"That's probably the nicest thing you've ever said to me."

"Don't get too used to it. And after this, I swear I'm never doing a musical again. They're terrible for your health."

THOUGH SHE WOULD NEVER have admitted it to her friends, Isobel was slightly disappointed that nothing else went amiss after Kelly got hold of Dan's prompt book. In fact, all things considered, the second performance went quite well. Isobel fumbled a lyric in the first-act finale, and Delphi almost missed her entrance as the hotel maid in act two, but overall it was a success and they acquitted themselves admirably in their new roles. For the first time since the ten-out-of-twelve, Isobel relaxed. Any initial misgivings about taking her Equity card vanished somewhere during the second-act love duet with Chris, when she finally internalized that the role of Jennie was now hers.

"Full company in the house, please," Kelly announced over the monitor. "As soon as you can, please change and come down. Thank you."

Talia paused with a makeup wipe in her hand. "Do you think it's the producers wanting to talk to us?"

"They didn't show," Isobel said.

Talia's face fell. "Were they ever coming?"

"Apparently they were and they canceled. It's probably just notes."

Delphi appeared in the doorway. "Are you heading down?"

"Yeah, give me a sec."

Isobel threw on her sweater and gathered her bags. She didn't really think it was notes. The urgency in Kelly's voice hinted at something more serious, and she had a pretty good idea what it was. Delphi's expression indicated that she had drawn the same conclusion. Either Talia didn't have a suspicious mind or she was playing dumb. Given what Isobel and Sunil had overheard in Price Chopper, she was inclined toward the latter.

They were among the last downstairs. Felicity stood in the aisle in front of the stage, talking to an unfamiliar man, while a sedately dressed woman lurked a few feet away.

Isobel nudged Delphi. "Detectives."

"Amazingly, I got that far myself," Delphi retorted.

Ezra, Jethro, Kelly, and Heather were down front, while the rest of the company, including Thomas and Dan, the tech director, were scattered throughout the auditorium. Talia followed a few moments later and joined Marissa, who had taken over several seats with her belongings. Chris was by himself a few rows behind. The orchestra sat off to one side, looking put out. Oliver was there, but Geoff was nowhere in sight.

Sunil made room for Isobel and Delphi as Felicity brought them all to attention.

"I wish a meeting of this kind weren't necessary, but unfortunately, recent events make it unavoidable." Her usually authoritative voice held a note of unsteadiness. "I'm not in a position to say more, so I'll turn it over to Detective Dillon."

Detective Dillon stepped forward. He had black hair, graying at the temples, hooded eyes, and a wide, friendly face. But the words he spoke were anything but warm.

"I regret to inform you that your colleague, Arden Claire Horowitz, did not die of natural causes. Preliminary toxicology reports indicate that she died of acute nicotine poisoning."

There was a collective gasp. As the memory of Felicity's words on the phone, "I don't think Arden smoked," ran through Isobel's mind, she scanned the theater to see who either looked unfazed or was overreacting. But it was a group of actors. They all looked like they were overreacting, even if they were pretending to be unfazed.

"We will need to interview all of you. I know it's late, and we won't be able to get to everyone tonight. Please check in with my colleague, Sergeant Pemberthy. She has a list of everyone involved in the production, and she will let you know if we'll be speaking with you tonight or first thing tomorrow." Dillon glanced at a piece of paper. "Where is Isobel Spice?"

"Here." Isobel's voice came out in a squeak.

Detective Dillon met her eye across the auditorium. "We'll start with you."

TWENTY-ONE

"I UNDERSTAND YOU WERE Arden's understudy," Detective Dillon said.

"That's right."

"And you've been eagerly learning her role."

Isobel leaned back too heavily in the padded chair in the small conference room next to Felicity's office and tipped backward. She steadied herself against the table, although she realized immediately the chair would never have gone off-balance. She, on the other hand, had, just a bit.

"How did you hear that? I thought I was the first person you were interviewing," she said.

"Please answer the question."

"I think diligently is a more accurate word. I was learning the role because that's what I was contracted to do. I can't help how it was perceived. And," she added, "it's a good thing I did, since I've had to take over."

Dillon turned his hawk-like eyes on her. "That's the problem, you see. In the strictest terms, you're the person who most obviously benefits from Arden's death."

Isobel folded her arms. "Have you seen the show?"

"Not yet," he admitted.

"Come tomorrow and see if you think this role is worth killing for."

Dillon cleared his throat. "Taking over the role enabled you to join the actors' union, which I understand can be hard to manage so early in one's career."

"Yes, and it was a difficult decision. I almost turned it down. Ask Felicity."

"She mentioned something of the sort. But let's be honest here." He leaned forward and his tie caught on a jag in the Formica, but he didn't seem to notice. "Wasn't that for show? You never had any intention of passing up an opportunity like that."

"I thought long and hard about it. I have exactly one other professional role on my resume, and it's an operetta in summer stock. Other than that, it's all college stuff. Now that I've shut myself out of non-union work, I'll probably languish in a stultifying array of offices slowly temping myself to death, while others of my type and talent level are cleaning up in non-Equity productions and preparing their resumes for the moment when lightning strikes and God bursts through the heavens to smite them with their union cards."

Dillon's eyes hardened. "Don't mock me, Ms. Spice."

"I'm not. I'm absolutely serious. Time will tell whether or not I made the right decision. The point I'm trying to make is that I very nearly made a different one."

He held her gaze a moment, then glanced down at his notebook. "You didn't get sick from the coffee the other night?"

"I poured a cup and then—" She blushed at the memory. "Hugh and I got distracted and I never drank it."

"Hugh Fremont. The musical director?"

"Yes. We're dating."

"Why would you sabotage the orchestra parts if it made more work for your boyfriend?" Dillon asked smoothly.

"Points for the segue," she conceded. "But I didn't. In fact, I helped fix them."

"A classic cover-up," Dillon said offhandedly. "And you also brought down the backstage curtain on Arden."

"It's called masking, and that was an accident, pure and simple," Isobel said, making a conscious effort to control her temper. She didn't want him to see that he was getting to her. It was one thing for her fellow actors to suspect her, but another thing when it was a cop. "Besides, I thought Arden didn't smoke."

"She didn't." Dillon leaned back.

His chair creaked comfortably without threatening to tip, which annoyed Isobel further. She felt better when she heard his tie rip a little as the movement tore it free from the jag in the Formica.

"It would be difficult to get a fatal dose of nicotine from smoking," Dillon continued. "We're talking about pure nicotine in concentrated form. Most likely administered in something she ate or drank. Did you happen to notice if she ingested anything right before she went onstage?"

Isobel was tempted to ask if he was finished accusing her and she was officially only a witness, but she refrained.

"Not that I observed."

"And you'd have been watching her closely, right?"

Nope, still being accused, she thought.

"Not backstage. I was only interested in what Arden was doing onstage. That's the job for which I was hired."

"Once it hits the stomach or the bloodstream, concentrated nicotine acts quickly on the nervous system." Dillon took the opportunity to examine the damage to his tie. "We're looking at the twenty minutes before she collapsed, tops. Did she drink from a bottle of water? Suck on a cough drop?"

"We all keep water in the wings," Isobel said. "I'm sure she drank some at some point."

"Do you label your bottles?"

"Sometimes, but not always."

"So, if most of the bottles are unlabeled, it's hard to tell whose is whose?"

"Right. You keep track of your own. Nobody's paying attention to anyone else's." She gave a dismissive wave. "But those bottles are long gone anyway. Either recycled or taken home, rinsed, and refilled, and nobody else has dropped dead. I don't think you'll find much joy there."

"Can you think of someone other than yourself who might have wanted to kill Arden?"

Isobel flashed Dillon her sweetest smile. "Let's be very clear about something. I did not want to kill Arden. And let me go one step further. I will probably figure out who did before you do."

"Excuse me?"

"Obviously, you're not much of a detective if you don't know who I am." Isobel was vaguely aware of an out-of-body iteration of herself hovering somewhere over her shoulder urging her to shut up, but she sped on. "I've worked with the New York City Police Department on three separate occasions, investigating murders that took place in my presence. In all three cases, I led them to the killer, having figured it out before they did. Don't be surprised if the same thing happens here."

Dillon took a moment to frame his response. "If you have any information about who killed Arden, you are obliged to turn it over to the police. Otherwise, you are withholding evidence, which makes you an accessory after the fact."

"Oh, I understand that. It's just that in the past, the police weren't particularly interested in what I had to say. But I'm happy to work with you, if you're willing to work with me." She saw him hesitate. "See? You haven't made up your mind yet whether or not you can trust me, since you've already predetermined—based on hearsay from an artistic director who got it from a bunch of jealous actors—that I killed Arden."

Dillon thrummed his fingers on the conference table. "You've been involved in three other murder investigations? Seems to me you're the common thread."

"I'd say you're right, except that they all led to convictions of people who weren't me." She leaned forward. "Considering all the sabotage that's gone on of late, here's the question you should be asking: who wants to keep the show from succeeding? By your own reasoning, it's not me, since as you pointed out, I've now got my Equity card. Goal achieved, level complete. I submit to you that Arden's death was a means, not an end."

"There are no plans to shut down the production at the moment, so not a very successful means, if you're right," Dillon said.

"Agreed." Isobel took the bold step of standing up, even though she had not been dismissed. "Look, as a show of good faith, I'll give you a few hints to get you started in the right direction. Talk to Geoff Brown, who wrote an original score that Jethro Hamilton chucked last summer and who was supposed to be the musical director. He wasn't in the house tonight, and I'm guessing he's not even on Sergeant Pemberthy's list, since he's not officially involved in this production. Look to the several women connected to the show that he dated, and don't forget Oliver, his brother, who stayed on as assistant musical director. Then there's the animosity between Ezra and Jethro, who have starkly different visions for the show. And finally, you might ask yourself who tipped off the *New York Post*'s theater columnist that the show was going to be a disaster, and what have they told him that prompted him to reserve seats through the weekend? Also, who invited New York producers, and why didn't they show? There. That should keep you busy for a while."

Dillon's jaw hung open in astonishment. Trying to conceal her satisfaction, Isobel continued, "This isn't going to end until you or Felicity shut down the show. And here's how I know. Even though Arden is dead, somebody took the trouble to hide the stage manager's book tonight, which almost caused the performance to be canceled. So let me put it to you this way: you got ninety-nine suspects, but this bitch ain't one. Can I go now?"

TWENTY-TWO

DELPHI CLAPPED HER HAND over her mouth. "You did *not!*"

"You quoted Jay-Z at the cop?" Sunil threw his head back and roared with laughter.

"Paraphrased, but yeah." Isobel pushed open the theater door and shivered in the cold air. It was well past midnight. Delphi and Sunil had been questioned also, while Isobel and Hugh, whose interview was scheduled for the next day, had waited for them in the lobby. They started down the street toward the condo, which was five blocks away.

"Only you, Isobel," Delphi said, linking arms with her.

Hugh trotted to keep up with them. "You might have made an enemy."

"Dear Hugh, ever my protector," Isobel said with a laugh. She squeezed his hand and was surprised when he drew back.

"I'm serious. I'm sure you were enjoying yourself immensely, but perhaps a little restraint was in order, under the circumstances?"

"I restrained myself as much as I could, considering he accused me outright of killing Arden."

"I'm sure he doesn't really think you did. He was just pushing your buttons," Hugh said.

"Yeah, and she beeped, loud and clear," Sunil said.

"My interview was quick, in and out," Delphi said. "I had my train receipt and the receipt from the cab, and they confirmed with Miriam in the box office that I was in the audience. Even though, as Dillon pointed out, I also benefited from Arden's death."

"He certainly seems fixated on that," Sunil said.

"He was forced to admit that in my case it was a stretch, and he let me go with a warning to watch my back," Delphi said.

"He must be warning you against me," Isobel said. "Guess I didn't convince him."

"Oh, and Kelly told me that once Arden's stuff is packed up, I can take her room."

"Don't leave me!" Isobel clutched her melodramatically.

"I won't. At least not right away. I don't mind my little pallet on the floor, or I can take the couch. Truth is, I'm not hankering to move into the other condo. I don't know those people at all, and what if one of them is a murderer?"

"Dillon isn't wrong that unless it's a crime of passion, the killer is usually someone who benefits from the death," Hugh said. "And I don't see what Marissa, Ezra, or Chris get from Arden's death."

"In my experience—" Isobel began.

Delphi groaned. "Here we go."

"Well, I have had some." Isobel allowed herself a flash of attitude. "And yes, usually the killer has something to gain. I think Dillon is missing the big picture, though. He's looking at this as a personal crime and trying to figure out who benefits from Arden's death, which even I have to admit is primarily me. I suppose it could be a crime of passion, although it seems premeditated. But I think he's barking up the wrong tree, because of all the other stuff. The ultimate benefit to the killer isn't from Arden's death—it's from the death of the show. I told him as much."

"I'm sure he loved that," Delphi said snidely.

"Dillon asked me about my relationships with everyone in the company, and he seemed stumped when he couldn't connect me to Arden in any meaningful way," Sunil said.

"That's because he can't," Isobel said. "You didn't have much to do with her."

Sunil paused on the steps leading up to their building. "That never stopped anyone from suspecting the dark-skinned guy."

He had his keys at the ready and opened the door. They crept up the stairs silently and entered the apartment. No light streamed from under Talia's door. She had left the theater as soon as she'd been released, obviously distraught, and must have gone straight to bed. Like Hugh, she was on the interview list for the following day.

An awkward silence descended as they stood in the foyer, each acknowledging the unfortunate truth of Sunil's statement, which still rang in their ears.

"Plans for tomorrow?" Isobel whispered finally.

"I'd like to check out the capitol," Sunil replied.

"Don't bother," Delphi said. "I grew up in upstate New York, and we had to go every year in elementary school. Trust me, it's a poor substitute for DC."

"How about a movie?" Isobel suggested.

"I'd like to join, but I have my interview with Dillon at eleven," Hugh said.

"We'll check the listings in the morning and pick a time when you can come." Isobel gave him a kiss. "We wouldn't dream of leaving you out."

There was nothing decent showing at the movie theater, and in the end, they spent the day hanging around the condo. When Hugh returned from his interview, they passed the afternoon playing Celebrity. They made it through all three rounds, frequently lapsing into gales of laughter despite their barely concealed competitive streaks. Although Delphi was irate over Hugh's lack of familiarity with *The Producers*, she cackled hardest at his attempts to convey Max Bialystock with the clues "a bagel without a hole" and "summer theater from hell." Similarly, he was irked that she'd never heard of Herbert von Karajan, but was impressed with her ingenuity in coming up with "luggage you bring onto an airplane." Isobel and Sunil trounced them handily, and they were still reliving their best moments when they got to the theater that evening.

"I can't believe you've never seen *The Producers*," Isobel said to Hugh, "but you've been in New York long enough to know what a bialy is."

"Seriously," Sunil added. "Your Yiddish education has some weird gaps."

"You should be glad I didn't put in Pussy Galore," Hugh said.

They cracked up anew at that, and then it was time to part ways to their dressing rooms. Kelly was waiting in the hall for Isobel.

"Got a sec?"

"Sure."

Kelly gestured around the corner, where the hallway continued several feet before dead-ending in a broom closet.

"I found my book," she said, a note of uncertainty in her voice. "It was on my table in the booth when I got in this afternoon."

"And my script page with the note was gone," Isobel guessed.

Kelly nodded. "I thought someone was trying to keep the show from going up on time last night, but it looks like they wanted to get rid of the note. Why wouldn't the person just grab the paper and throw it out?"

"Maybe they didn't have time to rifle through looking for it," Isobel suggested.

"But who even saw me put it there?"

"There were plenty of people standing around at the end of the dress rehearsal when I gave it to you," Isobel reminded her. "Did you tell Dillon about it?"

"It wasn't until I got the book back and realized all the papers in the front pocket were gone that I remembered it. I was so focused on finding a way to call the show last night I forgot it was even in there."

"What do you mean all the papers?" Isobel said. "What else is missing?"

"Directorial notes, old set renderings. The copies of your Equity contract. You'll have to sign them again."

"Oh!"

"But do you think I should tell Dillon now?"

Isobel pursed her lips thoughtfully. "Since we can't produce the note, maybe we should keep quiet. For now, at least."

"I was thinking the same," Kelly said, sounding relieved.

"Can I ask you something in confidence?"

"Sure."

"Who benefits if the show gets shut down?" Isobel asked.

Isobel waited expectantly, but Kelly only shook her head.

"Couldn't say," she replied. "Okay. We're at half hour."

Isobel returned to her dressing room, then changed her mind and knocked on the door of Delphi and Marissa's room. Delphi came out in her camisole and petticoat, shutting the door behind her.

"Stage manager's book turned up, but the 'Die, bitch' note is missing," Isobel said softly.

"Somebody is covering their tracks," Delphi said.

"I'm not sure." Isobel's brow furrowed. "If you were really planning to commit murder, why would you declare your intentions like that? It could only get you in trouble later."

"You don't think the note writer killed Arden?"

"No. Someone wrote that note out of anger—either at Arden or at me—and now that Arden's dead, she's afraid it'll look like she did it. And to be honest, if the person is discovered, she'll have a hard time convincing Dillon otherwise."

"You said *she*," Delphi pointed out.

"I did? I wasn't thinking about it. But yeah, it seems more like something a woman would do."

"Did you tell Dillon about the note?"

"No, and Kelly didn't either. We both forgot about it. But I'm glad I didn't. It would only feed the idea that Arden's death was the primary goal. My gut still says otherwise."

Thomas appeared to help Delphi into her costume, and Isobel returned to her dressing room, which she was relieved to find empty. Talia's street clothes were folded neatly over her chair, and her costume hanger was bare. Isobel could hear her vocalizing in the stairwell and wondered why she was the only one who ever thought to avail herself of the empty rehearsal studios upstairs.

The curtain went up on time, but the police interviews had taken a toll on the company. Everybody's energy was off. Chris fumbled several lyrics in his first song, and Isobel was so distracted thinking about her exchange with Kelly that she started to go onstage with Sunil for Emma's scene, and he had to push her back.

She hung in the wings and watched Sunil and Delphi play their scene. Delphi certainly looked lovely. Her skirt was hanging properly now. Either Thomas had done a better job jerry-rigging her fake bustle or he'd located a replacement. Isobel had to admit that Delphi was balancing Emma's vitality with the sweetness Jethro had chided Isobel for lacking. For all her contemporary gloss, Delphi had a natural way with period style. Chris made his entrance, and Sunil rejoined Isobel in the wings.

"That went well," he commented.

"She looks beautiful," Isobel said.

Sunil sighed. "Tell me about it."

The scene segued into "Song of the Sea" in its revised solo version. Although Isobel had enjoyed singing her part, she recognized the scene was tighter this way. And then she was back on.

"Oh, Jennie, you've made me the happiest man on earth!" Chris exclaimed. He reached for Isobel, who pulled away demurely. "Please? Not just a tiny kiss?"

On impulse, Isobel reached out to stroke Chris's cheek, a tender gesture that surprised both of them. She could practically see Jethro making a note, "Too forward!"

She snatched her hand away. "Not until we're married."

The band began "The Washington Post," and Chris spread his arms wide, singing:

> *I'll probably die if you don't kiss me,*
> *Yes, that's what I most want you to do,*
> *You simply have got to see it through!*

He pulled Isobel onto his knee, and she smiled sweetly at him as he continued to sing.

But suddenly, in place of Chris's face, perspiring under the lights, Isobel saw once more the image of Delphi's sleek silhouette, and her smile froze. She glanced into the wings, where Sunil gave her a thumbs-up. Forgetting where she was and what she was doing, she shook her head frantically.

Chris pulled Isobel to her feet and twirled her around, but she felt her body strain against his. He whirled her onto his knee again for the end of the song, and the lights dimmed as the orchestra struck up the gazouta. Isobel wrenched herself free, gathered her skirt, and ran into the wings, not caring that the audience could see her in the half light.

She had to stop Delphi from sitting down, before it was too late.

TWENTY-THREE

DELPHI PEERED INTO the mirror offstage left and secured a stray curl. Her scenes had gone well, although she was more disappointed about the loss of the duet than she was letting on. She went along with her friends' good-natured ribbing about her singing voice, but the comments stung. She wasn't classically trained like Isobel, but she'd always loved to sing, and all through high school she had sung in chorus and been in the musicals, often in a leading role. In college, she'd faced fiercer competition and landed mostly character parts like Snookie in *110 in the Shade* and Lily St. Regis in *Annie*. She'd always thought there would be a place for her in professional musical theater, but in the big leagues, even the actors with character voices sang better than she did.

Still, she was secretly grateful for this opportunity. When she'd hopped on the train to Albany, she'd been seeking escape. Jumping into the show had provided an even better distraction from her personal travails. With everything else going on, Isobel hadn't stopped to ask any difficult questions about what happened with Carlo, and Delphi was beginning to hope that when the time came, she would be able to relate the experience calmly, if not dispassionately.

"Delphi, thank God!" Isobel shrieked in her ear.

Delphi practically jumped out of her skin. "What the hell?"

"Is that Arden's bustle?"

"Yes, but why—"

Isobel yanked up Delphi's skirt and bunched it around her waist. "Hold this."

"Let go! What are you—"

"Just do it!" Isobel screeched.

"Shhh!" Heather hissed.

Flabbergasted, Delphi allowed Isobel to spin her around, and she felt Isobel's hands untying the waistband.

"Don't take my bustle off!"

Before she could protest further, Isobel had untied the wire frame and let it drop to the floor.

"I can't go onstage without it," Delphi protested. "My skirt will be a mess."

Isobel picked up the bustle by the waistband and shoved it into a dark corner behind the rigging.

"You're crazy, you know that?" Delphi whispered.

Isobel grabbed Delphi's hand. "I may be crazy, but I'm pretty sure I just saved your life. Come on."

The next thing Delphi knew, she was onstage for the first-act finale. She went through the motions and her mouth moved along with the words she had only recently learned, while her mind raced to figure out what Isobel was talking about. For the polka at the end, she had to hike up her skirt, which was dragging on the floor without benefit of Arden's bustle.

The curtain came down, but when Delphi looked for Isobel to ask what the hell was going on, she was nowhere to be found. Sunil materialized at her side.

"Your skirt looks like shit. Thomas is going to have a fit."

"Tell me about it. Come on."

Together they wound their way backstage to where Isobel had left Arden's bustle, but neither was there. They found Isobel in her dressing room, carefully layering the contraption into her cloth laundry bag. Isobel looked up as they came in.

"Shut the door," she commanded.

Delphi had never seen Isobel this agitated before.

"What if Talia comes in?" Sunil asked. "Isn't this her room?"

Isobel ignored his question and returned a different one. "Remember during tech when Chris pulled Arden onto his knee and her bustle stabbed her? She made a holy fuss about it, right?"

"Right," Sunil said.

"Chris had just pulled Arden onto his knee when she collapsed onstage," Delphi said, picking up Isobel's train of thought. She looked at the laundry bag in Isobel's hand. "You don't think…"

Isobel's expression was somber. "Concentrated nicotine. If someone dipped the exposed wire of Arden's bustle in it, and she sat down the way she did during rehearsal and it stabbed her, the poison would have gone right into her bloodstream."

"But Thomas fixed the wire," Sunil said. "And I don't remember her having a problem during dress rehearsal."

"Somebody unfixed it," Isobel said. "Anybody who saw what happened during tech could have gotten the idea and pulled it apart again."

Sunil rubbed his hands together uncertainly. "If you're right, then each successive person who wore the bustle could have been poisoned at the same time in the show, every night."

"Maybe that's what Roman Fried was promised," Isobel said, her voice trembling. "A body a night."

Delphi felt the room closing in on her. "I have to sit."

"Now you can. Put your head between your knees," Isobel instructed her. "How did you even come to have Arden's bustle in the first place? When I left you before the show, Thomas was fitting your roll."

"Heather came by with it right before places. The police brought Arden's costume back from the hospital," Delphi said, her head still down.

There was a loud knock at the door. "Is Delphi in there?"

Delphi sat up too quickly, making her head swim. "It's Thomas," she whispered. "He's going to want to know why I took off my bustle. We can't tell him! What if he's the one who poisoned it?"

"Put it on the shelf over the table. Carefully!" Isobel handed Sunil the laundry bag. "And push those wig heads in front of it." She knelt by Delphi. "Tell him you were feeling queasy, and the bustle was rubbing you funny—or something. Tell him you had to take it off and you dropped it offstage left by the rigging. He'll go looking for it, and that will buy me time to run it to Dillon. He's in the house tonight. I'll get one of the wardrobe girls to get a message to him to meet me upstairs."

Delphi nodded.

Isobel crossed the small room and flung open the door. "Yeah, she's here."

Thomas was through in an instant. "Girl! What happened to your bustle?"

Delphi felt herself slip effortlessly into performance mode, and in her most regretful voice said, "The tie around the waist snapped right before the finale. I didn't have time to try and fix it, so I took it off."

"Hmmm. In that case, I suppose I can't blame you for making me look bad." Thomas gave a theatrical sigh and held out his hand.

"Oh!" Delphi feigned surprise. "It's not here. I dropped it backstage."

"And you didn't retrieve it? Who taught you to take care of your costumes? Were you raised by monkeys?"

"Give her a break," Sunil cut in. "It's only her second performance, and everyone's on edge after the police interviews."

Thomas clucked at them. "You all change for act two. I'll get it."

He flounced away. Sunil retrieved the bundle and handed it to Isobel, who ran out of the room without another word. He started after her, but Delphi stopped him.

"Can you stay for a minute?"

"Of course. Still shaky?"

"Just wondering what I've gotten myself into."

"Join the club." They stared at each other in silence for a moment. "It does seem like Isobel has a knack for getting mixed up in stuff like this," Sunil said.

"Thomas will be back in a few minutes when he doesn't find the bustle. He'll be furious."

"Stick to your claim that you left it there. He can only blame you for being careless."

She sat up a bit straighter. "It'll be interesting to clock his reaction." The last of her queasiness drained away as her thoughts crystallized. "If he's the one who poisoned the wire, he'll freak when he realizes the bustle is missing. Let's see what he says when he comes back."

But Thomas didn't come back. When Kelly called places, and neither he nor Isobel had reappeared, Delphi retrieved the fake bustle roll from her dressing room and asked Sunil to pin it under her skirt. To her surprise, she wasn't embarrassed by the intimacy. On the contrary, she found herself hoping the task would take longer than it did.

TWENTY-FOUR

"GIVE ME A SECOND. I'll find it." Isobel leaned across the desk in Felicity's office, where the bustle was laid out before Detective Dillon and Sergeant Pemberthy. The policewoman's strong arm pulled her back.

"We'll examine it," Dillon said curtly. "I don't want you accidentally nicking yourself."

Pemberthy released her grip on Isobel. "If you're right, your friend was very lucky."

Isobel watched while Dillon, wearing rubber gloves, carefully turned over every inch of the contraption.

"No sharp edges that I can see," he said.

"Look again. There have to be."

Dillon waved his hand over the bustle. "There's nothing sticking out."

"There is. I'm sure of it. You have to look"—she turned her head sideways and tried to envision where it would have hit the back of Arden's thigh—"in this area here."

Dillon straightened and shook his head. "Nothing."

"Then the person bent it back in place," Isobel said.

"When would anyone have had time to do that? Surely somebody would have noticed a person fussing under Arden's skirt in the moments after she collapsed."

"Tonight, when you returned her costume. The bustle was handled by multiple people." She ticked them off on her fingers. "Heather and Thomas for sure, also probably Kelly, maybe even Felicity. Any of them could have seized the opportunity when nobody was looking. If you knew exactly where the wire was, it wouldn't take more than a few seconds to bend it back into place."

"It's pretty far-fetched," Pemberthy said.

Isobel gestured emphatically. "You can't figure out how the nicotine got into Arden's system, and I'm telling you: everybody saw her sit on an exposed wire during tech, and she collapsed onstage in the same spot opening night."

Dillon held Isobel's gaze for a moment, then gestured to Pemberthy. "Get this thing tested for traces of nicotine. Tell them to take apart all the wires and run every inch of it."

As the policewoman carefully bundled the bustle into an evidence bag, there was a frantic knock on the door, and Kelly burst in.

"There you are," Kelly panted. "It's places, and you're not changed."

"I know. I'm sorry—this was important. I'm coming now."

The bustle caught Kelly's eye, and Isobel saw her brows knit in confusion, but the exigency of the second-act curtain took precedence. Isobel let Kelly hurry her down the hall.

"You'll have to wear that for the opening of act two," Kelly said. "Thomas is already having a fit over Delphi's skirt in the finale. It's not his night, is it?"

They reached the stage door, and Kelly left to go up to the booth, where she called the show. Isobel took her place onstage in the gazebo next to Chris.

"Where were you?" he asked.

"The cops wanted to see me again," she said.

"In the middle of the show?"

"Their priorities are different from ours."

After the opening scene, Isobel changed into her emerald gown and returned to the wings to watch the seaside concert scene. While Talia sang her *Traviata* aria, Isobel caught sight of Delphi, whose skirt was once again draped awkwardly over the fake bustle roll. She was dying to know what Thomas had said when he couldn't find the bustle, but she knew she wouldn't have a chance to chat with Delphi until after the show. She did, however, find herself face-to-face with Sunil in the wings before her last entrance.

"What did Thomas say when he came back?" she whispered, first making sure nobody could hear them.

"He didn't."

"He didn't say anything?"

"No, he didn't come back. I thought that was weird."

"You know what else is weird?"

"What?"

"Kelly came to get me and saw the cops bagging the bustle, but she didn't ask Dillon why."

"Not everyone's as nosy as you," Sunil said.

"She didn't ask me, either, when we were alone."

"Maybe she thought you'd been caught red-handed?"

Isobel grabbed Sunil's arm. "I think either Kelly put the nicotine on the wire or she knows who did. And get this—the wire was bent back in place. So whoever did it tonight got their hands on it tonight and tried to cover their tracks."

"Or you're totally wrong and the wire is in place because nobody ever undid it again after Thomas fixed it."

"Wait, if Thomas didn't come back, who arranged Delphi's bustle roll?"

"I did," Sunil said proudly.

"You finally got up her skirt? Score! Ooh—gotta go."

Isobel made her entrance for the finale, and finally the show was over. After taking a moment to accept compliments from two of the chorus women, she raced back to her dressing room. She paused in the doorway, trying to figure out what was different. Delphi came up behind her and pushed past her into the room.

"We're switching," Delphi said.

"What?"

"Talia and I are switching dressing rooms. We started moving stuff during your long scene with Chris in act two. It was her idea. She said she could tell I was going to be in here all the time, and this would make things easier."

Isobel unbuttoned her bodice. "Did you check with stage management?"

"I asked Heather during intermission and she okayed it. I couldn't find Kelly."

"She was with me." Isobel filled Delphi in on what happened with the bustle. "Sunil said Thomas never came back?"

"Nope." Delphi braced herself against the dressing table and gestured with a makeup-removal wipe. "Do you think he figured out that *we* figured it out and made a run for it?"

"I don't know." Isobel looked down at her own bustle hanging around her waist. "Help me get out of this thing. It terrifies me."

Delphi untied it. "He's the costume designer. Nobody has better access than he does. And he must have flipped when he saw I took it off. I don't think he bought my story. Do you?"

"I don't know what to think."

There was a knock on the door. "Are you decent?" Sunil called.

"One sec," Isobel responded. They hastily finished undressing and threw on their street clothes. "Okay, come in."

He came in, closed the door, and leaned against it. "I have to tell you guys something."

"About Thomas?" Isobel asked.

"No, Chris."

"Chris?"

Sunil nodded. "Opening night before the show, I went outside to the alley in back of the theater to take a moment for myself. It's something I always do. Say a little prayer. We all have our rituals, right?"

"I take off my school ring, kiss it, turn it over three time in my palm, and then safety pin it to my underwear. Which is always purple," Isobel added.

"Um, that may have been TMI," Delphi said.

"Anyway," Sunil continued, "Chris was out there, too. I didn't see him at first because he was standing behind the dumpster. But then I saw a tiny flame, and I thought something was on fire. Chris claimed he'd been saying the rosary and was using a lighter to see. But there was enough low light that he could have seen well enough without it."

"Not to mention the difficulty of juggling a lighter and a rosary. Plus he has an iPhone with a flashlight," Isobel pointed out. "But go on."

"When Chris suggested we go back inside, I said I needed another moment. He looked like he didn't want me out there by myself poking around, but I didn't leave him much choice. And of course, that's what I did, the second I was alone."

"Did you find anything?"

"A charred photo of Arden."

Delphi gasped.

"You're only telling us now?" Isobel cried.

"I didn't want your imagination running amok now that you're playing opposite him, but between the note going missing and now this bustle thing, I think we need to tell someone."

"What did you do with the photo?" Isobel asked.

"I left it on the ground. If Chris went back and it was gone, he'd know I took it, and I didn't want to tip my hand. And besides, this was all before Arden was killed."

"We have to tell Dillon," Isobel said. "But first we should make sure the photo is still there."

"I'm sure it isn't," Delphi said. "I mean, if you were Chris, wouldn't you go back to retrieve it after the girl in the photo dropped dead on your watch and you were afraid someone saw you burning it?"

"You're probably right, but I think we should look."

They filed out of the dressing room and down the stairs to the wings. The light was switched off at Heather's desk. The cast had dispersed, and only a few crew members lingered backstage. Sunil pushed open the door that led to the alley and the loading dock.

"It was right on the ground behind the dump—" His hands shot out to either side, barring the way. "Holy fuck."

"What?" Isobel asked, her heart skipping a beat.

"Get Dillon. Kelly. Anyone." Sunil's voice was harsh and crackling.

"Is it the photo?" Delphi asked.

Sunil looked at them over his shoulder, his face slack.

"It's Thomas."

TWENTY-FIVE

"HERE, YOU NEED MORE whiskey." Isobel closed the living room door and refilled Sunil's glass with a healthy dram.

He brought it to his lips, hand shaking, and took a sip. "Poor Thomas. I've never seen a…you know…before."

Delphi moved closer to him on the sofa. "It's awful. But at least you weren't immediately swarmed by cops who thought you killed him, like I was my first time. But I know how you're feeling. It's not something you get over easily."

Isobel curled up in the armchair opposite and reflected that this was the fourth dead body she'd seen. Sunil had done his chivalrous best to shield them, but while Delphi had taken the directive to run for help, Isobel had pushed past his outstretched arm. Now the image of Thomas, his blood-soaked blond hair matted across the back of his head, was emblazoned in her mind. The other three victims she'd come across had either not been known to her personally, or, after a brief association, had been strenuously disliked. Thomas was different. She had enjoyed his flamboyant personality, and he had been unstinting with both his compliments and his gossip. Plus, he had taken care to make sure they all looked good onstage. All of which made her feel guilty for thinking him a possible murderer up until the moment they'd found his splayed corpse next to the dumpster.

Dillon and Pemberthy had returned to the theater to question those who were still there about their whereabouts during intermission and act two, but nobody had noticed anyone leaving the theater through the loading door, and, unsurprisingly, nobody confessed to coshing Thomas on the head with the blood-covered C-clamp found near his Bruno Magli-clad feet. Hugh wasn't feeling well and had gone back to the condo right after the show to go to sleep. It was a good thing he wasn't there. When Dillon asked what the three of them were doing in the alley, Isobel found herself answering with a lie.

"I lost an earring," she'd said. "I was out here before the show getting some fresh air and collecting my thoughts, and I thought I might have dropped it then."

Delphi had picked up her cue. "We were helping her look for it."

Sunil had remained silent during the interview, but now, bolstered by the whiskey, he confronted Isobel.

"What possessed you to say that about your earring? I was about to tell him what we were looking for."

"It was stupid, I know." Isobel examined her hands. "I wanted time to think."

"About what?" Sunil asked. "They need to know what Chris was doing out there. Especially now. Maybe Chris went back out to look for the photo and Thomas caught him."

"During the show? Impossible. Chris practically never leaves the stage."

"Sure he does. What about after Sousa's death scene? We're onstage for the entire finale without him."

"Chris wouldn't duck out and kill someone during the finale," Isobel said. "You're not thinking like an actor."

"No, I'm thinking like a murderer," Sunil returned. "Trying to, anyway."

"Fine, but how would Thomas even know Chris burned a photo of Arden?" Delphi asked. "He wasn't out there with you, was he? Say he was looking out the window or something, he wouldn't have known *what* Chris was burning."

"I don't know." Sunil threw himself back against the sofa in frustration. "Thomas always seemed to know everything."

"Isobel's right about one thing," Delphi said. "Whoever it was followed Thomas out there intending to kill him."

"But what was he doing out there?" Sunil asked.

"Looking for the bustle," Isobel said quietly. "We sent him on a wild goose chase. It's our fault he's dead." Tears leaked out the sides of her eyes.

"What? No." Delphi's face paled. "Sunil is right. Thomas must have known something."

"Not necessarily," Isobel said, her voice growing husky with anguish. "If the bustle wire was poisoned, the killer must have panicked when they saw you come on for the first-act finale without it. The person probably thought Thomas figured it out and got you to take it off." She wiped her cheek. "But it was me. I made you take it off. I don't think Thomas had any idea."

"There is another possibility." Delphi turned to Isobel. "I know you like to think you're a genius sleuth, but the poisoned bustle might be a figment of your imagination. Something else entirely could be going on."

Isobel hugged herself. "Like what?"

"Chris might have pricked Arden with some other sharp implement when she sat down. You couldn't see his hands. She did give him a nasty look, which indicates that it was something she knew he did, rather than sitting on her own costume. You should have let Sunil tell Dillon about the picture."

Isobel waved at Sunil. "Go ahead. No one's stopping you."

Sunil rubbed his forehead wearily. "Chris will deny it, unless we can produce the picture."

"It's probably not even there anymore," Delphi said.

Isobel unfolded herself from her fetal position. "Are you guys thinking what I'm thinking?"

"No," they said together.

"Yes, you are. You're both chickenshit. We have to go back for it."

"Now?" Delphi exclaimed.

"When else? We don't want to be seen poking around in the daytime."

"I don't think we want to be seen poking around at night," Sunil said. "Besides, don't you think they've found it by now? I'm sure they examined the ground thoroughly."

"Maybe they missed it," Isobel said.

"Or Chris went back for it yesterday and it's long gone," Delphi said. "Either way, the simple fact of his burning the picture doesn't prove he killed her."

"I know it doesn't, but it does indicate a depth of feeling that I, for one, had no idea was there. You're right that he was the only person in close proximity when she collapsed." Isobel stood up. "This might be our only chance. You guys can come with me or not."

Delphi and Sunil exchanged resigned looks.

Sunil pulled Delphi to her feet. "Come on. You know we're not letting her go alone."

They donned their coats, left the condo, and set out toward the theater in the frigid night.

"Shouldn't we tell Hugh?" Delphi asked.

"He really wasn't feeling well, and there's no reason to wake him up just to upset him," Isobel said. They walked in silence for another block before she spoke again. "Chris obviously hated working with Arden, but when I told him she was dead, he seemed genuinely distraught. I don't know how to factor that in with the photo."

"Relationships are complex," Delphi opined. "They obviously had a past of some kind."

Their steps slowed as they reached the theater.

"The street access to the alley is around here," Sunil said.

They followed him down the block, where the alley snaked along the back of the building to the loading dock. The area was marked off with yellow and black tape. There was nobody around.

Delphi rocked from side to side to keep warm. "Are you sure about this? We're disturbing a crime scene."

Isobel ignored her. "Where exactly was the photo?"

Sunil pointed to a spot on the far side of the dumpster. "Right around there. But it might have been kicked or blown away. I think Delphi's right. This is a bad idea."

"But it's my bad idea," Isobel said, ducking beneath the tape.

She was under no illusions: this truly was a bad idea. But she also knew it was their last chance to look for the photo. She knelt down next to the dumpster. To her surprise, the area didn't look as if it had been swept.

"Is this going to take all night?" Delphi called. "It's freezing!"

Isobel stood. "Are you sure this is where it was?"

"Positive."

She knelt down again and used the flashlight app on her phone to sift through the assortment of paper, dead leaves, bottle caps, and other detritus. Lost to herself for several minutes, she focused on her search but found no charred pieces of paper. She rose, empty-handed.

"Nothing," she said.

"Hello."

A deep voice broke through the stillness, and Isobel caught her breath. Detective Dillon emerged from the shadow of the loading dock, his hand extended.

"Looking for this?"

TWENTY-SIX

"I WAS WAITING TO SEE who would come back for it," Dillon said, stepping forward. "Thought it might be you. You see, when a person loses an earring, usually they're still wearing the other one."

"Wh-what?" Isobel stammered, her heart pounding.

"When I asked earlier why you came out here, you said it was to find a lost earring. But you weren't wearing earrings. You were looking for this, weren't you?"

He held up a plastic evidence bag, and Isobel saw the charred image of Arden's face, just as Sunil had described.

"So it was still here," she murmured.

Dillon put a hand on her arm. "Suppose we go down to the station, and you tell me why you were burning a photo of the actress you were understudying?"

Isobel flinched, but Dillon's grip held firm.

"I wasn't burning it. Chris was."

"Chris?"

"Chris Marshall, who plays Sousa. Sunil saw him." She hollered over her shoulder, "Sunil! They found the photo!"

There was no response. Dillon gave a nod, and Pemberthy appeared from behind him. She walked back out to the alley entrance and looked up and down the street.

"There's no one else, sir."

"What? Delphi and Sunil were here a minute ago! You've got to find them." Isobel clutched Dillon's other arm, suddenly terrified. "Something's happened to them."

"Are you sure they were with you?"

Isobel gaped at him. "Of course I'm sure!"

"They seem to have left you in the lurch," Dillon remarked.

Isobel's eyes blazed. "Okay, you're right. We came back tonight to look for the photo. Sunil told us about it after the show, and I insisted we come out here to look for it, and that's when we found Thomas."

Dillon eyed her. "If that's the case, why didn't Sunil come to us about the photo as soon as Arden's murder came to light?"

"I think he forgot about it until now."

Dillon gestured theatrically around the alley, empty but for the three of them.

"I would, but he doesn't seem to be here. Let's go." He led Isobel toward the alley entrance.

She stumbled along next to him, continuing her story. "We didn't want to tell you about Chris without having possession of the photo. He dropped it when Sunil surprised him in the act of burning it right before the show opening night. Chris pretended he'd come out here to say the rosary, but Sunil stayed outside after he left and found it. He was going to take the photo then and there, but he didn't want Chris to figure out he had it. And like I said, he only told me about it tonight. That's why we came out after the show came down, and that's why we came back now. Without the photo in hand it would have been Chris's word against Sunil's. I promise, if you test that photo, you'll find Sunil's and Chris's prints on it, but not mine."

Dillon shook his head in wonder. "Do you ever stop talking?"

"You're wasting your time with me. You should be questioning Chris."

"Hey! Let go of her!"

Isobel flushed with relief at the sound of Sunil's voice. He and Delphi sprinted toward Dillon's car.

"Where were you guys?" Isobel yelled.

"We walked around the block to keep warm," Delphi said, panting as they drew near. "We told you. Didn't you hear us?"

"No, I didn't. Sunil, tell Detective Dillon what you saw opening night," Isobel demanded. She tapped her foot impatiently as Sunil repeated, pretty much verbatim, what she had already told Dillon. When he finished, she turned to the detective. "Do you think you could let go of me now?"

Dillon obliged, and Isobel made a show of rubbing her arm, although he hadn't really hurt her.

"Tell me about Chris and Arden. What kind of relationship did they have?" Dillon asked Sunil.

"We were all annoyed by her diva act, but it seemed to get to Chris more than the rest of us. It got to the point where he'd pretty much stopped talking to her," Sunil said. "Beyond that, I couldn't say."

Isobel took up the question. "He seemed shaken up when he found out Arden was dead, which is a point in his favor, I suppose."

"And Arden was sitting on his knee—the way you do now in that song, the one with the inane lyrics—when she collapsed?" Dillon asked.

"They all have inane lyrics," Isobel said. "But yes, that's the one. Now that you've seen me do it, you can imagine it. One minute she was sitting there, and the next minute she was on the floor. But my idea about the bustle might be wrong. Chris could have injected her with something."

"The fact that the costume designer is dead makes me think you might be right, but we won't know for sure until the tests come back."

"That doesn't necessarily rule Chris out. He could have been the one who tampered with the bustle. Why don't you ask him why he was burning a photo of Arden an hour before he killed her?"

"Talk about leading the witness." Dillon opened the car door. "Get in. All of you."

Isobel crossed her arms. "Before you rush us to the station, my point—and I actually had one—is that now you have the photo. We came back here to find it to *bring* to you. So you got here first, whatever. The end result is the same."

"What are you talking about?" Dillon asked. "I'm giving you a ride home. It's freezing."

Chagrined, Isobel got into the car, and Delphi and Sunil piled in silently after her.

"Where do you all live?" Dillon asked.

"Four blocks down and one over."

"Theater put you up?"

"In a condo."

Dillon caught her eye in the rearview mirror. "Who lives there?"

"The three of us, Hugh, and Talia. Chris, Marissa, and Ezra live in another one. Arden lived there too. It's two blocks away from ours."

"That's it, up ahead on the right," Sunil said.

Dillon pulled over and turned around to face the back seat.

"See what else you can find out about Chris and Arden. What kind of history they had that would lead him to burn that photo."

"I thought you were going to question him," Isobel said, surprised.

"I am," Dillon said. "See what you can get from the others. You know, you're not doing too badly so far."

FELICITY BREATHED A SIGH of relief when the detective's car pulled away. She'd heard voices but couldn't identify them, and she didn't dare peek out the window to see who had shown up. She'd known there would be a continued police presence at the back of the theater, but she hadn't expected a mob. When the last security guards left the building for the night, she had shut the lights off. It didn't matter; she knew exactly where to find what she needed. Things were getting out of hand, she thought, as she stuffed the file into her oversized bag. If any of this got traced back to her, it would be all too easy for the police to draw the wrong conclusion. At this point, there was nothing to do but make sure there was no trail, paper or electronic. She glanced at her computer screen, which she had dimmed to a faint glow. One minute left. She examined her manicure and contemplated her endgame, but no clear path emerged. There were too many unknowns.

The computer chimed, and she nodded, satisfied, at her empty trash icon. Then Felicity switched her computer off and slipped out of her office, quietly closing the door behind her.

TWENTY-SEVEN

"WHERE HAVE YOU BEEN?" Hugh demanded.

"Now, don't go all Mrs. Weasley on us," Isobel said, shutting the front door. "We went back to the theater to check something out."

"You could have at least told me you were going!"

Delphi and Sunil exchanged a glance and slunk off toward the living room, but Hugh stood his ground in the foyer.

"I thought you were asleep, and as my mother says, bad news can always wait," Isobel said.

Hugh eyed her suspiciously. "What bad news?"

She swallowed. "It's Thomas. He's been killed."

He struggled to make sense of her words, but it was too incredible. "Thomas? How? When?"

"Someone smashed him on the head in the alley behind the theater, probably during the show. We found him after you left."

A wave of nausea overtook him, and he leaned against the wall to steady himself. "That's just awful. Bloody awful."

Isobel gave a little hiccup. "Possibly not the best choice of words."

"Lord, you're right. I'm sorry. And I'm sorry I wasn't there for you."

"It's okay," she said, reaching for his arm. "It's not like there was anything you could have done, and at least you didn't have to see what we saw."

He pulled away, gripped suddenly by a combination of fear, anger, and hurt as her actions sank in. "And you went back? Without telling me any of this?"

"You didn't honestly think something had happened—to all three of us?"

"I didn't know! And now with two people dead, it isn't exactly unreasonable to fear that whoever is knocking off members of our company is getting more efficient in his removal technique!"

To his immense annoyance, Isobel burst out laughing. "That's one of the things I love about you," she sputtered. "You can be mad as hell, but you still manage to turn a pretty phrase."

He grabbed her hand. "We have to talk."

She pulled back, her expression veiled. "We are talking."

"You know what I mean."

She gave an exaggerated yawn. "Look, it's late and it's been a difficult night. Can we talk in the morning?"

If he were back in Cambridge, if she were an English girl, he'd back off in an instant. Then again, things would never have come to this pass in the first place. Their native reserve would have kept their tempers in check, and eventually they'd simply have drifted apart. But Isobel was so confounding that he knew he had to be aggressive like an American or he might never have the guts to confront her again.

"Now." A wheedling note crept into his voice, and he despised himself for it. "Please?"

"Your place or mine?"

"Mine."

She followed him silently down the hall to his room, which was adjacent to Sunil's. She sat on his bed, and he felt her eyes on him, following as he paced.

"I've hardly seen you since Delphi got here."

"It's safe to say we've all been a bit busy since then."

He shook his head sadly. "It isn't that. It's like you've gone into full detective mode with your friends, and the whole reason we were excited to work together—so we could have some time alone—just went out the window."

"You once said you'd totally support me any time I wanted to investigate a crime."

"I do. But that doesn't mean I want to be left out completely."

She gave a tiny squeak. "You're jealous!"

He cringed and ran his fingers through his hair. "You make me sound like a year-nine girl. But all right, maybe I am. It's more than that, though. I don't know how to say this."

"Just say it."

This was the moment he had been dreading. Once he gave voice to the niggling doubt that had been plaguing him since they started dating, there was no going back. Either she would dispel his fears and their relationship would continue to grow, or she would confirm them and that would be the end. Then again, he had been the one to insist on this conversation. It was time.

"I'm never entirely sure how you feel about me." She opened her mouth to protest, but he held up a hand. "Let me finish. I mean, obviously you don't find me repulsive, but there are times when I feel…" He pulled off his glasses and rubbed them roughly on his shirttail. "I don't know how to say this and not sound like a total wanker…sometimes I think you're more attracted to my talent and to what you think I can do for you professionally than you are to me."

God, that sounded awful, he thought, but he'd made his point. He glanced at her to see how she'd taken it and realized he couldn't make out her expression without his glasses. He put them back on, but they were cloudier than before. Still, he was able to register her response, and the best way he could describe it was caught out. In an instant, however, this morphed into something aggrieved, but then, just as quickly, her lip twitched and she looked like she was about to cry.

"I don't know," she said finally. A single tear slid down her cheek.

His heart sank. He was right. But before he could say anything, she went on.

"I won't lie. Part of what attracts me to you is your talent. I mean, my God, you're amazing! But I also think you're incredibly attractive. I wouldn't be sleeping with you if I didn't think so. But the truth is…" A second tear chased the first, and she wrung his blanket between her hands. "I don't know if it's…"

"Love?" He felt the room swim a tiny bit. "I guess on some level I always suspected I felt more for you than you for me."

She rose and took his hands in hers. "Does it have to be a full-on serious commitment? Can't we be dating without having to make pronouncements and measure our feelings on some scale of indifference to marriage?"

He pulled his hands away. "You want to solve the murders, and I want to think. Maybe we should keep our relationship professionally friendly for the time being. When the show is over and we're back in New York, we can…reevaluate."

An expression that might have been relief flickered across her pert features, and she sighed. "Oh, Hugh. I don't want to hurt you. I'm sure we can find a way."

He nodded bravely. "I'm sure we can, too. Perhaps just not right now."

TWENTY-EIGHT

"LOOK AT THIS." Delphi shoved the *New York Post* toward Isobel. "Exactly what you'd expect."

Isobel scanned Roman Fried's column.

> *The* Post *has learned that Livingston Stage Company's leading lady and former Miss New York Arden Claire has passed away. Her able young understudy, Isobel Spice, steps into Ms. Claire's role as Jennie Sousa in "Sousacal," the biographical tuner now playing at LSC. One must wonder if Ms. Spice has watched "All About Eve" one too many times, especially since it appears her former role as Sousa's first love has been reassigned to her bosom friend, Delphi Kramer, who just happened to be in the audience opening night. Details of Ms. Claire's death have not been released. Watch this space.*

"He's falling down on the job." Isobel tossed the paper aside. "No mention of Thomas."

"He wouldn't have heard about that yet," Sunil reminded her. "I'm sure he'll be all over it when he does."

Isobel pushed away from the kitchen table and made a show of pouring herself more coffee. "I don't understand why he's so interested in a production in Albany. 'Watch this space'? Is there really nothing happening on Broadway? Or off, for that matter?"

"When you put it like that, it does seem strange," Sunil said.

"What seems strange?" Talia asked from the doorway.

Sunil offered her the paper. "The *New York Post* seems unduly interested in our offstage drama."

Talia took it with a shrug. "Not that strange. It's a new property, starring a former Miss New York..."

"Very former," Delphi said under her breath.

But Talia didn't respond. She was frowning at the page.

"What is it?" Isobel asked.

Talia looked up, somewhat guiltily, it seemed to Isobel. "Nothing. I guess it is a little strange."

Isobel took the paper from her and ran over the article again, but nothing new jumped out at her. She kept her eyes on the page as she spoke. "Chris seemed broken up about Arden, which I also thought was a little odd."

"What's so odd about that?" Talia asked.

Isobel looked up innocently. "I'd gotten the impression he was no more a fan of hers than the rest of us."

Talia's face reddened. "Speak for yourself. I thought Arden was okay. And she and Marissa were good friends."

She stalked over to the fridge, opened it and stared blankly at the shelves.

Delphi cocked her head toward Talia's back. Isobel cleared her throat.

"I'm sorry. That was insensitive. I didn't realize—"

Talia whirled around, tears glistening on her cheeks. "Didn't realize what? That not everyone wanted Arden dead so they could play her part? And she and Chris were engaged once, but she called it off—so no, it's not *odd*. The only thing odd about any of this is you!"

She slammed the refrigerator door and stormed out of the kitchen.

"I suppose you're going to pretend your goal all along was to piss her off so she'd say something interesting," Delphi said.

"People reveal a lot in anger," Isobel said defensively. "And now we know Chris and Arden had a past. That's unexpected, don't you think?"

"It explains his contradictory feelings," Sunil said. "He loved her, but she dumped him. He probably still loves her."

"Isobel!"

She turned to see Hugh standing where Talia had been a moment ago, sadness spreading across his face, and realized with dismay that he thought Sunil was talking about them.

"Talia just told us Chris and Arden were engaged once," she explained quickly. "We've been trying to get our heads around why he burned a photo of her but then mourned her death."

Hugh blinked. "Ah."

"That's why we went back to the theater last night. To find the charred photo to give to the police. Which we did."

She emphasized her final words to remind him that their actions last night had a measurable purpose. Somehow, she was more concerned about driving that point home than restoring equilibrium to her feelings about him.

"And you say Chris burned a photo of Arden?" Hugh asked.

"I saw him behind the theater opening night," Sunil said. "Of course it doesn't mean he wanted her dead, although it certainly makes him a suspect."

"It also explains the call I just got," Hugh said. "We're having an understudy rehearsal for you today."

Sunil's eyes went wide. "Me?"

"Chris has been taken in for questioning. Kelly wants to make sure you're on top of the part in case he's not released in time for tonight's performance."

"But I—I—" Sunil stammered.

They all stared at him.

"Please tell me you've been learning the role," Isobel pleaded.

"Yes, but I thought since I'm the second cover, it wasn't a super top priority for me to have it down, at least not this early in the run."

Isobel and Hugh exchanged a glance, united in their surprise.

Hugh recovered first. "What are you talking about? As far as I know, you're the only cover."

Sunil swallowed. "Um. I hope that's not true."

"Oh my God!" Isobel clapped her hand to her forehead. "I told you to work on it!"

"What made you think you were the second cover?" Hugh asked.

"Jethro told me after the first read-through."

"If you're not the first cover for Sousa, then who is?" Isobel demanded.

Sunil gave them a sheepish look. "Jethro."

"What?" Delphi exclaimed.

"Impossible," said Hugh.

"And it never occurred to you to check with Kelly or Ezra or Felicity, who's the person who hired you?" Isobel asked.

"How was I supposed to know he was making it up?" Sunil's voice rose angrily. "And maybe he wasn't! Maybe he really is planning to go on."

"He'll have to, if you're not prepared," Delphi said.

"Which is probably what he was counting on," Isobel said. "Except if that's the case…"

"What?"

"It means he was expecting to have the opportunity."

"You think Jethro framed Chris so he could go on as Sousa in his own lousy show? That makes less than no sense," Delphi said.

"Especially since Chris burning the photo doesn't have anything to do with Jethro," Sunil said. "No, I think he just wanted to reserve the option. And by telling me and nobody else, it ensured that if something did happen to Chris, I'd be underprepared and he'd get to go on."

"Not everyone would have taken Jethro's unsubstantiated word on the subject as a get-out-of-jail-free card," Isobel scolded him.

"Jethro is not going on as Sousa if I have anything to say about it," Hugh said firmly. "He's enough of a pain in the arse as the writer. I can't imagine what he'd be like to conduct."

"But I'm not ready," Sunil protested.

Isobel yanked Sunil to his feet. "Then you'd better get cracking."

TWENTY-NINE

As THEY ALL WALKED to the theater together, Sunil berated himself for being naïve enough to believe Jethro, especially since his contract was perfectly clear about his duties: "Cover: Sousa." He cast his mind back to that first day of rehearsal to see if he'd missed any signs that Jethro was having him on. Their conversation had taken place during the act break. Stage management had provided the customary first-day spread of bagels and coffee, and Sunil had been refilling his cup when Jethro's reedy voice startled him and he'd spilled powdered creamer all over himself.

"Nice reading of Swallow," Jethro had said.

"Thanks." Sunil had acknowledged the compliment while ineffectively brushing granules of creamer off his favorite sweater.

"Sorry you don't have more to do in the show. I mean, you've got the Pawnee chief, but I'm guessing you're not exactly thrilled about that," Jethro observed shrewdly.

Sunil responded with characteristic self-deprecation. "It's a step up from Halal Guy Number Two. And at least I've got Sousa to work on."

Jethro whistled through his teeth. "You'd have to knock off both of us, though. And that's not likely, is it?"

"I don't follow."

"You're the second cover for Sousa, after me, right? Something would have to happen to both Chris and me for you to go on. You don't need to spend all your coffee breaks cramming. You can explore our lovely state capitol building and its environs."

"But my contract doesn't specify second cover."

"They never do."

Like an idiot, he'd taken Jethro's words to heart and blown off learning the role, although he hadn't taken him up on the sightseeing. Still, he wondered now at his reluctance to explain to Isobel why he wasn't bothering to study up. He remembered almost telling her during the ten-out-of-twelve, but somehow they'd gotten off the track. Did he know on some level she'd call bullshit? And why hadn't he double-checked with stage management? Why had he eagerly accepted Jethro's permission to avoid learning Sousa's part?

He knew the answer. The material was downright embarrassing, and Sousa had the lion's share of it. He had taken refuge in his supporting role, knowing there was a better chance of avoiding ridicule the less he had to do. Unlike Isobel, who seemed thrilled to expand the parameters of making a fool of herself, he shrank from it, despite the egotism that fueled every actor's desire to take center stage. Perhaps it was because so often he *was* relegated to Halal Guy #2 or, to his mother's horror, Terrorist #1, that his threshold for feeling foolish was lower than Isobel's.

Of course, he should have known better. He should have acted like a professional and done the job he was hired for, regardless of the alleged line of succession. And now he was completely behind the eight ball. He'd have to learn the entire role in a day—unless Jethro was somehow able to strong-arm the powers that be into letting him go on. Sunil hoped he had absorbed most of the words by osmosis, and as far as the blocking went, the others could always propel him in the right direction if he got in some chorister's way.

Who was he kidding? He was totally unprepared, and that was nobody's fault but his own. It was going to be an intense day, followed by a nerve-racking performance that he'd have to get through with as many notecards and mnemonic devices as he could devise. One thing was for sure: he'd never be this irresponsible again.

When they walked into the lobby, Sunil was surprised to see Ezra, Felicity, and Kelly standing in front of the theater doors, which were firmly shut.

"I have no idea what it is," Kelly was saying. "Or where it's coming from. It seems to be everywhere."

"Well, call someone," Felicity demanded.

"Who? What kind of person deals with this?"

"What's going on?" Hugh asked.

Kelly jerked a thumb at the theater doors. "Smell for yourselves."

Hugh opened the door, and Sunil, Isobel, and Delphi followed him inside.

Delphi clapped her hand over her nose. "Oh my God. It's worse than South Street Seaport after Hurricane Sandy."

Sunil nodded, trying to hold his breath. The stench was overpowering. He couldn't imagine where it was coming from. Undeterred, Isobel bolted down the aisle toward the stage, where the curtains were drawn and a work lamp was set up.

"It's worse down here," she called through her fingers.

Sunil gasped for air, felt his stomach churn ominously, and ran back into the lobby. Hugh and Delphi were close on his heels.

"Ugh!" Hugh coughed. "That's awful. What is it? What can be done?"

"I don't know," Kelly said. "I mean, who do you call to fix a smell?"

"It's your job to figure it out. And fast," Felicity snapped. "There's no way we can allow an audience in there with the theater smelling like—I'm not even going to say it." She stalked away down the hall.

Kelly gestured helplessly. "I'm open to suggestion."

But Sunil's mind was racing in the opposite direction. This could be the reprieve he hadn't dared hope for. If they couldn't rid the theater of the putrid smell, they'd have to cancel the performance. And by tomorrow, Chris would be back, unless they'd arrested him of course, but in any case, with an extra day, he'd have time to nail down the role before he had to perform it. Unless…

He darted back into the theater, with Delphi calling after him, "What are you, crazy?"

"Isobel?" he cried. "Isobel!"

She poked her head out from the wings and called back, "I'm over here. I think I've figured out—"

"Shhh!" He galloped down the aisle waving his arms frantically and sprinted up the side stairs to the stage. "Tell me. Quietly."

She eyed him curiously and then hefted the bottom of the curtain. "Look at the stitching. It's been opened and rebasted." She gritted her teeth. "Dare me?"

He nodded, and she ripped it open. The smell instantly intensified, and she turned the hem of the curtain inside out. About two dozen shrimp tumbled onto the floor.

"Eeeugggh!" Isobel plugged her nose.

"What made you even think to look?" Sunil asked, trying to breathe through his mouth.

"I read about it on the internet. A jilted wife sewed shrimp into the curtains of her house before leaving it to her ex. The smell drove him so crazy he sold it back to her for peanuts but took the curtains with him, and she got the last laugh. I'm sure it's urban legend, but it occurred to me our prankster might have decided to try it, proven or not." She stood up and gazed into the house. "I wonder if it's only in the curtains. The smell is everywhere."

Sunil grabbed her arm. "Let's keep this quiet for now."

"What? Why?"

"I've been an ass. You were totally right. I should have been learning my role all along, whether or not Jethro was telling the truth. I was hired to understudy Sousa. Lesson learned."

"Better here than on Broadway," Isobel said.

"I marvel at your continued faith in me. Lord knows I don't deserve it. But right now I need to buy some time. There's no way I'll be ready to go on tonight. Let's hold off telling anyone what you found, okay?"

Isobel bit her lip. "I don't know if that's a good idea."

"At least until this afternoon when it would be too late to get rid of the smell in time. Please?" he begged.

"You really can't be ready by tonight?" she asked reproachfully.

He winced. "It'd be dicey. And do you want to play opposite Jethro?"

"Sold." She glanced at her watch. But only on one condition."

"Anything."

"That you start working on Sousa right now."

"Deal." He pointed to the shrimp. "What about those?"

Isobel used the material to scoop them back inside the hem and rolled up the bottom of the curtain to secure it. "If we throw them out anywhere, the smell will spread, and they'll figure it out." She stood up. "Let's leave by the stage door and go around to the lobby that way. We don't want anyone wondering why we've been in here so long."

He pushed the door open cautiously. "Coast looks clear."

Isobel followed him out, but they were stopped almost immediately by the sound of Felicity's voice. She was speaking softly, but the intensity of her tone propelled her words around the corner to where they were standing.

"I don't take kindly to blackmail, Mr. Fried, and I don't know where you got that information," she said.

Isobel inhaled sharply, and Sunil put his hand over her mouth. He shook his head ever so slightly.

"Publish whatever you like. I'm sure you will regardless."

Isobel mimed talking on the phone, and Sunil nodded.

"As I said, you can't prove anything. Speculation is just that, and you'll look foolish when you're proved wrong."

There was a longer silence, and when Felicity spoke again, it was clear that she'd hung up on Roman Fried and placed another call. Their eyes widened as they heard her speak.

"Magnus? Destroy your files. All of them."

THIRTY

"ARE YOU SURE you heard her correctly?" Delphi asked.

They were in the third-floor studio, on a break from Kelly putting Sunil through his paces. It hadn't yet been determined whether or not the show would go on. In the meantime, Sunil was rehearsing, just in case. Isobel was pleased to note that he knew the role better than he thought. Kelly and Hugh had gone off to consult with Ezra about "Song of the Sea," since it would save time if he didn't have to review the new solo version with Sunil. Isobel was relieved that Hugh was out of the room. He had been perfectly gentlemanlike all day, but Isobel knew he was still upset by their conversation the night before. She was, too. And she wasn't sure if he wanted to be included in their discussions of what was happening at the theater.

"Earth to Isobel." Delphi snapped her fingers. "Did Felicity really say that? It sounds pretty melodramatic to me."

"Sorry." Isobel returned her attention to Delphi. "Yes, we both heard it."

"I can't quite believe she would say something that sounds right out of a B movie," Delphi said.

"If you need to tell someone to destroy evidence, how else are you going to say it?" Sunil said. "She didn't know anyone was listening."

"She could have sent a text," Delphi said. "People are always lurking around a theater. And if not people, then ghosts."

"Don't tell me you believe in theater ghosts, too?" Sunil asked.

"Yes, I do." Delphi prodded his chest. "And so should you."

"Not everyone texts," Isobel pointed out. "That guy Magnus, the president of the board, doesn't look like he's first in line at the Apple store for the next-generation iPhone. Besides, then it would be in writing."

"But what's going on? What does Fried think he has on her?" Delphi asked.

"That's the question, isn't it?" Sunil agreed.

Isobel stood up abruptly. "If that's the question, then we should ask it."

"What?"

"We should ask Roman Fried."

"What, you mean, like, call him up and say what did you know and when did you know it?" Sunil asked.

Isobel turned to him. "Exactly."

Sunil held up a hand. "Wait a minute, let's think this through."

"Does either of you think Roman Fried killed Arden and Thomas?" Isobel asked.

Sunil and Delphi shook their heads.

"Neither do I. But somebody told him to cover *Sousacal*, and now he's threatening Felicity. He's got information, and I want it."

"What makes you think he's going to give it to you, even if you ask nicely?" Delphi asked.

Isobel stretched her right leg onto the ballet barre bolted to the studio wall. "Information trade. He's a gossipy theater columnist. I give him what he wants, he gives me what I want."

"That's a terrible idea." Delphi elbowed Sunil. "Tell her it's a terrible idea."

"It's reckless, and potentially dangerous, but not necessarily terrible," Sunil said slowly.

"You're a big help," Delphi grumbled.

Sunil ambled over to the barre. "What information are you going to give him?"

"Nobody knows about the shrimp."

"The what?" Delphi asked, trailing him.

"See, you don't even know," Isobel said. "Um, could you help me with my leg? I can't...quite..."

Sunil gently lifted her foot off the barre. Isobel lowered her right leg, shook it out, and decided against repeating the exercise with her left.

"Thanks." She hobbled two steps toward Delphi and said softly, "We know what's making the theater stink, but we aren't telling anyone until Sunil is ready to go on or Chris gets released."

"What is it?"

"Shrimp sewn into the curtains."

Delphi's eyes widened. "Why would someone bother with a silly prank like that after killing two people? I mean, we know why they hid the stage manager's book—to get rid of the incriminating note. But this? What's the point?"

"To keep the show from going on."

Sunil gazed thoughtfully at the ceiling. "Isn't it curious that with two people murdered, rotten seafood might be the thing that finally keeps the curtain from going up? Shows you how messed up people's priorities are."

Isobel paced to the piano and ran her fingers over the keys. "Except that whoever planted the shrimp had to have done it before today. It takes time before it starts to smell. It may even predate the masking."

"Okay, but it accomplishes the same thing."

"It does, but..."

"What?"

Isobel shrugged. "I don't know. Something seems off, and I don't just mean the smell. I'm not sure what I mean."

The door burst open and Hugh and Kelly came in. She returned to the table, and he joined them at the piano.

"'Song of the Sea' is still in, tempting though it is to take this opportunity to scrap it completely. But this way if Chris is released in time for the show and they clear the smell, we aren't scrambling to put it back." Hugh turned to Isobel and Delphi. "You guys can take a break for about two hours. I'm going to run music with Sunil, and then Ezra wants to do scene work."

"That's fine," Isobel said, rushing to gather her things. "We've got stuff to do."

She caught Sunil's eye and after a slight hesitation, he nodded his approval.

When they reached the hall, Isobel clutched Delphi's arm.

"Roman Fried," she said.

"I don't know about this," Delphi wavered.

"I don't either, but it's all I got."

Their heels clacked against the slick floor as they headed toward the stairwell.

"How are you going to find him?" Delphi asked.

Isobel pulled out her phone and tapped until she had pulled up the phone number for the *New York Post*. "I'll call his office."

"But he isn't there. He's up here somewhere."

"I learned a few things temping at Dove & Flight Public Relations, one of which is that most reporters leave their cell phone numbers on their outgoing voicemails. And a gossip columnist wouldn't want to take the chance of being scooped because he missed a tip." She dialed and waited a moment until the operator answered.

"Roman Fried, please."

There was silence while she was connected. "Get ready to remember a number," she whispered to Delphi. She held up a finger as she repeated the digits aloud.

"Okay, hit me."

Delphi rattled off his cell number as Isobel dialed. He picked up after two rings.

"Mr. Fried?"

"Yes?"

"I want to thank you for my first real review in the New York press. But I take issue with your *All About Eve* comment. I had absolutely nothing to do with Arden's death."

There was a moment of silence.

"Who is this?"

"Isobel Spice, of course. Can we meet?"

THIRTY-ONE

SUNIL WAS SURPRISED to discover he enjoyed singing "Song of the Sea."

"That's much more gratifying than the marches," he remarked when he finished.

"That's because it's an actual song set to actual lyrics, which is infinitely more satisfying than singing words shoehorned into melodies that were never intended to carry them," Hugh said.

"It works nicely with the one verse," Sunil said. "I feel disloyal saying this, but I don't understand how Delphi could have moved to New York thinking she was competitive. She sings on pitch, but it's all scoopy and her vibrato is so fast and throaty."

"I'm sure you wouldn't have minded too terribly much singing a love duet with her."

Sunil raked his fingers through his hair, then smoothed it down. "I've pretty much given up. She's not interested."

"All the more reason to enjoy it onstage when you can," Hugh said.

Sunil tried to catch Hugh's eye to communicate an opening in case Hugh wanted to confide in him. Delphi had told him earlier that Hugh and Isobel had had a bit of a falling out. But Hugh's gaze was fixed on the music.

"Thinking about how much better Geoff's score must have been?" Sunil asked.

Hugh gave an amused sniff. "No, actually. I was thinking how strange it is to be around Isobel when she's in detective mode." He turned a candid eye on Sunil. "I once told her I'd back her one hundred percent, but the truth is I don't like it."

"You're concerned for her safety," Sunil said. "I get it."

"That's part of it, of course it is," Hugh said, "but she gets so focused that…"

"She gets a little single-minded?"

Hugh leaned on the piano and rested his forehead on his arms. "I'm not expressing myself well. I suppose I feel left out. You seem like the three musketeers, all for one and all that, and she's choosing you over me." He raised his head. "I can't believe I just said that. I sound completely selfish and stupid. Forget I said anything."

"Nobody's leaving you out on purpose. I think it's probably because we're all in the acting company, and you're on the creative team. We're thrown together more. We'll totally make an effort to include you."

Hugh sighed. "That's not it either. We're imbalanced as a couple, for want of a better word. We've decided to keep things professional for the time being. Do you want to try the song again? I don't know what's held Ezra up."

"I'd rather run 'The Washington Post' again if you don't mind."

"Not at all. But you sounded fine on it."

"That's not the problem. I have to make sure I don't slip and sing my parody lyrics."

"Oh!" Hugh brightened. "Let's hear them."

Sunil launched into his version of the song. "*I'll die if I ever have to sing that! I'll fall off the stage and land on my head, and then I'll be just as good as—*"

Sunil stopped when he saw the color drain from Hugh's face. He turned to see Jethro looming in the open doorway.

"*Dead.* Isn't that what you were going to sing?" Jethro strolled over to the piano. "You don't want to telegraph the rhyme like that. It's the sign of a lazy lyricist."

Sunil glanced at Hugh, who was watching the exchange warily. "I'm…I was only playing around. It's not…I'm not…"

"You're not ever going to have to sing it, because you're the second cover. I'm going on tonight as Sousa."

Hugh stiffened on the bench. "Does Ezra know this? Does Felicity?"

"Of course they do. Sunil was only ever the second cover." Jethro cast a disdainful look at him. "We can't possibly have Sousa played by someone who isn't white."

Sunil's temples started to throb. He took a breath and tried counting to ten. He made it to three.

"You did not just go there," he said through gritted teeth.

"Benjamin Swallow is one thing—people have never heard of him. But John Philip Sousa is a beloved historical figure everybody knows. You're a contingency plan. Worst-case scenario. You understand. This sort of thing must happen to you all the time."

Hugh put out a restraining arm, but Sunil shoved past him toward Jethro, his fists clenched at his sides.

"You know, for someone whose name actually is Hamilton, you're pretty fucking clueless about the way shows are being cast these days. You're lucky you're not my actual employer and I can't sue you for discrimination. But fine. Go ahead. Nothing will sink this piece of shit faster than you going on as Sousa. You know what? That's the best thing that could happen. That way no more people will die. Literally and figuratively."

Sunil looked over his shoulder at Hugh, whose lips were pressed tightly together.

"Good luck, mate." Sunil saluted him and left.

THIRTY-TWO

"YOUR CALL WAS UNEXPECTED," Roman Fried said. "What was it you wanted to discuss, and why couldn't you tell me over the phone?"

Isobel took a sip of her Diet Coke and leaned back against the banquette in the bar of the Hilton Garden Inn. "I'm offering an information trade."

"I don't work like that," Fried said curtly.

"Let me put it this way," Isobel said. "Judging from your column, I know a lot more about what's going on at Livingston Stage than you do. Unless you're sitting on the good stuff."

"If you mean the fact that Arden was murdered, well yes, I'm sitting on that."

"Why?"

Fried waved her off. "Not relevant."

Isobel snorted in disbelief. "Not relevant?"

"Not to my overall story, no," Fried said. "And don't bother asking me what *that* is, because I'm not telling you. So unless you have another information bomb, enjoy your soda on me."

He pushed his chair away from the table and stood up.

A sardonic smile spread across Isobel's face, and she applauded slowly.

"Nice exit line, but your delivery needs work. I don't think you're going anywhere. If you were planning to give up that easily, you wouldn't have bothered to meet me." Isobel folded her arms. "Let's cut the drama, which we both know is best left to the professionals. Do you want to know what I know or not?"

After a long moment, Fried sat down again.

"Ground rules. You tell me something, then I tell you something. If I already know yours, you don't get mine. Deal?"

"Deal."

"You first."

Isobel paused for effect. "The show might or might not go on tonight."

"That is a completely content-free sentence."

Now it was Isobel's turn to stand. "Okay, bye."

"Please don't play games with me, Ms. Spice. You will lose. I have far more experience at this than you do. Sit down and tell me whatever it is you're dying to tell me."

Isobel was happy to comply. "There might not be a show tonight, because there's a terrible stench in the theater. If they can't figure out what it is and get rid of it in time, it will be impossible for the show to go on."

Fried let out an exaggerated sigh. "That's not much of a tip. Knowing that it might not happen will be irrelevant as soon as it either does or doesn't."

"But I know what's causing the smell."

"Because you're responsible for it?"

"No, because I figured it out. But for reasons of my own, I am choosing to keep it to myself. So if Felicity is forced to cancel the show, you'll be able to tell people why. And if the show does go on, you'll be able to spill the beans and reveal the problem after Felicity thinks she's made it go away."

"What's causing the smell?"

"Somebody sewed shrimp into the curtain. And if I had to guess, other places in the house as well. The smell is pretty pervasive."

Fried's lip curled into a smile. "That would do it, I suppose."

"Now I get to ask you a question," Isobel said. "Who told you to cover *Sousacal*, and why do you have tickets all week?"

His jaw twitched. "That's two questions. And what makes you think I have tickets all week?"

Isobel cocked her head. "Seems to me that's a new question. If I answer, will you answer both of mine?"

Fried paused. "Fine."

"The box office told me."

"Why were you asking about me?"

"Uh uh uh," Isobel said in a singsong voice. "That's another question."

Fried regarded her. "Look. This is a little ridiculous, don't you think?"

Isobel nodded vigorously. "I couldn't agree more. What do you say we lay our cards on the table? I've already told you something you didn't know, so it's your turn."

Fried beckoned to the waitress.

"I'll have a Bushmills, neat."

"That's my whiskey of choice too," Isobel remarked as the waitress scurried away to fill the order. "You see? We were meant to be friends."

Fried folded a cocktail napkin neatly in half. "Why are you so interested in this?"

"You pretty much accused me in print of being out for blood to get Arden's part," Isobel said. "Some people will take that very seriously. I have a vested interest in figuring out what happened in order to protect my reputation, not to mention my life."

"Fair point."

The waitress brought Fried's whiskey, and he signed it to his room. He knocked back a healthy gulp, then set the glass down.

"I got a call from your costume designer, Thomas Falk. He told me a few things that interested me. How much do you know about how Livingston Stage is funded?"

"Nothing at all," Isobel said, trying to hide her surprise.

"It's partially funded by the state," Fried said. "For years, educational outreach was an important component of their business model. But that ended five years ago, when management claimed the theater was hemorrhaging money and couldn't keep the program operational. The state rolled back the funding gradually, and then two years ago, it dried up completely."

"So they're hurting for money?" Isobel asked.

"That's what's odd," Fried said. "The theater's bottom line didn't take much of a hit, and Thomas started speculating that Felicity Hamilton had been diverting the state's money all along."

"Embezzling?"

Fried took a more measured sip of his whiskey. "That's what Thomas thinks. He claims there's evidence of unnecessary expenses like meals and hotels—mostly on visits to New York for auditions. And he hinted there might be something else going on, but he wouldn't get specific."

"Why haven't you put all that in your column?"

"That alone would not interest my readers. But when he told me Felicity Hamilton was dumping money from one or more anonymous donors into a new musical that was embarrassingly awful—and penned by her unknown, unproven nephew—I thought there might be something in it."

"Why buy tickets for the whole week? Why not see it once, write about it, and leave?"

Fried's face clouded. "Thomas called me the day before you opened and said there was a series of incidents that would amuse me. But frankly, there's nothing amusing about an actress being murdered. That's why it's not relevant. Even I have my limits."

Isobel nodded. "He was talking about the stuff that happened before Arden died."

"What stuff?"

"During our ten-out-of-twelve, somebody untied the masking backstage and it fell. It happened to fall on Arden, but I don't think it was necessarily intended for her." Isobel held up her fingers and counted off. "Then somebody put a laxative in the coffee, and we had to end our tech early because everyone had the runs."

Fried's face flooded with gleeful approval. "That is positively devilish."

"But wait, there's more," Isobel said. "Somebody snuck into the theater later that night and put random cuts in all the orchestra parts, which rendered our dress rehearsal useless from a musical point of view. I think that's the stuff Thomas wanted you to write about."

"But how would I have found out about that? He would have had to tell me, and he didn't."

"That's a good question," Isobel acknowledged. "Maybe he was waiting to tell you after you witnessed whatever happened opening night, but Arden's death wasn't what he was expecting."

Fried downed the rest of his whiskey. "Going back to your initial question about why I'm here, I have a theater with inklings of fiscal wrongdoing pumping money into a musical of dubious quality by the artistic director's nephew, and a staff member who seems to know—in advance—that misadventures will befall the production." He let out a snide chuckle. "Trust me, that's a lot more interesting than the string of revivals opening on Broadway this season."

"And I just gave you tomorrow's column. The shrimp. You're welcome."

Rather than offer his thanks, Fried looked perplexed. "I haven't heard from Thomas since he called to tell me Arden was murdered."

Isobel sat back. "I can tell you how she was murdered, and I can tell you why Thomas hasn't told you. But you have to promise me something in return."

"What's that?"

"If you find out where the money is coming from for *Sousacal*, will you tell me?"

Fried looked into his empty glass. Then he met her eyes and nodded. "Yes, I will. Now tell me why I haven't heard from Thomas."

"If he told you Arden was murdered, then he probably told you she died of acute nicotine poisoning. This next bit hasn't been confirmed yet, but I'm willing to bet my brand-new Equity card that an exposed wire on her bustle was treated with the stuff. When Chris pulled her onto his lap during 'The Washington Post,' it stabbed her and injected the poison into her bloodstream."

Fried took a moment to collect himself. "Well. That would explain why I haven't heard from Thomas. A poisoned costume piece? He must be in police custody."

Isobel set her mouth in a grim line. "That's not why he hasn't called you."

THIRTY-THREE

"I DON'T KNOW WHO I feel sorriest for," Isobel said to Sunil. "You, Hugh, or myself."

"Oh, Lord." Delphi rolled her eyes. "It isn't always about you, honey!"

"I know Jethro was heinous to Sunil, and poor Hugh has to coach him, but if he goes on as Sousa, I'll have to kiss him, for God's sake," Isobel protested.

"Maybe not," Delphi reminded her. "We still don't know if there's going to be a show tonight."

Sunil flopped onto the living room sofa. "As infuriating as that racist, talent-free boor is, his behavior pales in comparison to what you're telling us about Felicity, plus the fact that Thomas was Roman Fried's informant. Where do we go with that?"

"Well, we know Thomas didn't bash his own head in," Delphi said. "But Felicity might have had to shut him up."

"And Arden? Why would she kill her leading lady?" Isobel asked.

"It also begs the question where she was getting the money to dump into this piece of shit production," Delphi added.

"No, it doesn't," Isobel said.

"Of course it does," Delphi said. "Where did she get the money, and what in God's name made her think she could promise a return on the investment?"

"No, you're not using the phrase 'begs the question' correctly. It doesn't mean raises the question, it means you're asking the speaker to support the premise behind the question. It's another way of asking 'What's your point?'"

"What's *your* point? That I'm a moron? Seriously, Isobel, I know you're a grammar freak, but can we stick to the actual question at hand, which fine, I will fucking well ask: where did she get the money and why did she bother?"

"I think the better question is how do we find out?" Sunil said in placating tones.

"Fried is working on that," Isobel said.

Delphi looked skeptically at Isobel. "And you're cool with that? I've never known you to not follow up on a lead. Or are you still obsessing about having to kiss Liver Lips Louie tonight?"

Isobel paced over to the window. "There's too much here that doesn't make sense. I'm having trouble reconciling..." She pulled the curtain aside.

"Reconciling what?" Sunil asked.

"Never mind. We have company." Isobel turned from the window. "It's Detective Dillon."

"Here?" Delphi asked.

"Anyone have a guilty conscience?" Sunil canvassed the room. "Then we should be fine."

"You think Jethro called the cops on you?" Isobel asked him.

"With Hugh as my witness, I didn't threaten him, and he provoked me with a blatantly racist insult. I stand by every word I said."

Dillon rapped sharply on the front door.

"Company behavior, everyone." Isobel went to answer it. "Detective Dillon. Sergeant Pemberthy. What brings you here?"

"I want to know how you knew," Dillon said bluntly.

"I know a lot of things. To which are you referring?"

"That the nicotine was on the bustle wire," he said. "Can we come in, please?"

Isobel felt her stomach drop. As much as she liked to be right, she was deeply unsettled that in this case she was. It could so easily have been any of them. What if the bustles had gotten mixed up?

What if the bustles *had* gotten mixed up?

Dillon reached out to steady her. "Are you all right?"

"Um, yeah. Come in. Delphi and Sunil are here, too."

"How did you know the nicotine was on the bustle?" Dillon repeated as he and Pemberthy followed Isobel into the living room.

Delphi clutched Sunil's hand, and he pulled her closer in response.

"It just seemed logical to me," Isobel said, sinking into her favorite armchair. "Arden had made a big public fuss about an exposed wire the day before, and she keeled over at the exact same moment. It wasn't much of a stretch."

"How badly did you want Arden's role?" he asked.

Isobel caught Delphi's warning glance. "If I had killed Arden, why on earth would I have told you how I did it? And to tell you the truth, with Jethro Hamilton going on for Chris tonight, I'm inclined to call in dead myself."

"We let Chris go," Dillon said. "We dropped him off at the other condo before we came here."

"Is there even going to be a show tonight?" Isobel asked.

Dillon's eyes narrowed. "What do you mean?"

"There's a horrible smell pervading the theater, and nobody can figure out what's causing it," Sunil said. "If they can't get rid of it, we can't perform."

"How bad can a smell be? Can't you open all the doors?" Dillon asked.

"It's stomach-churning, believe me," Delphi said.

Dillon surveyed them all. "This may seem like a glib question, but I'm serious. Has anyone gone missing?"

"You think it could be a dead body?" Sunil shot a sideways glance at Isobel.

"It was more like the worst garbage you ever smelled," Isobel said quickly. "It reminded me of when I was in Florence the summer after I graduated, waiting in line to visit the Uffizi, and there were open grates into the sewer. That's more what it smells like. Sewage. Fishy sewage, to be exact."

"Thank you for that evocative description, but we can't rule anything out until the source is discovered." He turned to Pemberthy. "Get over there and see what the deal is. We may need to get involved."

She nodded and left.

"I honestly think it's another prank," Isobel said.

"We'll find out soon enough."

Isobel decided it was time to change the subject. "Has Felicity Hamilton ever been investigated for embezzling state funds from the theater?"

Dillon whipped out his notebook and pen. "Care to explain where that question came from?"

"Thomas told a friend of his that there were rumors of misappropriated state funds for personal use. And now Thomas is dead. Sunil and I overheard Felicity on the phone earlier today instructing the president of the board to destroy his files."

"Who is Thomas's friend?"

Isobel shook her head. "I can't reveal my source. I made a promise."

"I can make you, you know."

"Why don't you follow up on my lead first and see if there's anything there?"

"What else have you got for me?"

"Felicity also dumped a fair amount of money into *Sousacal.* Where did that money come from?"

"I think you just answered your own question. If she's been stockpiling state funds, maybe she's been saving up to back the show."

"My gut tells me there are two different things going on," Isobel said.

"Do you have any idea yet who killed Arden and Thomas?" Sunil asked.

Dillon looked momentarily pained. "There's a surprising lack of physical evidence. Whoever did this knows what they're doing."

"Then we're all in danger," Delphi said. "What if he or she strikes again?"

"It's a possibility," Dillon said soberly. "We've beefed up security around the theater, and we're on the lookout."

"But for what?" Delphi pressed. "We have one poisoned bustle and one bloody C-clamp. Do you even know what to look for? Why haven't you shut the theater down?"

"We have little else to go on except to watch closely and hope our killer makes a false move," Dillon said. "If we shut down the theater, everyone scatters and our chances of solving the murders diminish. We spoke with Felicity Hamilton about this at length, and she agreed. At least for a little while longer."

"Felicity is on board with this?" Isobel asked. "Pretty convenient if she's the murderer and she isn't finished yet."

"What about our costumes? Our props? Scenery? How do we know we're safe?" Sunil asked.

"Well—" Dillon was interrupted by the sound of a key in the lock.

A moment later, Hugh appeared in the living room. "I hope I'm not interrupting."

Dillon rose. "I'm finished."

"There's no show tonight," Hugh said.

"But Chris is back," Isobel said. "They've let him go."

"It's the smell. An exterminator is coming, but Felicity opted to cancel now so there would be enough time to alert ticket holders."

"Sergeant Pemberthy may get to the bottom of it first." Dillon returned his notebook to his coat pocket. "But it looks like you get an unexpected night off."

"You didn't answer Sunil's question. How do we know we're safe?" Isobel repeated.

Dillon met her gaze steadily. "I'm afraid you don't. But unless you want to quit—and, I gotta tell you, after seeing this show I wouldn't blame you—you're going to have to stick it out until we catch the killer. Stay alert. I'll show myself out."

When he was gone, Sunil clapped his hands together cheerfully. "Who feels safe? Yeah, didn't think so."

"At least we have the night off," Delphi said.

"Jethro nearly exploded, he was so furious. He was absolutely raring to go. Ezra was beside himself. He said this was the first he'd heard of Jethro covering." Hugh plopped onto the sofa. "I wonder what *is* causing that smell."

"We know what it is," Isobel admitted.

Hugh sat up. "You know and you haven't told?"

"We only just found out that Chris was let go. Did you really want to do the show with Jethro? Or an unprepared Sunil?"

"Thanks a lot!"

"No, and I'm perfectly happy to have a night off," Hugh said. "But what is it?"

"Shrimp sewn into the curtain."

Hugh grimaced. "It's going to take a while to get that smell out. Felicity was right to cancel. But you are going to tell her tomorrow, right?"

"We won't have to." Isobel grinned. "Roman Fried will."

THIRTY-FOUR

BUT TO ISOBEL'S SURPRISE, Roman Fried didn't write about the shrimp and the canceled show. In fact, he didn't write about anything.

Isobel handed the paper across the kitchen table to Delphi. "He doesn't seem to have filed a column today. Don't you think that's funny?"

"I don't know. I don't read the *Post*."

"His column appears every day. Page six."

Delphi squinted at the paper. "It's an ad encouraging people to subscribe."

Isobel rose and paced to the sink. "That means his decision not to file was last minute. If it was a planned miss, they'd have substituted other editorial. That's what the *Times* does when a columnist is on vacation."

"Are you seriously comparing the *Post* to the *Times*? I thought you were better than that."

Isobel filled a glass with water and returned to the table. "No, really. Even if he decided not to write about the shrimp, why didn't he offer a replacement column?"

Delphi buttered her toast, spraying crumbs in Isobel's direction. "He probably didn't have any other gossip worth gossiping about."

"As if that's ever stopped him. If there isn't real gossip, he makes stuff up." Isobel swept the crumbs off the edge of the table into her hand and brushed them onto Delphi's plate. "I think something's wrong. He was like a bloodhound on the scent yesterday."

"Why don't you call and ask him why he didn't file?"

"Very funny."

"I'm serious. If you really think something's up, call him. You have his number."

Isobel pulled her phone from her pocket and scrolled back until she found it. She glanced questioningly at Delphi, who crunched her toast and nodded. Isobel dialed. She frowned and hung up.

"It says his mailbox is full."

"Probably fans calling demanding to know where his column is. Doesn't mean anything."

"Morning, ladies," Sunil said from the doorway. "What's the news?"

"None, as it happens," said Delphi. "Roman Fried didn't write about us."

"He didn't file a column at all, and his voice mailbox is full," Isobel added.

Sunil poured himself a cup of coffee. "So he chose not to reveal the secret of the surreptitious shrimp?"

Isobel shook her head. "What should we do?"

Sunil took a sip and swore. "Crappy coffeemaker. I don't know. I guess at this point we should 'fess up."

"You say that as if we were the ones who did it," Isobel said.

"You know what I mean. Tell them we identified the problem. We don't have to say we figured it out yesterday, but we can say that we remembered reading about a similar prank and suggest that might be it."

Isobel rustled the paper absentmindedly. "I'd be surprised if the exterminator didn't get to the bottom of it. I mean, it took us what, like, five minutes? You just follow your nose."

"And yet, Felicity canceled in advance, knowing help was on the way," Sunil mused. "Almost makes you wonder if she just plain didn't want the show to go on last night."

"You think she would purposely deny her beloved nephew the chance to star in his own so-called musical?" Delphi asked.

Isobel paced to the kitchen window and looked out, half-expecting to see Detective Dillon watching her from his unmarked car, but there was only the usual intermittent traffic.

"I'm still trying to figure out who put money behind it in the first place and whether it's connected to the embezzling or not. Fried said Thomas told him trips to New York, meals, hotels…"

"I don't see why the two things wouldn't be connected," Sunil said. "And as you correctly point out, all of this turns on the question of Felicity's taste. I don't care how much she loves Jethro like a son, business is business."

"Business is business, but love is blind," Delphi said.

"I'm with Sunil," Isobel said. "The woman is running a theater, possibly into the ground for all we know, and she's got to know this is no cash cow. So what is she up to?"

"And where is Roman Fried?" Delphi finished.

"Did you try his hotel?" Sunil asked. "You know where he's staying, right?"

"Oh! Of course." Isobel searched for the number of the Hilton Garden Inn and dialed. "Hello, may I speak to Roman Fried, please? He's a guest."

There was a pause on the other end.

"I'm sorry, he's checked out," said the clerk.

"When?"

"Yesterday evening."

"Can you tell me if he was always scheduled to check out then, or was that an early departure?"

"One moment, I have to look up his reservation." After a minute, she returned. "He was originally booked in through the weekend. Is there anything else I can help you with?"

"No, thank you."

Isobel hung up and turned to the others. "He's gone. Checked out yesterday ahead of schedule."

"I wonder why," Delphi said.

"We can add that to our list of questions," Isobel said. "I hope somebody's keeping a log."

"Is this a private meeting, or can anyone join?" Hugh said from the doorway.

"We're just discussing the case." Isobel waved him in. "Join us."

She noticed his hesitation, but he accepted the olive branch and entered the kitchen. She glanced behind him.

"Do you know where Talia is?"

"She just left to go to the market." Hugh poured out the rest of the coffee and joined Isobel and Delphi at the table.

"It's time to take stock," Isobel said. "I'm confident that none of us is responsible for any of the hijinks, fatal or not, that have ensued. I'm sure we all have thoughts banging around our heads, so let's compare notes and see where we stand. Suspects?"

Three pairs of eyes blinked uncertainly back at her.

"Come on, really?"

Hugh cleared his throat. "I keep coming back to Geoff and, I hate to say it, Oliver. That prank with the orchestra parts seemed very pointed to me, not to mention the fact that whoever did it knew exactly how to wreak the most havoc with the fewest crotchets."

"What the hell is a crotchet?" Delphi asked.

"Sorry. A quarter note. You can take the boy out of Cambridge…" Hugh said with a laugh. "But seriously, Geoff must be furious that Jethro tossed his score aside."

"I agree that the musical prank implicates Geoff," said Isobel. "But do you think he would actually murder an innocent person, bitch though she was, RIP—"

"Talk about circular logic, but go on," Delphi said snidely.

"It damages the show and Jethro going forward, so if that was his goal, maybe," Hugh said. "Who would touch a musical with that kind of bad luck? Though murder is extreme, I grant you."

"I'm giving you Geoff," Isobel said.

"What do you mean?"

"Find Geoff and chat him up. Find out what happened between the first workshop and opening night. Will you do that?"

Hugh opened his mouth to object but then nodded. "All right, but I want to make sure you all know exactly where I'm meeting him and when, so that if I don't reappear...you know."

"Good idea." Isobel looked around. "Any other suspects?"

"Now that we know you're making assignments, I pick Chris," Sunil said. "The cops may not have had enough to hold him, but if he and Arden were engaged, and his love turned to hate, and then he was forced to endure her abuse while playing opposite her—well, that seems like a perfect storm."

"Great. Hugh's ground rules apply. Make sure one of us knows when and where you're meeting. We don't know what we're stepping into, so we all need a lifeline. Like that game show."

"Great, now we're playing *Who Wants to be a Murder Victim*," Delphi grumped.

"You're next. Who's your pick?"

"Do I have to? I'm the new kid."

"Yes. There are more of them than there are of us."

Delphi blew an exasperated raspberry. "Okay. I guess Kelly."

"Why Kelly?"

"She's the stage manager. Nobody else has unimpeded access to every element of the production. And I still think it's weird that her book went 'missing' with your note," Delphi said, applying air quotes.

"You think she pretended to lose her own book to get rid of the evidence?"

"And throw suspicion on someone else, yeah," Delphi said.

"I can't imagine a stage manager sabotaging her own ability to call the show," Sunil said. "I think even if her brain wanted her to do it, her body would resist. It goes too hard against the grain."

"Not even if her ultimate objective was to shut the whole thing down?" Delphi asked.

"But what motive could she possibly have?" Hugh wondered.

Delphi winked. "When I find out, I'll let you know."

"I love confidence in a woman. It's hot," Sunil said.

Delphi ignored him and jutted her chin at Isobel. "You're up."

Isobel gazed at the ceiling and gathered her thoughts. A strange idea was taking shape in her mind, and she wasn't quite sure what it meant. She had three people in mind, none of whom had been mentioned. But for now, she could only pick one. In the interest of dispatching the least likely suspect, she made her choice.

"Ezra."

"Oh, that's interesting," Sunil said. "His name is attached to this piece of crap, and he can't be happy about the result."

"The question is, would he resort to murder to keep the show from having a future?" Isobel mused. "Would anyone?"

"Someone did," Delphi said.

Isobel pushed away from the table. "Let's go find out who."

Sunil and Delphi left the kitchen, heads together, chattering. Hugh held back.

"Isobel."

She smiled expectantly, praying he wasn't about to launch into another relationship conversation.

"No matter what we decide after this is all over, I want you to know I appreciate being included. I know that sounds silly, and like I've reverted to primary school social games, but I think you know what I mean."

Isobel nodded.

"I also wanted to say that you're simply lovely as Jennie. But then, I always knew you would be."

"I did, too," she said impishly. "But it's much better hearing it from you."

THIRTY-FIVE

"IS THIS OKAY?" Hugh gestured to a small table by the window in Starbucks.

Geoff lifted his shoulders laconically. "Fine with me."

Hugh figured that in addition to having alerted Isobel to his plans, sitting in full view of the street wasn't a bad idea. Not that he thought he was in imminent danger. Even though he'd picked Geoff, imagining him to be a cold-blooded killer seemed as impossible as imagining himself capable of such an act. They were both artists: composers, conductors, pianists. Birds of a feather. Now, sitting across from him, Hugh decided there was no way Geoff had killed Arden and Thomas.

"Did you kill Arden and Thomas?"

The words were out of his mouth before he could stop them, and he realized to his consternation that he was channeling Isobel.

Geoff paused with his coffee midway to his mouth. "You don't mince words, do you?"

"I figured we'd bazooka the elephant in the room so we can talk about what really interests me," Hugh punted, wondering what had possessed him to say such a thing.

"Which is what?"

"Excuse me?"

"What interests you? Why did you want to meet?"

Hugh took a long sip of his chai before answering. "I've been having a rather rotten time of it. Jethro is constantly putting in his oar. I prefer my writers dead. Present company and self excluded, of course," he added quickly.

Geoff opened the plastic lid and tapped more sugar into his coffee. "What kind of stuff do you write?"

"Theater songs, art songs. Music and lyrics. I'm working on a musical."

Geoff crumpled the empty sugar packet. "Everyone in New York is working on a musical."

"That's what I wanted to ask you about. I've got very little experience with getting a show produced. I know you had a bumpy road with *Sousacal*—"

Geoff snorted. "That's the understatement of the century."

"But I thought perhaps I could learn from your experience."

"You mean how not to spend several years of your life collaborating on a piece and then having your contribution kicked to the curb?"

Hugh felt his face go warm. "Yeah, that."

"Mmm." Geoff sipped his coffee. "First piece of advice, choose your collaborators wisely."[1]

"What made you pick Jethro?"

"I was musical director for *A Colonial Christmas Carol*, and Felicity introduced us opening night. She wanted him to meet me because she knew I was a composer, and Jethro had been wanting to write a musical about John Philip Sousa for years."

"And you honestly thought that sounded like a good idea?"

"Anything's a good idea if you're getting paid."

"Wait, Jethro paid you to collaborate?"

"Not Jethro. Felicity."

Hugh took another sip of tea and tried to look nonchalant. "I suppose you had to return the money when Jethro scrapped your score?"

"No chance! I did my job. I turned in a score—a damn good one, I'll have you know."

"So what happened?"

Geoff took the lid off his coffee again and to Hugh's disgust tapped in another packet of sugar.

"We did a staged reading up here, and then a workshop in New York. Ezra had been recommended to me as a director, and I brought him on for that. He had a pal at the Donnelly Group and got some bigwig there to see it. Apparently, Donnelly, or whoever it was, made the mistake of commenting to Jethro afterward that it seemed strange to write a musical about Sousa without any of his music, so out went my score. I said no way was I going to MD what I was certain would turn out to be a disaster—no offense—and I walked away."

"But Ezra stayed on. Why?"

Geoff shrugged. "A job's a job? Who knows, maybe he has gambling debts or something."

Hugh wondered briefly if this was more than a casual suggestion and filed it away to tell Isobel.

"Jethro must have pulled the score together pretty quickly, because I was brought on only a few weeks later, or so I was told."

"They didn't have a score in place when they were holding auditions," Geoff said.

Hugh sat back. "Let me get this straight. Felicity paid you to write a score for Jethro's Sousa musical, presumably because she didn't think he had the talent, and then your score got scrapped because of an offhand comment by Donnelly, so Felicity held auditions for a show that had no music?"

"More or less. I mean, I don't know for sure, but I would guess Jethro must have shown her something to reassure her that he was on the right track and would get it done."

Hugh shook his head. "That's almost worse. I mean, listening to any of it would send any sensible producer screaming for the hills. The idea of lyricizing Sousa marches is completely daft."

"You still don't get it," Geoff said. "This was never about quality. Jethro is the son Felicity never had. I wouldn't say she's blind to his imperfections, but she's certainly willing to make allowances."

"Even if it goes against her best interests?" Hugh asked.

"*If* it does. More likely she has some interest in the show that nobody knows about." They sat in silence for a moment. "Want something else? I'm craving a donut."

"No, I'm good, thanks."

Hugh watched him saunter up to the counter to increase his already shocking sugar intake. Geoff was so confident, so full of swagger. Hugh wondered how talented he was. Maybe his score wasn't as good as he thought. On the other hand, it couldn't possibly be worse than what they'd ended up with.

"You must have been pretty angry when you got cut loose," Hugh observed when Geoff returned, glazed donut in hand.

"At first, yeah. But I calmed down. I mean it's not like this was ever going to put me on the map."

"It seems the Donnelly Group has lost interest now." Hugh stirred his tea. "Any idea why they didn't make it opening night?"

"Oh, probably a little birdie told them it wasn't worth the gas."

Hugh looked up. "You?"

"I hadn't seen it yet. I didn't know," Geoff said innocently.

"Oliver must have told you."

"Oh, he did. But I never make recommendations on someone else's word. Even my brother's."

"Why did he stay on after what happened to you?"

Geoff's expression softened. "Ollie's young. He's still building his resume, and this was his first contract with Livingston. I think you've been good for him. You're a talented conductor."

Hugh felt a rush of pleasure. "Thanks. You've seen it then?"

"I was there opening night. Pretty shocking." Geoff took a longish sip of coffee as if it were a bracing whiskey.

"Did you know Arden well?"

Geoff smacked his lips. "Didn't know her at all. She came on board after I was thrown over. I mean, I knew who she was. Miss New York and everything. But we never met."

"Then who did the workshops?"

"Talia."

"As Jennie, I mean."

Geoff licked honey glaze off his fingers. "Yeah, as Jennie."

"And she was bumped for Arden?"

For the first time, Geoff appeared uncomfortable. He shifted in his seat and glanced into his lap before he answered. "Arden was a draw, obviously, but beyond that, Talia isn't much of an actress."

"And she was willing to stay on in a smaller role after originating the lead?"

"I got Felicity to put her on an Equity contract. Talia wanted to join the union and get a solid theater credit on her resume. Thinks it'll make her more marketable. I don't have the heart to tell her it won't make a difference unless she takes some acting classes."

"And Felicity was willing?"

"She felt bad about drop-kicking me, so yeah."

"Did you ask for anything else?"

Geoff laughed. "A royalty point. Didn't get that, though."

"So you and Talia, what's the deal?"

"We went to grad school together. Dated a little, off and on. You know."

"Are you on again or off again right now?" Hugh asked.

Geoff smiled cryptically. "Yes."

"What does that mean?"

He took a bite of his donut and wiped a stray crumb from his chin. "Exactly what you think it means."

Hugh sighed. "Yeah, that sort of sums up Isobel and me, I guess."

"That girl's got talent," Geoff said appreciatively. "And sangfroid, the way she jumped into the fray. She must have been a Girl Scout."

"I was proud of her." Hugh consciously tamped down a twinge of sadness. "But listen, I have to ask you. If you don't care about the show and what's happened to it, why did you bother to come back to see it?"

Geoff's face drew in on itself as if he'd sucked a lemon. "I don't know what makes you think I don't care. I put two years of my life into this show, and I wanted my work to see the light of day. That's a lot of wasted time. Put yourself in my shoes. You'd feel the same way." Geoff glanced at his phone and stood up abruptly.

"Actually, I have put myself in your shoes," Hugh said. "If it were me, I wouldn't go anywhere near it, especially if I was sure it would be a disaster. Let them fail on their own and good riddance."

"Everyone's different. That's what makes horse racing, as my grandma used to say. I gotta run. It's been nice chatting with you. Good luck with, um…everything."

"Thanks. You, too."

Hugh watched him swing through the door. On the sidewalk, Geoff flipped up the collar of his peacoat, ducked his head against the wind, and walked away.

It wasn't a stretch for Hugh to understand Geoff's seemingly contradictory response to the way he'd been treated on *Sousacal*. But he still didn't have a sense of how far he was willing to go to get revenge for that lost time and opportunity. Sabotage? Murder?

And just like that, Hugh realized that Geoff had never answered his first question.

THIRTY-SIX

ISOBEL AND SUNIL WALKED the few blocks to the other condo to look for Ezra and Chris, but nobody answered the buzzer. They doubled back to the theater, where they found the doors to the auditorium flung open. Giant fans were set up in the aisles, and theater staff moved through the rows, bending down and straightening up as if they were planting seeds.

"Looks like the jig is up," Isobel said.

"I blame Pemberthy."

Heather straightened up and called out, "Got one."

"I'm coming," Dan, the tech director, responded.

He came around to Heather and held out a giant trash bag. Plugging her nose, Heather dropped a shrimp into the bag. Onstage, one of the stagehands was spraying the curtain hem with Febreze.

"Do you see Chris?" Sunil asked.

Isobel scanned the house. "No. I don't see Ezra either."

"I'm going to head back home. I don't want to get roped into active duty."

She considered going with him, but while there wasn't any particular reason why Chris would be hanging around the theater, Ezra might well be there somewhere. She decided to stay and take a look around, but first she sent a group text to the others: *Shrimp discovered, show tonight.*

"Hey!"

Isobel realized she'd taken a step backward into Marissa. "Oh, sorry!" She gestured to the shrimp-pickers. "Looks like they figured out the smell."

"Yeah, I came to help clean up."

"Oh, um, me too," Isobel said. "Let's go in."

Ezra could wait. Ever since Arden's death, Marissa had been avoiding Isobel, and an opportunity for chitchat while de-shrimping the theater was too good to pass up. Even now, Isobel caught a flicker of annoyance cross Marissa's face, and she knew instinctively she'd made the right decision.

Kelly waved at them as they entered the theater.

"Oh, hey, Isobel! I didn't know you were—"

"Many hands, light work, and all that," Isobel said quickly, ignoring Marissa's suspicious glance.

"Come grab a pair of scissors, and you guys can take the last few rows."

Isobel strode down the aisle and accepted two pairs of scissors. "What exactly are we doing?"

Kelly sighed heavily. "Some bozo sewed shrimp into the seats and the stage drop. We've got the curtain emptied out, but we need to go over every seat. They've probably been there a few days, so it's easy to nose them out. Fortunately, whoever did it was pretty sloppy, so you'll see a small, badly basted seam in the front under the cushion. Between the seam and the smell test, you should be able to identify which seats need surgery. If you find a live one—meaning a dead one—open the seam and remove it, and call for Dan. He's circling with a trash bag."

Weapons in hand, Isobel and Marissa made their way toward the back of the house. Isobel set to work at an industrious pace, waiting to see what direction Marissa's conversation would take. She didn't have to wait long.

"How did you know about the shrimp?" Marissa asked.

Unless you put it there yourself, Isobel silently added Marissa's unspoken thought. She decided it was best to stick to the truth as much as possible. "I came down looking for Ezra, but when I saw what was going on I figured I'd pitch in. What about you?"

"I was with Heather earlier when she got the call."

"I guess we're back on tonight," Isobel said.

"I'm sure you're pleased."

Isobel let Marissa's snarky comment hang in the air. A moment later, Marissa spoke again.

"Sorry. I'm still upset about Arden."

"I didn't realize how close you were."

"I wouldn't say close, exactly. It's complicated."

Isobel made a noncommittal sound, hoping Marissa would elaborate, which she did after taking a hair longer than necessary to inspect a seat. It seemed she was as reluctant to exist in silence as Isobel normally was. Today, however, Isobel was finding it surprisingly easy to keep quiet.

"We knew each other a little growing up. Our parents met on a cruise when we were both in high school, and our families got together a few times afterward. They thought Arden and I would hit if off, because we both wanted to be actors." Marissa pulled self-consciously on her loose-fitting top. "She had no interest in me, of course, but I used to have dreams about being her friend. That she'd transfer to my high school, and one of the girls who mocked me all the time would start up and Arden would spring to my defense. Just a dumb loser high school fantasy, you know?"

Isobel nodded. She was beginning to understand.

"Anyway," Marissa continued, "I hadn't seen her or thought about her for years, but when rehearsals started for *Sousacal*, she acted like we were long-lost besties. It was almost like she was clinging to me. It was kind of like my dream come true, when a person you admire suddenly wants you, maybe even more than you want them."

Isobel sat back on her heels, mindful of the need to encourage Marissa's confidence without saying the wrong thing. "People change and grow."

"Yeah, I know, but it seemed more like she didn't feel she could trust anyone else. It seemed situational, not personal. You know what I mean?"

Isobel suddenly remembered Marissa inexplicably bursting into tears when Kelly's book went missing.

"You wrote the note," Isobel said.

Marissa's round face went dark red. "It was stupid of me. A step too far. I did it to impress Arden, but when I told her about it she was horrified. I only meant to get you to back off, send you a message, but after she died, I realized it would look like I was threatening her and not you. I saw you give the note to Kelly, so I hid her book and got rid of it."

"Why didn't you grab the note out of the book while nobody was looking?"

"I thought if I took the whole book, everyone would think it was another prank. Then nobody would guess it was me."

"Unless they thought you were responsible for everything."

Marissa looked aghast. "But I'm not!"

"I believe you," Isobel said sincerely.

Marissa bit her lip. "You're cutting me a lot more slack than I cut you. I know you were just doing your job. I don't know what came over me. And I haven't known what to do." She sniffed back tears. "I've been wanting to tell you, but I was scared, and now I feel like a complete fool. I'm sorry."

"I did something like that once," Isobel admitted. "In high school. There was a girl I desperately wanted to be friends with who had the piano lesson after mine. She had mentioned casually that she hadn't practiced that week, so during my lesson I put a pencil on the edge of the piano lid, knowing it would fall in as soon as someone put the top down. I don't know what I thought would happen, but my teacher's husband had to unscrew the lid, and he wound up scratching the wood badly, just to open it up and get the pencil out. I was absolutely mortified. All I'd done was succeed in damaging a beautiful instrument. Because of course the other girl still had to have her lesson, and I couldn't ever tell her, and we never became friends." Isobel blinked at Marissa. "Anyway, I recognize the impulse. I mean, we never truly escape our high school selves, right?"

"Except when we change and grow," Marissa said through her tears.

Isobel laughed. "Touché."

Marissa made a face. "Ugh, I think I found a shrimp." She cut open the seam. "Yuck! Dan!"

Dan came over with his trash bag, accepted the decomposed offering, and left to answer a call on the other side of the house.

"Who do you think is responsible for the other stuff?" Isobel asked. "Any ideas?"

"I don't know. What about you?"

"There's a lot banging around in my head, but I can't quite connect it." Isobel's phone buzzed in her pocket, and she pulled it out to see a text from Hugh. She stood up. "Sorry, I have to go."

"Thanks for not freaking out at me," Marissa said.

"Thanks for telling me the truth. Kelly and I never told the police about the note, and there's no reason to tell them now, is there?"

Marissa smiled gratefully. "You're actually pretty cool, you know that?"

"You are, too."

Isobel hurried out of the theater. Hugh had certainly gotten more information out of Geoff than she'd expected him to. And as she scanned his words again, one of the fractured thoughts in her head suddenly took shape.

THIRTY-SEVEN

DELPHI EMERGED FROM the bathroom in time to see Isobel flying through the lobby. "Hey! Where are you going in such a rush?" she asked.

"Have to see a man about a shrimp," Isobel said hurriedly. "What are you doing?"

Delphi crossed the floor and spoke in a low voice. "I was going to talk to Kelly, remember? But I haven't been able to get her alone."

Isobel gestured impatiently. "Forget Kelly. She's not important. Talk to Heather."

Delphi felt herself deflate, disappointed to have her choice of suspect dismissed. "About what?"

"Ask her what instrument she plays, but be discreet."

"How do you know she plays an instrument?"

"I just do." Isobel brushed past her and left the building.

Delphi yanked a stray curl in annoyance. She was tempted to run after Isobel and ask her to fill in the blanks, but Heather appeared, wiping her forehead with her sleeve.

"Run, save yourself," she joked to Delphi. "I've got to get some fresh air."

"Oh, I was…" Delphi paused, struck by sudden inspiration. "I was looking for Hugh or Oliver or someone to plunk out some notes on the piano for me. There's a bit in the opening number I'm sure I'm singing wrong. Maybe you can help me?"

Heather looked puzzled. "Me?"

In a flash, Delphi realized what Isobel was getting at. "You don't read music?"

"Nope. I took Suzuki violin in fourth grade for six months until my parents decided the arts weren't important."

"Really?" Delphi asked, shocked.

Heather laughed. "No. They couldn't stand the skritch-a-skritch of me practicing. So no, I don't read music."

"And you never picked up another instrument?"

"After the violin debacle, I took visual art instead of music every chance I got." She jerked a thumb back toward the theater. "Marissa's in there. She could give you a hand. Or ask Kelly. She plays clarinet, I think. Or sax. I forget which, but I'm sure she could bang something out for you."

Delphi nodded her thanks. Heather was almost to the front door when Delphi remembered the other part of Isobel's assignment. On impulse, she decided to come at it from a different angle.

"I was wondering," she began. Heather turned, her hand on the door. "Did Kelly ever date Geoff Brown?"

Heather's face went pale. "Did she?"

"That's what I'm asking you."

"What makes you think that?" Heather's hand dropped and she took a step toward Delphi, who instinctively moved backward.

"Nothing. I—I don't know. You dated him, right?"

"Why are you asking all these questions? What do you know?"

Delphi blinked. "I don't know anything, honest. I was just curious, that's all."

"Oh my God, is that why he's ghosting me?" Heather shook her head. "No, not Kelly. She wouldn't. She knows—"

"Knows what?"

"How I feel about him," Heather said breathlessly. "She knows better than anyone."

And with that, she turned and ran outside. Delphi dialed Isobel.

"Hey. I'm not sure if I succeeded or failed, but I've got something for you. Where are you?"

"At the condo," Isobel said. "Come back."

Delphi hung up and followed Heather's path out of the building, practically knocking over Jethro, who was rushing up the steps. He steadied himself by grabbing her arm. Startled, she met his eyes, which were shining with excitement.

"There's a show tonight!"

"Um, yeah," Delphi said. "Can I have my arm back?"

He let go and hurried past her into the theater. Bemused, she continued back to the condo, where she found Hugh and Isobel sitting next to each other on the couch in the living room. It was the closest she'd seen them in several days. Sunil was seated in one of the armchairs.

"Close the door," Isobel instructed.

"Did you guys all talk to your people?" Delphi asked.

"I talked to Geoff, and Isobel talked to Marissa," Hugh said.

Delphi glanced at Isobel. "I thought you were supposed to talk to Ezra."

"No longer relevant."

"What about you?" Delphi asked Sunil.

"I couldn't find Chris."

"What did you get?" Isobel asked Delphi. "Let's see if it jibes with what we've got."

Delphi perched on the chair nearest the sofa. "You were wrong. Heather doesn't play an instrument. But Kelly does."

"Kelly?" Isobel repeated, nonplussed. "Are you sure?"

"Yes, and when I asked if Kelly and Geoff ever dated, Heather got upset and said Kelly would never do that to her because Kelly knows her feelings for Geoff. I assume you thought Heather messed with the orchestra parts on Geoff's behalf. She played Suzuki violin for two minutes, but you know with Suzuki you don't learn to read music. But if Kelly was also a Geoff girlfriend, then maybe it was Kelly, not Heather. I mean the note did go missing from her book."

Isobel gave a dismissive wave. "Marissa wrote the note."

"Marissa? Why?"

"She and Arden go way back, but Arden was fabulous and Marissa was…Marissa. She wrote the note—to me, after all—in an attempt to impress Arden with her loyalty. Then when Arden died, she realized it could be misconstrued, so she stole Kelly's book to make it look like another prank and dumped the note."

"Did Marissa date Geoff too, then?"

"I don't think so. She says she didn't do any of the other things, and I believe her."

"If I'm following you correctly," Delphi said, "you think Geoff's girlfriends were acting in concert to sabotage the show?"

"Not acting in concert, competing," Isobel clarified. "Whoever is willing to go furthest wins his favor. Except I'm guessing Geoff doesn't give a shit about any of them. He puts each girl up to it separately, and it isn't until other stuff starts happening that she realizes she's not the only one. Already knowing Geoff's reputation with the ladies, plus the rumors and gossip, she figures it's a battle for his affections."

"It still doesn't answer who did what," Hugh said.

"Oh, easy. Heather rigs the masking. She also slips into the green room and puts the Ex-Lax in the first pot of coffee and drinks a cup herself to divert suspicion."

"I don't know how you thought Heather could have done the orchestra parts if the whole point of the laxative was to get everyone out of the theater, including her. And Kelly was sick, too."

Isobel gave a decisive nod. "That was Geoff. Who else would derive that kind of personal satisfaction from defacing the parts? The rest of it he could delegate, but not that."

Sunil started to laugh. "If Isobel and I had more devious minds, we might have prevented the shrimp."

"What are you talking about?" Delphi asked. "Who did the shrimp?"

There was a knock on the living room door, and Talia poked her head in.

"Hey, Isobel. I got your text. What's up?"

THIRTY-EIGHT

TALIA LOOKED DOLEFULLY around the room. "How did you figure out it was me?"

"Sunil and I saw you and Geoff in the frozen food aisle at Price Chopper," Isobel said. "We overheard part of your conversation, but it didn't make sense until we found out that you were the original Jennie and got bumped for Arden. And that you and Geoff had a thing."

"I didn't kill Arden," Talia insisted. "You have to believe me."

"People keep telling me I have to believe them," Isobel said to Delphi.

"And do you?"

"In this case, I'm not sure." Isobel turned to Talia. "Tell me why I shouldn't believe you killed Arden in revenge for her taking your role. After all, you were perfectly willing to believe it of me."

Talia flicked a strand of silky, dark hair behind her ear and sighed. "Geoff wrote the role for me. In his score, Jennie was a coloratura soprano. Lots of wonderful period-sounding parlor songs, an impassioned love song to Sousa, it was great stuff. His score really made the show. There was a gorgeous duet where Jennie accused Sousa of loving the band more than her, but Jethro made him take it out. Nothing could tarnish the image of his sainted Sousa." Talia snorted in disgust. "Then we did the workshop for the Donnelly Group—"

"Wait, it was mounted just for the Donnellys?" Isobel asked.

"Not just for them, but they were the big fish. Otherwise it was a lot of random people. I remember one woman with witchy hair and wild eyes telling me she was going to invest twenty thousand so she could come to the opening night party on Broadway. Which was crazy, because at that point Broadway was a long shot."

"And it became an even longer shot when Geoff's score got junked," Hugh said.

Talia nodded. "But the Donnelly Group was enthusiastic, and Felicity raised a bunch of money that day, but next thing we heard Jethro was revising the score and they were recasting Jennie. Geoff was crushed. I mean, I don't know how much he let on to you, but he really was. I was, too. Marjorie Moody was always a character singing the opera arias, and Geoff got Felicity to let me play her. So I agreed to do it in return for my Equity card."

"I can relate." Isobel gave Hugh a triumphant look. "And then what happened?"

"Well, it looked for a while like the show might be kind of good."

Delphi stifled a squawk.

"On what planet?" Isobel asked incredulously.

"It was a quality cast. Say what you will about her, Arden had star power. You guys are so good and you weren't even playing big roles, and Chris has the right energy. This was at the beginning. I was excited." She sighed. "Maybe I just wanted it to be good."

"*I* can relate," Hugh said, returning a look to Isobel.

"Anyway, I said something along those lines to Geoff, and he blew up at me. He said no way was this show going to succeed without him." Talia took a deep breath. "He asked me if I would help him sabotage it, and I said no."

"So he enlisted another ex-girlfriend," Isobel said. "One so mousy and unprepossessing nobody would ever suspect her."

"Heather," Talia confirmed. "He never cared about her, but she mooned around after him like he was Beethoven. I think sometimes he preferred her adulation to my challenging him on musical matters. Our bond is based on mutual talent. With Heather, he could pretend he was special."

"You knew what Heather was up to?"

Talia sighed. "Yeah. When I refused, he said fine, no problem, he was sure Heather would be willing to help. I was sure, too, so I put it out of my mind and tried to stay out of the way. First the masking fell, and then the thing with the coffee happened." She blushed a bit. "You all know how sick I was. That pissed me off. That's why I let slip to you guys that it might be Geoff. I told him you can't hurt people trying to bring down the show."

"What did he say to that?"

"You had your chance, and you chose not to help. Sorry if you were collateral damage."

"Harsh."

Talia sighed again. "Harsher still, he and Heather got back together. And I have to admit, I was jealous. When you saw us in the store, he was giving me the chance to help him out again, and this time I did, but I made him promise to dump Heather. We bought the shrimp that day, and then he and I were able to sneak back into the theater early the next morning because Heather had made him a set of keys."

"Why did you even bother with the shrimp after Arden was dead? If that wasn't going to kill the show, the shrimp wasn't."

Talia couldn't resist a smile. "That's where you're wrong. The shrimp did shut down the show, albeit temporarily." She sobered. "Besides, at that point we didn't know Arden had been murdered. If we'd known that, we never would have done it. At least I wouldn't have."

Isobel leaned forward. "I don't think you killed Arden any more than I did, and I don't see Heather going that far either, but how can you be certain Geoff didn't?"

Talia's face whitened. "He wanted the show to fail, but he wouldn't kill anyone."

"How well do you know him? How well do we really know anyone? What about Oliver?"

Isobel could feel Hugh's disapproving gaze on her, but she kept her eyes trained on Talia and saw doubt play across her delicate features.

"But don't you think the person who killed Arden is the same person who killed Thomas?"

"Yes, of course," Isobel said.

Talia looked palpably relieved. "I know who killed Thomas. I saw him."

"What? Who?"

Talia shrank back into her chair. "I'm not sure if I should say."

"I'm not sure if you're being coy or if you're legitimately scared, but I don't care," Isobel said. "Let me put it this way. Geoff is figuring pretty high on our list of suspects right now. If you can provide a credible alternative, I suggest you do. Otherwise, my next phone call is to Detective Dillon. About *all* of it."

"Fine." Talia clasped her hands in her lap and steeled herself. "It was Chris."

Delphi gasped, Sunil made a "hunh" sound, and Hugh exclaimed, "Chris?" but Isobel remained silent. If Talia was telling the truth, Isobel was spending most of the show alone onstage with a murderer. Anything could happen—had already happened—in full view of the audience, and she would be powerless to protect herself.

"You don't believe me," Talia said when Isobel didn't respond. "It was right at the top of act two, during the chorus bit, before the seaside concert scene. I had ducked into the bathroom offstage left to check my makeup. When I took my place in the wings, I saw Chris off to the side, near the alley door. He looked a little wild. He was tucking his shirttail into his pants, and there was a splotch of blood on it."

"Wait, you didn't actually see him kill Thomas?" Isobel asked.

"Well, no. I never left the building. But he must have just come back inside after having done it."

"And then what happened?"

"At the time, I didn't know about Thomas, so I put it out of my head. Then we went onstage."

"Did you tell anyone else?" Isobel asked.

Talia shook her head. "I didn't, because of the other stuff. I was afraid that would all come out somehow. My involvement. And Geoff's."

"And Heather's," Delphi added.

"I don't give a shit about Heather," Talia said hotly. "If she hadn't gotten her claws back into Geoff, I wouldn't be involved at all. And he's only using her. He and I have something special."

Isobel resisted the temptation to roll her eyes and instead cast her mind back to the night Thomas was murdered.

"I don't remember anything off about Chris. It was my second performance, and he was pretty attentive. Not distracted or anything."

"All that means is he's able to compartmentalize," Talia said.

"He didn't the night Arden was killed," Hugh said. "I was watching him from the pit. He looked completely freaked out when she collapsed."

"He would have to, wouldn't he?" Isobel pointed out. "He was in full view of the audience. If he'd been all 'oh, yeah, dead soprano, no biggie,' people would have pinned it on him immediately. Don't forget, he's an excellent actor."

"And he killed Thomas because...?" Sunil asked.

Isobel turned to him. "Because Thomas figured out how Arden was killed."

"Which was how?" Talia asked.

"Remember she sat on an exposed wire during tech?"

"Yeah, but Thomas fixed it."

"Someone unfixed it and dipped it in pure nicotine. Pretty effective way to deliver a fast-acting poison."

Talia blanched. "What? How?"

"Chris must have gotten the idea when she complained about it during tech," Sunil said. "You told us Chris and Arden used to be engaged. Do you know what happened between them?"

"No, but whatever it was, it ended badly."

"Obviously," Delphi said.

Talia shot her a look. "I mean before this."

"How did you even hear about them? Did Chris tell you? Arden?"

"Marissa told me. She may know more. You'd have to ask her."

"Dillon brought Chris in for questioning but didn't keep him," Isobel said. "I wonder why."

"Not enough evidence, probably," Sunil said.

"I wonder..." Isobel began.

Sunil jumped suddenly, and like a ripple effect, the others started in response.

"What the hell?" Delphi yelped.

"Sorry, my phone buzzed." He pulled it from his pocket, and a curious expression took over his face.

"What is it?" Isobel asked.

"A text from Kelly." Sunil looked up. "Chris is sick, and Ezra vetoed Jethro. I'm on as Sousa tonight."

THIRTY-NINE

"THANKS FOR GETTING back to me, Detective. Finally." Isobel muttered this last bit after she hung up. She set her phone down on the dressing room table.

"What did he say?" Delphi asked.

"He reiterated that they have no physical evidence linking Chris to the murders."

"What about the blood on his shirt?"

Isobel examined herself in the mirror and swept more blush onto her cheekbones. "Traces at best. You know wardrobe has to wash shirts after every show."

"They can't bring him in for more questioning?" Delphi persisted.

"Not without evidence."

"I don't think he's sick. I think he's gone." When Isobel didn't respond, Delphi asked, "Don't you?"

"I'm not convinced."

"But you think Talia's telling the truth?"

Isobel turned her head to one side, squinted, and then examined the other side. "I think she's telling the truth about what she saw, but she didn't witness the actual murder. Don't you think it's possible Chris went out there and simply discovered the body?"

"Why would he have gone out there?"

"Same reason we did. To retrieve the photo."

"During the show, though?"

Isobel stood and removed her act one costume from the rack. "I didn't think so at first, but on the other hand, when better? He's offstage at the top of act two when the ensemble is on. He knelt down to see if Thomas was alive and got blood on his shirt. If you bashed someone on the head, you'd be spattered with blood. It wouldn't be a splotch on your shirttail."

"That's a good point." Delphi positioned her bonnet atop her pile of curls and skewered it with a lethal-looking hatpin. "If it wasn't Chris, then who was it?"

"Talia will defend him until the cows come home, and I'm sure Heather will too, but my money's on Geoff. He wanted to shut down the show, and as Talia pointed out, Arden's death didn't do the trick. It didn't even make a difference when foul play was discovered. It took a cache of rotting shrimp to get Felicity to cancel, and that was only for one night."

"How would he have known about the loose wire on the bustle? Nobody saw him around during tech."

"He heard about it from Talia or Heather. Or Oliver. He asks, 'How's it going?' 'Oh, Arden is a total diva, she was bitching about sitting on a wire,' and the light bulb goes off.'" Isobel smoothed her bodice. "I'm going to go warm up."

"You're not nervous about tonight?"

Isobel laughed. "I think yesterday put the fear of God into Sunil. Haven't you noticed him cramming Sousa every spare moment he has? Besides, I'm betting he always knew a lot more of it than he was letting on."

"I didn't mean Sunil. Aren't you afraid Geoff will try something else?"

Isobel paused with her hand on the doorknob. "He doesn't need to right now. The shrimp did its thing, and with Chris out, that's more trouble afoot. Events have overtaken him, so I think he'll lie low. At this point, he knows the show is in trouble. In fact," she added cheerily, "I'd say tonight is probably the one night we can count on a smooth sail."

Isobel let the door close gently on Delphi's worried features, and as she hurried down the hall and into the stairwell, she tried to convince herself that she meant what she'd said. Logically, it made sense, but privately she shared Delphi's sense of unease. What Talia was missing, and Heather probably was too, was the fact that Geoff had set them up brilliantly. Their pranks were easily traceable to them, and they could swear up and down that Geoff was behind them, but with the astonishing lack of physical evidence, it would be hard to prove that one or both of them hadn't killed Arden and Thomas. Who knew what Geoff had up his sleeve that would implicate both Heather and Talia? Possibly some DNA evidence he could plant somewhere.

Isobel opened the door onto the third floor and found the rehearsal studio empty, as it always was this time of night. She shut the door behind her and flicked on the light. Humming softly, she made her way to the piano and gave herself a starting pitch for her scales. As she warmed up, she continued to ponder the situation. There really was no reason for Geoff to cause mischief tonight. Word had gotten around yesterday that Sunil wasn't ready, and as far as anyone knew, he might not be any more ready now. The police investigation clearly wasn't progressing. Isobel wondered if they had any suspects at all. Maybe instead of suggesting they bring Chris back, she should have urged Dillon to bring Geoff in.

She was an idiot. That was far and away the most sensible thing to do. If nothing else, it would ensure they would all stay safe tonight with Geoff off the premises. She mentally smacked herself for not thinking of it sooner and reached instinctively for her phone, but she'd left it in her dressing room. The clock over the door said seven forty-five. She still had time to call if she was willing to abandon her warm-up.

"Mi-mi-mi-miiiii—okay, that's good."

She lowered the lid over the keys, which she always did even though nobody else ever bothered, and shut off the light behind her. As she turned toward the stairwell, she realized voices were coming from one of the other, smaller studios. The studios were pretty soundproof, but whoever was in there hadn't closed the door all the way. As she drew closer, she realized it was Ezra and Jethro.

"I know why you're still here," Jethro said. "You're not going to leave until you've finished what you came to do."

"I'm here because there are more revisions to be made on this deeply flawed piece of material," Ezra responded. There was an iron edge in his voice that Isobel had never heard before.

"You can't fool me. I know what you're really trying to do."

"Then you know I don't intend to stop now," Ezra countered.

Isobel heard furious footsteps pounding toward the door, and she looked around for someplace to hide. She darted into the costume shop and stood behind the door, panting. Ezra. Her initial impulse to question him stemmed from her desire to dismiss him as a suspect, but she'd been distracted by her conversation with Marissa. Now she was glad she had avoided a run-in with him. It seemed he would stop at nothing to make sure the show died a quiet death in Albany, no matter who else had to die with it. A noise in the costume shop made her jump, bringing her back to reality, and she realized it was seven fifty. She lurched into the hallway—and ran smack into Jethro.

"Isobel! What are you doing up here?"

"I, uh...I'm warming up."

His eyes narrowed. "In the costume shop?"

"Oh! No, I needed a safety pin."

"Did you find one?"

"Yeah, I'm good."

"You'd better get downstairs. It's almost places."

Jethro gave a curious glance behind Isobel and then closed the door to the costume shop. She followed him to the stairwell, and they proceeded down in silence.

At the theater level, Jethro rested his hand on her shoulder. "I want you to know, as far as I'm concerned, it was always you. Arden was never anything but a publicity draw. That's why I kept harping on your Emma. I wanted the rest of the creative team to see that your natural qualities were better used elsewhere." He smiled goonily at her through his flop of ginger hair and opened the stage door for her.

"Um, thanks. I think," she said.

Kelly flew at her. "Where have you been? I called places, and nobody knew where you were."

"Sorry, I went upstairs to warm up. I was watching the time."

Kelly turned to Jethro. "And you're not supposed to be backstage after half hour."

"Yes, you've all made that clear." Jethro winked at Isobel and retreated.

"Come on," Kelly said, hustling Isobel into the wings. "There's enough weirdness tonight without you disappearing on me."

There was no time for Isobel to ask what Kelly meant, but in principle, she agreed.

FORTY

SUNIL FELT HIS FIRST performance as Sousa warranted a repeat of his opening night ritual, but going out to the alley seemed like bad karma, even though the crime scene tape had been removed. He briefly considered going upstairs to look for an empty rehearsal room like Isobel did, but he didn't relish the idea of wandering around the building where he couldn't hear the monitor. He let the wardrobe mistress fuss with his costume a bit longer—Chris had a huskier frame—but as soon as Kelly called five, he grabbed his script, now dog-eared, and left his dressing room in search of solitude. He ran into Hugh, who was coming up the stairs from the pit.

"You okay?" Hugh asked.

"A little nervous," Sunil admitted. "I want to grab a few moments for myself. I think I'll go downstairs."

"You're going to be great. Remember to watch me coming out of the *ritard* at the end of 'The Washington Post.'"

Sunil continued down to the vom. That was the perfect spot. No actors or stagehands, just the comforting cacophony of the musicians warming up on the other side of the wall.

"Like spirits beyond the veil," Sunil muttered to himself. As soon as he said it, he felt his skin crawl. Jewish superstition. It was inbred, the flame fanned further by his mother, whose lengthy rites to keep away the evil eye had first spawned the idea of an opening night ritual.

"Get a grip," he told himself. "This is no time to freak yourself out for no reason."

Chairs and a few old set pieces were stacked against the wall. He stood next to them and closed his eyes, praying silently. His standard message combined English, Hindi, and Hebrew, and the familiar words flowed through his head, calming him. His stomach unclenched, his shoulders lowered, and his jaw released. Even if he didn't turn in the kind of slick performance Isobel gave her first time out, he was at least confident that he wouldn't embarrass himself. Maybe he would even be good. Despite his misgivings about the piece, his actor's ego started to kick in, and he felt a rush of adrenaline at the prospect of being the star.

As he opened his eyes, he saw a flash of gold shimmer and then disappear around the far side of the vom. Even though he was stage left, where he needed to be for his first entrance, he crept around to the other side and peered up the stairs. A figure in a black and gold cape was sweeping up the last two steps. Curious, he followed, but when he emerged, there was nobody there. He wondered who it was. Nobody wore a costume like that. Mark, the props guy, strode into the wings from the stage and took his place by the long table, where each prop sat in its labeled spot.

"Who was that guy who just came through?"

Mark looked blank. "What guy?"

"He looked like he was wearing a cape."

"Nah, didn't see anyone."

Sunil looked past him onto the stage, where the ensemble members were taking their places for the opening number, chattering among themselves. There was always a buzz of excitement when an understudy went on, and normally Sunil would have allowed himself to enjoy the attention, but given the recent murders, somebody lurking around backstage who shouldn't be there took precedence.

"Places!" Kelly's voice echoed over the monitor.

He crossed the stage, barely hearing the well wishes from his colleagues. Delphi was waiting for him on the other side. She clasped him in a bear hug, which he was also too distracted to appreciate. She pulled back and held him at arm's length.

"Are you so nervous you won't even hug me back?"

"I saw someone wandering around backstage who shouldn't be here."

"Who?"

"I didn't see his face. A guy in a black and gold cape was going up the stairs from the vom stage right."

"Nobody wears anything like that."

"I know."

They heard a burst of applause, which died down a moment later as Felicity stepped in front of the curtain. Sunil heard his name over the monitors as she informed the audience that he would be playing the title role and Matt Hurd would be taking on the roles of Benjamin Swallow and the Pawnee chief. Felicity's exit was accompanied by whispers and scattered applause, but Hugh cut them off with the overture.

The resounding brass brought Sunil back to himself, and he determined to forget the figure in the cape. This was his chance to show them all what he could do. He caught sight of Isobel pacing in the wings stage right. He tried to catch her attention, but the moment she looked up, the curtain rose and the ensemble began to sing.

ISOBEL TRIED TO CATCH Sunil's eye, but he became distracted as soon as the curtain went up. She had hoped to spend a few moments with him before the show to wish him luck and relish the surprising reward of going on opposite one another in the leading roles. When they'd accepted their contracts, neither of them expected it to happen, yet that slim hope was what made them both sign on the dotted line (that and the fact that, no matter how you sliced it, it was a bona fide regional theater job). And now here they were. With Delphi and Hugh, no less. Isobel knew enough about show business to realize that the likelihood of a confluence like this ever happening again was small. But she'd been too preoccupied by the argument she'd overheard between Jethro and Ezra to make Sunil a priority.

Ezra. She'd dismissed him earlier, but something there didn't add up. Mostly he was genial and warm, but he had a short fuse. Sometimes he seemed to enjoy his job, and sometimes he seemed like he was there under duress. Putting in understudies didn't strike her as enough of a reason for him to stay. That kind of thing happened all the time, and it was the stage manager's job to oversee the transition. Once a show was open, it belonged to the stage manager, not the director, and Kelly had proven herself more than competent. So what *was* Ezra still doing in Albany? Of course, there was the continuing tussle over "Song of the Sea." Could Ezra have stuck around just to make sure Jethro didn't sneak the duet version back in, or to finish the job and cut it entirely? Or was it more sinister, like maybe he wanted to make absolutely certain the show sank without a trace, so nobody would ever connect his name to the flotsam. Even if it meant weighting it down with a body or two.

Suddenly, Isobel was on. Hearing her entrance cue brought her immediately back to herself. And there was Sunil as Sousa, gazing at her as if he really were falling in love with her. They sailed through their first scene, then their second. Before she knew it, "The Washington Post" duet was upon them. She saw him hesitate for a millisecond before pulling her onto his lap, but the move passed without incident. They finished the number to an enthusiastic ovation. But while they were holding for applause, Isobel saw the color drain from Sunil's face.

It was all she could do not to break character and ask what was wrong. He turned back to her and continued with the dialogue that led into the first-act finale, but the lines came out detached and robotic, devoid of the warmth and charm he usually radiated. Overcompensating, Isobel's voice soared into singsong territory, but she couldn't stop herself. It was as if she and Sunil were having an entirely different conversation underneath Jennie's and Sousa's lines. This, she realized, was what acting teachers were getting at when they talked about subtext.

The first-act curtain came down at last. She turned to Sunil, the question poised on her lips, but he answered before she could voice it.

"The theater ghost. I saw him," he said throatily. "Wearing a black and gold cape. He was there, and then he wasn't."

FORTY-ONE

Isobel drew away from him, agog. "You've got to be kidding me."

Sunil knew he sounded stupid, but he also knew what he'd seen. "He was in the vom before the show, and then I saw him again in the wings after 'The Washington Post,' dressed in Revolutionary garb. It was the ghost of Robert Livingston."

"I don't doubt there's a ghost in the theater. What I can't get my head around is you admitting you saw it."

He grabbed her hand. "Come on. We have to find it."

She pulled free. "That's not how ghosts work. They find you. Besides, we have to change for act two." She hurried into the wings, calling over her shoulder, "By the way, you're amazing!"

He rushed after her, but suddenly Delphi was there, throwing her arms around him. "You are absolutely magnetic! I can't take my eyes off you when you're onstage!"

"Thanks, but I can't right now." He patted her shoulders and pushed past her, not before noticing the flash of hurt on her face.

In different circumstances, he might have seized on the unexpected encouragement to press his suit, but he could only file away the compliment for quiet enjoyment and hope to recapture the moment later. Right now he had other fish to fry, and exactly fifteen minutes to do it.

First thing was to return to the scene of the initial sighting. He scurried downstairs to the pit, where musicians were milling about the entrance. Sunil slowed his pace and crept quietly into the vom. It was empty, except for the stacked chairs near the stage left stairs. He leaned against the wall where he had prayed earlier and half-closed his eyes, waiting for a shadow to pass again. Nothing happened. He continued around to the other side of the stage and yanked open the door to the stage right bathroom, but it too was empty. He climbed the stairs where he had seen the figure retreat earlier, but the wings were now a bustle of activity as the running crew set up for act two. The black and gold cape was nowhere to be seen.

As Sunil hurried back to his dressing room to change, he realized it was unlikely the ghost would make an appearance during intermission when there were so many people around. He didn't know why, but he felt certain the ghost wanted him, and him alone, to acknowledge its presence. When he returned to the wings stage left costumed for act two, he realized the only place he hadn't looked was the one he had been too scared to visit before the show. He steeled himself, opened the side door, and silently crept out into the alley.

ISOBEL HAD MASTERED buttoning herself into her second-act costume in under five minutes, and she was changed and gone before Delphi returned to their dressing room. A truly bizarre thought had taken hold, and she had exactly ten minutes to check her theory. She stuffed her phone and her kid gloves into the little drawstring purse she carried in act two. In the wings, she waited until Heather was otherwise occupied, and then Isobel opened the stage door into the lobby.

She realized her folly immediately. The lines for the bathrooms snaked around the corner, and she was in full view of most of the female and a handful of male patrons. Passing them to get to the main stairwell would draw unwanted attention.

"Oh, honey! You have such a lovely voice," a woman called.

"Muriel, look, that's the girl playing Jennie!" exclaimed another.

Isobel gave a feeble wave. Her mission would have to wait. She had a solid twenty-minute break midway through act two from the scene between Mrs. Blakely and Sousa through the international touring medley, where Talia sang her second aria. That was a much safer bet. She took refuge backstage, thinking back to the end of act one. Sunil was certainly acting strangely. Last summer, when she'd seen the ghost onstage at the Galaxy Playhouse, he never believed her, in spite of mounting evidence in support of her claim. To this day, he refused to acknowledge her brush with the supernatural. And now he was claiming one himself? Impossible. He was up to something, and whatever it was he didn't want her involved.

Fine, she thought, if he was going to be that way. But it wasn't like him, and she had to admit she was curious. She glanced at her phone. Five minutes to go. Just in case he was telling the truth, she circled behind the set and descended the stairs to the vom.

"Hello?" she called. "Show yourself! I'm a welcoming spirit. A friend."

"I'm jolly glad to hear that."

Isobel clapped her hand over her heart. "Hugh, you scared me!"

"What are you doing back here? I was on my way back to the pit, and I hear you carrying on like a bacchante."

"I was looking for the theater ghost. Sunil claims he had a sighting here earlier, but I don't believe him."

"I should hope not. He never did you the courtesy of believing you." Hugh came toward her and took her hand. "Beautiful job tonight, as always. You and Sunil are quite magical together. You have real chemistry." For a moment, she was afraid he might kiss her, and she didn't want to have to deal with that in the middle of everything else. But he brushed her fingers with his lips instead. "Now, go slay them in act two!"

She winced. "Maybe not the best choice of words."

Hugh gave a pained shrug and continued to the pit. She looked down the empty passage. Even if the ghost decided to turn up now, there was no time left to pursue it. She sighed and tromped back up the stairs. As she came to the top, she heard a muffled banging. It seemed to be coming from the door to the alley. She wrenched the door open, and Sunil stumbled into her arms.

"What were you doing out there?"

"Nothing, it was stupid. I thought…I don't know what I thought. Anyway I got locked out. Thank God you came along."

"Someone would have heard you eventually, or Kelly would have flipped out when she called places and you didn't show." A shadow crossed Isobel's face. "Did anyone see you go outside?"

"I don't think so. Why?"

Before she could answer, her phone buzzed in her purse. She scanned the text and felt a flash of terror before reason took over.

"What is it?" Sunil asked.

She darkened the screen and palmed the phone. "Nothing important."

"Places," Kelly called.

"If you say so." He sounded unconvinced. "Meet you at the double bar line."

Here's hoping, she thought as he took his position in the wings. She turned her phone over and reread the text from Roman Fried.

Enjoy your last performance.

FORTY-TWO

ISOBEL BEAMED AT SUNIL as he sang to her. He seemed to have set aside his preoccupation with the ghost of Robert Livingston and was once again fully committed to his portrayal of John Philip Sousa. Isobel's head, however, was spinning, trying to find a place for Fried's text in her working theory. It didn't *not* fit; it only suggested a link she had missed somewhere. There was time to work that out later. In the meantime, she tapped her toe impatiently along with the music, waiting until she was sprung for her hiatus and she could resume her aborted intermission investigation.

She marveled anew at Sunil's glorious tenor. He really was exceptionally gifted. He was also a wonderful actor and so attractive. She couldn't for the life of her understand why Delphi wasn't interested in him, especially when his feelings for her were so obvious. Isobel hoped her friend would wise up and see what a catch she had in Sunil.

He must have felt her gaze on him, because he turned toward her in a spot where Chris usually interacted with one of the ensemble men. Of course, this was Sunil's first time on for Sousa, and minutiae like shifting one's focus was not the kind of thing a director specified. A movement like that was solely at the actor's discretion, but as Sunil caught her eye, she saw something she didn't expect.

Fear.

And in a flash, she understood everything. She willed the song to end, but it seemed to her that Hugh was slowing down the tempo deliberately, when it was more important than ever that she get back upstairs.

Finally the audience was applauding. She gave her exit line and left the stage, trying to keep her walking pace normal. But as soon as she reached the wings, her boots skittered across the floor.

"Where are you going?" Heather's urgent hiss followed her out the stage door. "You can't go out there in the middle of the show."

"I'll be back in time for my entrance, I promise."

"Isobel, wait!"

Ignoring her, Isobel ran into the hall, now empty of full-bladdered patrons, knowing Heather wouldn't dare leave her post during the show to come after her. Isobel paused for a moment and pulled out her phone again. Closing the text from Roman Fried, she opened her browser, navigating quickly to Amazon. She found what she was looking for and knew for certain she was on the right track. She had to act quickly.

Taking the stairs as nimbly as she could in a bustled evening gown and high-heeled boots, Isobel emerged finally onto the third floor. She hurried down the hall past the rehearsal studio and flung open the door to the costume shop.

"Where are you?" she asked, her voice above a whisper but not quite conversation level.

There was no answer. She glanced nervously over her shoulder and tried again louder.

"I heard you before. I know you're in here."

And there it was. The same scuffling noise she'd heard when she'd taken refuge in the costume shop before the show.

"Keep doing that. I'll find you."

She pulled on her kid gloves as she followed the sound to a closet in the far corner of the room by the window. She opened it and gasped.

"Oh my God, are you okay?"

Chris blinked groggily at her. His hands were tied behind his back, his ankles bound together with duct tape, and he was propped up against several bolts of material.

"Drugged?" Isobel asked.

Chris nodded in slow motion.

She knelt beside him and spoke quickly. "I need you to stay here for another forty-five minutes or so, okay? I promise you'll be safe, but we can't let him know I found you. I have a plan, but I have to leave you here. Please don't hate me."

"He killed them," Chris croaked. "Arden and Thomas…"

"I know."

"But not me."

"No, not you. I promise we'll get you out of here. Just not yet. This is the best way." She searched his face earnestly. "Do you trust me?"

Chris worked his lips together slowly and closed his eyes.

"Stay quiet and sleep it off if you can." Cringing, she closed the closet door again.

She glanced at her phone. Thirteen minutes before she was due back onstage. There was no time to waste. She closed her eyes and ran through the rest of the show in her head, trying to anticipate his next move, but her mind was spinning in circles.

Then she remembered. The banquet scene, which was also the next time she was onstage. The running crew would have preset the props offstage right on the banquet table during intermission, because it was a complicated set change. That meant the wings stage right would be clear—now.

Isobel had never run so fast in her life. By the time she came flying through the stage door again, she was panting and gasping. But if Heather expressed surprise, Isobel didn't stick around to hear. There was one more set of stairs, the ones leading down to the vom. She stumbled on the last step but caught herself before she fell. The figure was lurking at the foot of the stairs on the right side of the passage, the gold and black cape grazing the floor behind him. She righted herself and took two steps forward.

"Mr. Livingston, I presume?"

FORTY-THREE

THE FIGURE STIFFENED. Clearly, he had not expected to be disturbed. Isobel saw him hesitate, deciding whether to confront her or continue up the stairs to execute his diabolical plan. She couldn't risk that happening.

"Jethro," she said, her heart pounding with fear, "I love you."

Slowly, he turned, the tricorn hat casting his face in shadow.

"What did you say?"

She moved toward him, and her college acting teacher's words filled her brain. *Work with whatever you're feeling.*

She grabbed his hand and put it to her breast. A bolt of electricity seemed to shoot through him.

"Feel my heart, it's beating like crazy at the thought of what you've done for me. At what you're about to do."

He pulled her hand, still clasped around his, to his mouth and began to smother it with kisses. Isobel moaned in disgust, knowing Jethro would interpret it differently.

"You know, and you don't mind?" Jethro asked huskily.

"How could I mind?" she whispered. "You wanted us to be together, right? And this was the only way?"

"The others couldn't see it," he said breathlessly. "You were Jennie. It had to be you, and they wouldn't let it be. It was never going to work with anyone else, so I had to kill her. That was the only way it could be perfect. But of course it wasn't perfect—not quite. I had to be up there with you for the final, glorious consummation of my mission!"

"The interloper upstairs," she said urgently. "He must be stopped."

He flicked his cape dramatically. "I am on my way."

It was do or die time. For Sunil, literally.

"Oh, darling," Isobel breathed, "you've risked everything for our happiness. Let me do this one last thing for you. For us."

She could hear the applause as the international touring medley finished. In a moment, the running crew would be setting up the banquet. She threw her arms around Jethro's neck and before she could think too hard about what she was doing, kissed him fully and deeply on his meaty lips. When she pulled away, his eyes were glazed with ecstasy.

For the second time tonight, she asked, "Do you trust me?"

He nodded eagerly and reached for her again, but she stopped him.

"There's no time. Later. I'm all yours for the rest of the performances."

She sent up a prayer of thanks to Roman Fried, whose text meant she could make that promise unreservedly.

"Give me the poison."

Jethro stuck his hand inside his cape and withdrew a small, stoppered bottle. He was about to hand it to her when he suddenly became aware of the furniture moving above his head. The color drained from his face.

"It's too late! They're already setting up the banquet."

Isobel could see the storm brewing on his face. "I have a better way. A more dramatic ending. One for the history books." She held out her hand. "We must act now or all is lost!"

He shoved the bottle into her gloved hand. "Nicotine," he whispered. "One drop will do it."

"Yes, my darling, I know." Isobel gingerly settled the bottle in her drawstring purse and pointed to the wooden chairs stacked by the stage left stairs. "Sit there and wait for me. If you're not there when I come back, I will never allow my womanly treasures to be yours, do you understand?"

Jethro's lips quivered. "Yes, my love. Now, fly. Fly!"

As Isobel fled upstairs, she wondered if that last bit had been too much. Then again, when you were dealing with full-on crazy, there was probably no such thing.

FORTY-FOUR

THE LIGHTS CAME UP on the banquet scene. Sunil turned to deliver his first line to Isobel, but she wasn't there. His blood froze. It wasn't like her to miss an entrance, and he hadn't told her the truth about what happened in the alley. The door had been propped open slightly, and when he'd looked out, he'd seen the ghost's cape on the ground. He'd taken a step outside, when he was knocked forward, landing on his knees. He'd felt the cape being swished away next to him, and then he'd heard the door slam and lock behind him. The ghost had locked him out. On purpose. And now Isobel was missing.

He glanced into the wings stage left, but there was no sight of her. Next to him, Marissa gave him a quizzical look. He cleared his throat and ad-libbed.

"Ah, Mrs. Blakely, I'm glad we resolved our differences so you could join this celebration of the band."

Marissa blinked at him.

"Mrs. Blakely?" he prompted.

"I'm not Mrs. Blakely in this scene. She's dead," Marissa muttered.

Jesus, thought Sunil. Does she not know the basic rules of improv?

"Pardon me, madam, it's just that you very closely resemble the litigious widow of my late partner. But of course she is *dead*," he spat the word, "and you are obviously someone else." He smiled wickedly. "What is your name?"

"Oh!" Marissa started. "I'm Mrs....um...Miss..."

She was saved by the appearance of Isobel, who fluttered in from the wings and cried, "Darling!" She threw her arms around Sunil and hissed in his ear, "Had to make a call."

Before he could respond, she drew back and jumped into the scene.

"Oh, Philip, what an honor."

Relieved, Sunil picked up his cue. "And tomorrow I launch my new venture in Philadelphia. Jennie, dear, I only wish you could join me."

"If you had not established your silly 'no wives on tour' rule, I could. Hoist by your own petard once again, you darling old meddler."

The scene continued without further incident, but the moment the lights came down, Isobel grabbed his arm and steered him into the wings with surprising force.

"It's Jethro, and you're next."

"What are you—"

"Play dead in the next scene."

"Well, it is my death scene."

She yanked him closer. "No, I mean *really* dead. Your life depends on Jethro thinking you, Sunil, are dead."

"Oh, shit," he breathed.

"One other thing. When Delphi leans over you to check your pulse, tell her to scream, 'Oh my God, Sunil is dead.'"

"What the hell?"

"I'll explain later."

"What if she won't?"

"Make her."

DELPHI PACED BACKSTAGE in her maid's costume, waiting for the crew to set up the Philadelphia hotel room. Isobel and Sunil had been on edge all night, but there was nothing she could put her finger on beyond the obvious. Although now that she thought about it, she'd hardly seen either of them backstage during the show. And then Isobel was late for that last scene, which wasn't like her at all. Delphi heard the ad-libbed exchange between Marissa and Sunil over the monitor. Sunil had seemed off during the act one finale, not that she could blame him since it was his first time going on as Sousa. But again, it wasn't like him. Even when he didn't know exactly what he was doing, Sunil's confidence never seemed to falter.

The scene change seemed interminable tonight, but finally the lights came up. Sunil was sprawled on the bed in a strange position, with his head upstage, the opposite of the way he'd been blocked. It meant that when she bent over him, she'd be giving the audience a charming view of her backside. Sunil must have realized that, the swine. He'd done it on purpose. She'd make sure to give him grief for it afterward.

She strode onstage, breakfast tray in hand, and paused outside the wooden doorframe.

"Mr. Sousa? I've got your breakfast."

She sighed and set down the tray, then knocked on the door and slowly nudged it open.

"Mr. Sousa, you ordered your toast for nine o'clock."

She approached the bed and bent forward at what she knew was an unattractive angle and put her fingers on his neck. To her surprise, he grabbed her hand and pulled her close.

"Scream, 'Oh my God, Sunil is dead,'" he whispered. "Just do it."

"What? Why?"

He opened one eye. "Isobel."

Delphi screamed.

ISOBEL HOVERED ON THE STEPS to the vom, directly above the spot where Jethro, if he was following orders, was sitting on his chair, waiting for her triumphant return.

She was prepared for the gasps and shrieks from the audience when they came, but she put the sound out of her mind. She had to focus. It was imperative that this next scene play out according to the script in her head. She glanced behind her and then took the last few steps at a bound.

"It's done! Did you hear? Just like I promised!"

Jethro was seated, his head bowed, his hands before him as if in prayer. His hat was in his lap, and when he looked up, his eyes glittered feverishly and a foolish grin overtook his pudgy features. In that moment, he resembled an overgrown child granted his greatest Christmas wish.

"You've killed the impostor," Jethro said in awestruck tones. "Then you do love me?"

"I've proven it, haven't I? I gave your poison to him. Now it's only you and me, Jethro."

"Philip!" he snapped. "I'm John Philip Sousa!"

Of course you are, in a Robert Livingston costume, thought Isobel. Ah, well, first rule of improv.

"Yes, and I am your Jennie. How did you arrange it?" she asked wonderingly.

"I got rid of the people in the way," he said. "I killed that tart and the meddling costumer. And now the two impostors are gone." He grabbed her arm. "I had to kill them so we could be together, my dove, and now we are!"

"We'll perform in your masterpiece as ourselves, in love, as we were always meant to be," Isobel said, although the words made her sick.

"Yes. Yes!" Jethro crowed. "We'll be together in death as we never were in life."

Over the monitors, the clamor of the audience was reaching a fever pitch.

"Wait—what?" she stammered.

"I said we'll be together in death. For all eternity!"

Jethro lunged toward her. Isobel stood, horrified and rooted to the spot, as strong arms grabbed her and threw her roughly to the ground.

FORTY-FIVE

ISOBEL WAS LUCKY she landed on her ass. If she had landed face down, her drawstring purse would have hit the floor and the nicotine bottle would have smashed and drenched her. Even worse, her iPhone would have broken. Ironically, it was her wire bustle that protected her, although it made for a painful landing. Sergeant Pemberthy helped her to her feet while Detective Dillon and another officer pinned Jethro against the wall and cuffed him.

"I'll take that," Dillon said, prying a nasty-looking switchblade from Jethro's trembling hand.

"You okay?" Pemberthy asked Isobel.

She rubbed the back of her thighs under her skirt. "I'll mend. Even though I knew you guys were behind me on the stairs, when he said that about being together in death…" Her breath caught. "I'm just glad you were backing me up."

"It's a good thing we were already on site to pick up Felicity Hamilton when you called. Otherwise we would never have made it in time," Dillon said as he jerked Jethro away from the wall. "Come on. Let's go join Auntie in the lobby."

"What exactly did Roman Fried find?" Isobel asked.

Dillon gave a snide chuckle. "Yeah, your secret source. He called me a few hours ago. He found evidence that Felicity and the board president were in the habit of raising more funds than were budgeted for every show and siphoning money off the top. It's been going on for years apparently, but she made a few mistakes with this one. When the state funds dried up, some muckety-muck New York producers—"

"The Donnelly Group?"

"I think so. They had seen the show or something and were interested, and they ran their own numbers to see what it would cost to produce. Then Felicity came back to them and gave them something so wildly inflated that they went back and looked at another show of hers they'd put money into— some musical about Starbucks, if you can believe it—and realized she was planning to take them for a ride. They called Fried and asked him to check it out."

"Why did they call Fried and not the cops?"

"They didn't have evidence. But I gather he's something of a dirt-digger, and even if he couldn't prove it, he could always print something in the paper damaging enough to the theater's reputation that it would get the Feds interested."

"I can't believe the Donnelly Group was ever actually interested in this show," Isobel said.

"Apparently, they only wanted it if they could get someone else to write the story."

"You mean the score—the music and lyrics," Isobel clarified.

Dillon shook his head. "No, apparently they loved the music, but they thought the play part was sappy and didn't have enough dramatic tension. I gotta say, I thought the whole thing was a snore."

"That's a lie!" Jethro bellowed suddenly. "They wanted the book! They hated the music. They wanted my story! They wanted my Sousa!"

"Doesn't matter now, does it? Come on, big boy."

The other officer led Jethro up the stairs. Dillon paused next to Isobel.

"You were very impressive. Really kept your cool. Even with me, which is saying something."

"Thanks," Isobel said, secretly pleased. "Though my heart hasn't stopped pounding."

"You know, if the acting thing doesn't work out…" He winked. "Send Sergeant Pemberthy the recording of your little encounter with Jethro, but keep it on your phone as backup, please. We'll be in touch."

He followed Jethro up the stairs. Isobel handed Pemberthy her drawstring purse.

"The nicotine is in there. I had my gloves on the whole time. Jethro's prints should be the only ones on the bottle."

"Dillon's right. You are a cool customer," Pemberthy said with admiration. "You got Jethro to say exactly what we needed. Between his recorded confession and the nicotine, we've got pretty solid evidence. What put you onto him anyway?"

"The ghost of Robert Livingston. Jethro was the only one who claimed to have seen him in *this* theater, although Kelly saw him at the old vaudeville house. Ghosts haunt places, not people. If there really is a ghost, he's still there, playing to an empty house. When I remembered Jethro wrote historical mysteries, I searched them on Amazon and confirmed that Robert Livingston is his fictional detective."

"How come only Sunil saw him?"

"Jethro knew Sousa's track by heart. He waited to show himself when he knew Sunil would be alone. I think he must have been hiding out in the stage right bathroom. There's less room on that side. That's why most of our entrances and exits are blocked from the left."

"I still don't see how you made the connection."

"It was something he said to me on the stairs. About how much he wanted me as Jennie all along, and I remembered how he described my first time in the role as uncanny. When rehearsals started, he told me to look up Jennie Sousa online, and I do resemble her quite a bit. When I thought about Chris disappearing and Sunil seeing this crazy ghost, his motive finally clicked. Jethro wanted everyone else out of the way so he and I could do the show together. Speaking of Chris, is he going to be okay?"

"I think so. He was knocked out with chloroform. I wonder why Jethro didn't kill him."

"You'd have to ask him, but I think he actually admired his performance. And I don't think Jethro much cared what happened after tonight. It's clear he was planning a *Liebestod* kind of thing."

Pemberthy frowned. "A what?"

"Tristan and Isolde? An apotheosis in love and death?" Isobel tried again.

"Oh, I see. I think."

"Anyway, by the end, I think he believed he was Sousa and I was Jennie. He was going to kill me and then himself so we could be together forever." Isobel shuddered. "And he would have killed Sunil. First Jethro tried to spook him and get him out of the way by dressing as the ghost of Robert Livingston, and then he locked Sunil outside. That's what made me suddenly remember the noises I heard in the costume shop. The banging wasn't as loud, but it was a déjà vu moment."

"Good thing, too," Pemberthy said. "If Chris had passed out, we might never have found him. But how did you know what Jethro was going to do?"

"I had a hunch he'd go back to nicotine, and I calculated that his best opportunity was to spike Sunil's glass in the banquet scene. But I managed to distract him long enough for the crew to get the props onstage before Jethro could do it."

"And Thomas?"

Isobel's heart twinged. "I blame myself for that. Jethro saw that Delphi had taken off Arden's bustle during act one that night. I sent Thomas on a wild goose chase looking for it in the wings by the alley door, but of course it wasn't there, because I'd brought it to you. Jethro must have assumed Thomas removed the bustle because he'd figured out how the nicotine had been delivered, so Jethro lured him outside and killed him. Thomas was the one feeding information to Roman Fried, but the irony is he knew nothing about the poisoned bustle. And he was killed for it anyway."

"What about all the other stuff? I mean, I get that Jethro was hoping the masking would fall on Arden and kill her, but why did he bother putting a laxative in the coffee, and messing with the music, and sewing the shrimp into the curtains?"

Isobel paused. "I don't think that was Jethro."

Sergeant Pemberthy cocked her head to the side. "Then who was it?"

Isobel thought a moment. "I might be wrong about the ghost. Maybe when the company left the old vaudeville house it did move in here. You know, I think it must have been the ghost." She blinked innocently. "Because I can't for the life of me think of another explanation."

"WILL YOU HURRY UP?" Delphi shouted up the stairs. "We're going to miss our train!"

"I'm coming! Hold your horses!"

A moment later, Isobel came galumphing down with her suitcase. "Okay, I've got everything."

"The boys are already in the cab. Come on."

They let the front door slam behind them, and Isobel rolled her suitcase down the path.

"Wait!"

Isobel turned to see Talia flying down the sidewalk toward them. "I thought you already left," Isobel said.

"I'm taking the four o'clock. I just went over to Geoff's to say good-bye. A real good-bye, as in good-bye and good luck."

"Ah."

"Listen, I wanted to thank you for not ratting us out to the cops."

"There was no point. Felicity would have had to press vandalism charges against you, and considering they've shut down her theater and she's facing prison for fraud, she isn't in a position to make a fuss. But I don't think I would have in any case. If ever a show was worth sabotaging, this was it."

Talia smiled sheepishly. "I'm sorry I thought you had it in for Arden. You were honest about everything the whole time, and we all treated you terribly."

"Thanks." Isobel gave Talia a hug. "Maybe we'll see you in the city. You know, I never said, but you have a beautiful voice."

"Thanks. So do you!"

The cab driver honked his horn, and Delphi yanked Isobel's arm. They slammed the trunk shut over Isobel's suitcase and piled in.

"Train station, please," Hugh said from the passenger seat.

In the back, Delphi slid closer to Sunil. He put his arm around her, and Isobel noticed that she didn't object. His brush with death had wrought a subtle change in Delphi's attitude over the past twenty-four hours. Nothing had happened between them yet as far as Isobel knew, and they might well revert to their old sparring, but she hoped Delphi was finally coming to her senses. At the same time, Isobel realized that once they were home, there was no more putting off the conversation she and Hugh needed to have, and the prospect of where they were headed saddened her.

Isobel's phone rang. Her spirits lifted when she saw the number.

"Mr. Fried," she said. The others turned to her with interest.

"Ms. Spice. Well done on your end."

"I might say the same."

"Sorry for going AWOL like that, but I didn't want you caught in the crossfire. There seemed to me a real possibility that Felicity was behind the murders as a way of covering up her fraud. I was able to hightail it back to New York and get the confirmation I was looking for, but I didn't want to put you in any further danger."

"Thank you. But of course it was Jethro who killed Arden and Thomas."

"A very disturbed young man, it seems."

"Is it true that the Donnellys wanted Felicity to throw out Jethro's book and keep the score, and not the other way around?"

"Oh yes, I heard it from Irv Donnelly himself. He fell in love with Geoff Brown's score. Thought it was fantastic. It was what they were most excited about. But when Felicity balked at junking Jethro's script, Irv started asking colleagues if they thought he should take a chance on a show with a great score, but a crappy book. He happened to ask a friend who'd put money into *Baristas*. This guy lost money, even though the show was successful, so Irv started asking Felicity some tough questions. She got nervous and decided Irv's snooping wasn't worth his backing. She saw a way to disengage from the Donnellys by doing the opposite of what they wanted."

"How did you get involved?"

"When Irv heard they'd trashed Geoff's score, he became even more curious. He called me, and I started digging around. I have to confess, I told a little white lie when we met at the Hilton. Thomas didn't find me; I called him. When you want to know what's going on at a theater—"

"Always ask the costume shop," they finished together.

"But what about Donnelly coming to see the show opening night?" Isobel asked. "Felicity seemed to think it was because they were interested."

"Yes. Irv called and told her he was reconsidering and wanted to see what she'd done with the piece. I was always going to be his date."

"Why didn't he come with you?"

"So Delphi could have a seat," Fried quipped.

Isobel chuckled. "Seriously."

"The most mundane reason in the world. He got the flu."

"If the Donnellys didn't pump money into *Sousacal*, then who did?"

"Felicity Hamilton. Whatever money she'd saved up from skimming all those years went into the show. She was apparently devoted to Jethro. Somewhat misguidedly, as it turns out."

"So I was wrong and the two were connected," Isobel admitted. "I guess sometimes the obvious explanation is the right one."

"Occam's razor, my dear."

"What?"

"Look it up."

"Train station," barked the cabbie.

"I have to go," Isobel said. "But thank you."

"Oh, you've read it? Good! Bye, now."

He rang off, and Isobel stared at her phone with a confused expression.

"Come on." Delphi nudged her. "You can fill us in on the train."

They tumbled out of the cab, pooled their money to pay the driver, and reorganized themselves and their bags. Inside the train station, they scanned the board for their platform.

"Hang on a sec," Isobel said. She ran over to a newsstand, where the *New York Post* was prominently displayed between the *Times Union* and the *New York Times*. She plunked down her money and grabbed a copy, flipping to Roman Fried's column.

> *And so, a respected regional theater is consigned to an untimely demise by a dishonest producer. There's a shocker. But one good thing came out of this misguided concatenation of history, ego, and strict march tempo: the opportunity to become acquainted with the enterprising talent of one Isobel Spice, who rose above the circumstances to deliver a charming performance of mediocre material. She's one to keep an eye on.*

A shiver of delight ran down Isobel's spine. She extracted the page and shoved the rest of the paper over the counter.

"Here, you can recycle this."

"Don't you want it?" asked the clerk.

"Only page six. I'm going to frame it next to my first Equity contract."

She waved the newsprint in his face and ran off to join her friends.

ACKNOWLEDGMENTS

It turns out my friends are more devious than I, so for pranks and other nefarious suggestions, my thanks to Geoff Gaebe, Peter Büchi, Seth Christenfeld, Emilie Storrs, Aileen Itani, Christianne Tisdale, Matt Conroy, and Liz Reddick. (And if I ever share the stage with any of you again, I will be sure to watch my back!) Gratitude always to my stalwart support team, editor Kira Rubenthaler of Bookfly Design, designer Linda Pierro of Flint Media, and agent Kari Stuart at ICM, as well as my trusted betas, Helen Lessner, Tim Peierls, and my very own Hugh (but without the British accent), Joshua Rosenblum.

About the Author

Joanne Sydney Lessner is the author of *Pandora's Bottle*, a novel inspired by the true story of the world's most expensive bottle of wine (Flint Mine Press). *The Temporary Detective, Bad Publicity, And Justice for Some* and *Offed Stage Left* (Dulcet Press) feature aspiring actress and amateur sleuth Isobel Spice. No stranger to the theatrical world, Joanne enjoys an active performing career in both musical theater and opera. With her husband, composer/conductor Joshua Rosenblum, she has co-authored several musicals including the cult hit *Fermat's Last Tango* and *Einstein's Dreams*, based on the celebrated novel by Alan Lightman. Her play, *Critical Mass*, received its Off Broadway premiere in October 2010 as the winner of the 2009 Heiress Productions Playwriting Competition. Joanne is a regular contributing writer to *Opera News* and holds a B.A. in music, *summa cum laude*, from Yale University.

Look for the next Isobel Spice novel, coming soon!

Sign up for updates at
joannesydneylessner.com